DOORS

ED McBAIN

DOORS

WARNER BOOKS

A Time Warner Company

The poem on page 16 originally appeared in *The New Yorker*, Copyright ©
1963.

WARNER BOOKS EDITION

Cover design and illustration by Tony Greco

This Warner Books Edition is published by arrangement with HUI
Corporation.

Warner Books, Inc.
1271 Avenue of the Americas
New York, NY 10020

Visit our web site at
http://pathfinder.com/twep

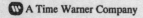 A Time Warner Company

Printed in the United States of America

First Warner Books Printing: December, 1995

10 9 8 7 6 5 4 3

This is for Ingram Ash—
who I think might have enjoyed it.

ONE

They were sitting at a table in the back room of Henry's jewelry shop in the Bronx. There was a big black double-door Mosler on one wall, and all of the windows were barred on the outside. At the front of the store, both plate-glass windows had been covered with metal grilles for the night. Alex had noticed them on the way in.

He watched now as Henry rose and walked ponderously to a wall cabinet opposite the safe. He took from it two glasses and a bottle of whiskey, and then carried them back to the table with him. Henry was an enormously fat man, dressed in a black suit, a white shirt open at the throat, no tie. There were rumors that he had once done time in a German concentration camp, but Alex couldn't believe a man so fat had been through such an ordeal. Henry spoke with a marked German accent though, so maybe the stories were true. He set the glasses down on the table and poured a generous amount of whiskey into each.

"Have you ever been arrested?" he asked.

"Twice," Alex said. "The first time when I was eighteen. I got off with a suspended sentence. The last time was three years ago. I did eighteen months at Sing Sing."

"Ah, too bad," Henry said, and shook his head and lifted his drink. He wore thick rimless spectacles. His eyes behind them were a watery brown, magnified by the lenses.

"I learned a lot there," Alex said.

"Drink, please," Henry said, and raised his own glass in encouragement. Sipping at the whiskey, he said, "You are working with someone else now?"

"I usually work alone."

"I do not mean on the job," Henry said. "I am talking about receiving."

"I have two fences," Alex said.

"Do they also finger jobs for you?"

"One of them does. The other is strictly a receiver."

"I hear very good things about you," Henry said. "You are a good burglar."

"Thanks," Alex said. "What's this job you have in mind?"

"Well, let's talk a little more, eh?" Henry said. "Or are you in a rush?"

"I'm not in any rush," Alex said.

"How well do the police know you?"

"They come around every now and then. Whenever there's a job they can't dope out, they figure I did it. They don't worry me, they can come around as often as they like. I've got a lawyer, and also a bondsman who'll go to twenty grand if it's necessary. But so far, I've only been inside a station house three times since I got out of Sing Sing."

"You have your own lawyer, eh? And a bondsman, too?"

"That's right, I don't count on fences for that kind of help. All I want from anybody who receives the goods is quick cash."

"Well, naturally, no one wants to keep fourteen television sets in his basement, eh?"

"I hardly ever steal home appliances," Alex said. "That's for your junkie burglars."

"Then you are not on narcotics, eh?"

"No."

"That's good. How old are you, may I ask?"

"Twenty-five."

"What has been your biggest score?" Henry asked. "More to drink?"

"A little, thanks. The biggest I ever got, my end of it, was forty-two thousand. That was after I got out of Sing Sing."

"Where was that? A hotel, a residence?"

"An apartment house. I'm a crib burglar. I don't work hotels, I don't work offices or stores. Strictly apartments, and strictly during the day."

"You are opposed to working at night?"

"Yes."

"Why is that? I know some very good burglars who work at night."

"Not me. I work percentages. If you're stealing from stores or offices, you do it at night because that's when the people are supposed to be home in bed. If you're stealing from apartments, you do it during the day, when the people are supposed to be at work. I don't want to see anybody when I'm inside a place. If I so much as hear a pussycat fart, I'm out in a minute. What exactly do you have in mind here?" Alex asked. "Tommy told me you needed a good burglar, that's why I'm here. Is this a regular thing we're talking about, or just a one-shot?"

"It would be a regular thing," Henry said. "Provided it works out."

"The only way it wouldn't work out is if I got busted," Alex said. "I don't intend to get busted ever again."

"So," Henry said, and smiled.

"So what's the job? Or ain't you interested anymore?"

"I am, of course, still interested," Henry said. "Did Tommy tell you what percentage I work on?"

"No, what is it?"

"I pay twenty-five percent of the value," Henry said, and peered at Alex from behind his eyeglasses.

"That ain't enough," Alex said, and rose immediately from the table.

"Sit down," Henry said. "Please. What are you accustomed to getting from your other receivers?"

"Thirty percent."

"That's high," Henry said.

"It ain't high, it's standard."

"Yes, but these other men do not finger jobs for you."

"One of them does, I already told you that. And he gives me a straight thirty, and that's what I work for. If there's a man along as helper, if that's what the job calls for, then I'll give him ten percent of my end. But that's it."

"Still, thirty percent . . ."

"Look, we're wasting time here," Alex said, and started for the door.

"Sit down," Henry said again. "I think we can maybe do business together."

They began talking about the job then.

Alex thought he had handled himself fine.

That bullshit about the twenty-five percent was strictly for crude burglars, your goddamn window men, if they got *even* that. Windows were from hunger, amateur night in Dixie. You took any punk, he could wrap a towel around a brick and smash in a window, and reach up for the latch. He was usually some junkie, he had a habit as long as your arm to feed. He stepped over the fire escape, he tried the window next to it cause people usually locked the window right *on* the fire escape, but they didn't bother locking the one alongside it. If it was unlocked, the guy was in free and clear. If it wasn't, then he'd try the window on the fire escape, slip a knife up between the window frames, turn the latch that way. Those window latches weren't worth a shit. A chimpanzee could open any one of them in thirty seconds flat.

But sometimes the latch and even the window itself was painted shut, and that's when your crude burglar would smash it in with a wrapped brick. It depended on how crude he was, whether or not he'd tape the window first. If he taped it, the glass wouldn't make so much noise cause it'd stick to the tape, and then he could lift out the pieces until he had a big enough hole to get in through. Sometimes, though, if he was a desperate junkie, he couldn't be bothered with taping, he was just interested in getting in there fast and getting out. So he'd wrap the brick and smash out the whole pane of glass, and in he'd go, never mind about noise, never mind about maybe cutting himself in the bargain. He was only going to be in there three, four minutes, anyway. He'd grab whatever he saw around, it didn't matter, he was only interested in getting enough for his next fix. He never had a big score in mind, cause he stole from people living in cheap neighborhoods, so what could he expect to get? A portable radio? A toaster? A guitar if it was a Spanish neighborhood? Three or four bucks somebody left in a bureau drawer? Small-time shit.

Your crude burglar, he hit in the daytime like most crib burglars, but he wouldn't know a diamond from a piece of glass, and anyway he didn't expect to find any diamonds in those cheap dumps he made. He had to keep busy, that was it, he had to make as much as two hundred bucks a day to support his habit, depending on how long it was. That meant he had to rip off a lot of places each and every day of the week, cause you had to figure he'd get cheated on the value of what he stole. Usually, he wasn't connected with a finger or a fence. His pusher took the goods from him, and the pusher discounted it for whatever the traffic would bear. If the guy was real sick, the pusher would take from him a portable black-and-white TV worth a hundred and fifty bucks, and instead of giving him what he'd give a pro, which was fifty bucks, or even what he'd give a rank amateur, which was fifteen bucks, he'd give him instead a dime bag of heroin, and the junkie burglar would run around the corner to shoot up, and half an hour later he'd be looking for another score.

You either know what you're doing or you don't, Alex thought, it's just like any other profession. A junkie don't know what he's doing, he's driven all the time. He's got to have that fix, he'll steal his own mother's wedding band to get the bread for it. When he ain't shooting up or nodding, he's stealing. But he doesn't figure the odds, that's the trouble. He goes into a place and steals a typewriter which, if he's lucky, he could get thirty bucks for, but if he gets caught he's going to get hit with a burglary three rap, and that's a class-D felony for which he can get a minimum of a year or a maximum of anywhere from three to seven. That's if they didn't throw the book at him and charge him with possession of burglar's tools, or even criminal mischief. The criminal mischief would be if he'd damaged any property while he was inside the place, which a lot of these junkies did because they were in such a hurry. One to seven, that was it, but Alex always liked to figure it as strictly seven because he never knew what kind of judge he'd be coming up against if he ever got busted again.

If you were a real pro, you had to operate on percentage,

just like he'd told Henry. You had to know the risk you were taking, and you didn't go after cheap crap that could get you the same time in prison a big score would get you. That was what the crude burglars didn't realize. A man could steal a $3,500 mink jacket or a $25 portable radio, and it would still be seven years if that was what the judge felt like handing out that day. The *value* of what the man stole added grand or petit larceny to the burglary charge, but breaking and entering was still the basic beef. If a burglar made a hole only big enough to stick his hand inside a building, that was breaking and entering. He didn't have to put his whole body in there, he didn't even have to step over the windowsill. Just poke his pinky or even a tool into that little hole he made, and that was breaking and entering, and that could be seven years if he came up against a judge who didn't like the color of his eyes.

A man didn't even have to *steal* anything while he was in there. Just going in there, even if he went in with a key— which Alex had done any number of times—was enough. He could go in there expecting the Hope Diamond, finding instead an empty room without a stick of furniture in it, and if they caught him and could prove he intended to commit a crime in there, that was it, the charge was burglary three. Of course, if they couldn't prove he was planning to rip off the place, then the charge was only criminal trespass, which was a bullshit violation—fifteen days or a $250 fine. But if anyone was banking on criminal trespass, he'd better not have anything on him that even faintly *resembled* a burglar's tool. That included a credit card, even if it was made out in his own name, because a credit card or any similar piece of plastic could be used to force open a door lock.

Yeah, he felt pretty good about the way he'd handled himself with that fat Kraut, who was probably a Jew besides—

not that Alex ever rated a man by his color or his religion or anything except whether he was good at what he did. Archie Fuller, for example, was one of the best burglars he knew, and he was black. Some of the best burglars he'd ever met were either Jews or Italians, but he knew guys who said Canadians couldn't be beat. He knew some old-timers, too, who remembered back to before Castro, and they'd told him Cubans used to be the best around. It didn't make any difference to Alex. Still, that fuckin Henry shouldn't have tried to Jew him down by five percent.

The job looked like a good one, but it bothered him a little because it took away the element of surprise. Before he'd made this connection with Henry today, he'd had only one other fence who also fingered jobs for him, and that was Vito. He had to have fences, of course, what the hell was he supposed to do with a hot wristwatch? Stop a stranger on the street and whisper in his ear that he had a bargain for him? Bullshit. He knew one burglar who'd done that, and the stranger turned out to be a detective from Midtown North. Anyway, that was the same thing as being a salesman, and if Alex had wanted to be a salesman, he'd have taken a nine-to-five, like a square. And maybe miss a chance at that big score he was always looking for.

That's what bothered him about this job—he knew just what was in there, he knew just what he would net. Whenever he was on the prowl for himself, he never knew what to expect. Forty percent of the time, he'd come away with goods worth somewhere between a hundred and five hundred dollars. One time out of twenty, he'd get lucky and score between a thousand and five thousand. On a job that hadn't been set up in advance, he considered anything over five thousand a tremendous score. But there was always the chance of going in some place and stumbling upon that treasure trove, that half-a-million-dollar score, or maybe more. He'd heard stories of guys who'd done that. That's what was missing from this job.

Still, he felt pretty good.

Henry had told him he was a good burglar.

On Monday morning Alex went to work.

The building was on the corner of Sixty-ninth and Madison, across the street from the Westbury Hotel. The neighborhood was a good one, and he was dressed for it. He was wearing a gray suit, a white shirt with a dark blue tie, blue socks, and black shoes. And, because this was April and still a bit chilly, he had on a light topcoat. A copy of *The New York Times* was tucked under his left arm, and in his right hand he held a dispatch case he had bought at Mark Cross on Fifth Avenue. He wore no hat. His hair was blond, and he had often thought this a disadvantage, but had never once considered dyeing it a less identifiable color. Henry had told him everything he needed to know about the job, but Alex never went into a place without first checking it out himself; if he got caught in there, it would be *his* ass, not Henry's. The information had been pieced together from two sources, Henry himself and the maid who worked for the Rothmans. It was Henry who knew exactly what kind of loot was inside there. Henry *had* to know because he was the one who'd sold the ring to the Rothmans four months ago, just before Christmas.

They had come all the way to his shop in the Bronx because they'd heard he dealt in exceptional pieces, most of them antiques purchased from European estates. That was true enough. He also dealt in stolen jewels, but the Rothmans hadn't known that. They certainly hadn't known that the diamond ring they'd bought from him was marked for theft four months later. He had sold them the ring for thirty thousand dollars, explaining that the six-carat marquise diamond was flawless and the setting extraordinary—notice the way the two tapered baguette diamonds are set into the platinum, please, this ring belonged to a countess in Germany, you do not find this sort of workmanship anymore.

He had been telling the truth, old Henry. You did not find this sort of workmanship anymore, and come Thursday the *Rothmans* wouldn't find it anymore either. Come Thursday it would be back in Henry's fat little hands, and he'd remove the stones from their extraordinary setting, maybe shave a bit off the top of the big diamond to reduce the number of carats, and then ship all three diamonds back to Europe, where they would get lost on one or another of the diamond exchanges. He had told Alex the ring was worth thirty, but he'd probably shaved *that* a bit, too. Still, Alex could expect nine thousand for the job, plus thirty percent of whatever else happened to be in the wallbox.

The maid had been cultivated by a black gambler Henry knew. She was a girl in her twenties, just up from the South, dumb as the day was long. The gambler had been supplied with only her first name, which the Rothmans had casually mentioned on the day they were buying the ring, but it hadn't taken him long to find out which Gloria in the building was the one employed by the Rothmans. He had made her acquaintance in a coffee shop on Lexington Avenue, after following her from the building on her way home one night. He'd begun dating her in February, and had since learned everything there was to know about the habits of the Rothmans, without ever once indicating that he was in any way pumping the girl for information. She had seen him only last week. She didn't yet know she would never see him again. For that matter, she didn't even know his real name. On

Thursday, when the ring was delivered, Henry would give the gambler three thousand dollars for his part in setting up the burglary.

According to the maid, Mr. Rothman worked as a stockbroker down on Wall Street. He left for work at nine each morning, in time for the market's opening at ten, and generally got home earlier than the usual square; the market closed at three-thirty, and most days he was home by four-thirty or five. Mrs. Rothman did not work—she was sixty-one years old—but she was generally out of the apartment between ten and twelve in the morning, when she went over to Central Park for a brief stroll. That was on good days. On rainy days she never budged from the apartment, a fact about which her maid had complained bitterly to the gambler. But aside from that two-hour-long Central Park constitutional, Mrs. Rothman rarely ventured outside on *sunny* days either, which meant Alex had to hit the place between ten and twelve. That was cutting it very thin, even though he knew exactly where the box was.

Henry had told him there was a doorman and an elevator operator in the building. Alex wanted to check that out, of course, but he also wanted to see whether the maid had been right about Mr. Rothman going off to work at nine, and Mrs. Rothman going down for her stroll at ten. He had been given a fair description of what the Rothmans looked like, but he wasn't about to base his calculations on maybe identifying the wrong people. There were easier ways of checking on whether the apartment was indeed empty between ten and twelve on Thursdays. Alex had already decided on Thursday for the hit; Thursday was the maid's day off.

He arrived at the apartment house at seven-thirty on Monday morning, walking past it on the other side of the street, just to get a feel of the place. The doorman was standing on the sidewalk outside the glass entrance doors, under a green awning that ran to the curb. There was very little activity at this hour of the morning. Alex walked down to Park Avenue, crossed the street, walked uptown to Seventieth, and then circled the entire block, walking past the building on the same side of the street now, not five feet from where the doorman still stood inside the glass entrance doors. The doorman was a man in his sixties, brawny, redfaced, very fat in the behind. He was wearing a gray uniform with a narrow blue stripe down each outside trouser leg. He scarcely glanced at Alex when he went past, but Alex knew he couldn't go by the building too often without attracting his attention sooner or later.

He circled the block again, this time walking downtown to Sixty-eighth and coming up to Madison that way. Then, instead of going into the street again, he crossed Madison Avenue and positioned himself on the corner diagonally across from the building, where he could study the building and the street without being noticed by the doorman. The time was seven-forty-five A.M.

As he stood on the corner, he occasionally raised his newspaper toward an approaching taxicab, but only if he could tell the cab was already carrying a passenger. Whenever an empty cab approached in the distance, he kept his newspaper under his arm. Every now and then, he glanced at his wristwatch, as though fearful he would be late for work. He did all of this unobtrusively, even though he knew nobody in New York gave a damn about anyone else in New York. As far as any of the passers-by were concerned, he could be turning cartwheels trying to get a taxi and none of them would have noticed. Still, he tried to keep track of the people going by because he didn't want some little old lady to notice he'd been standing on the same corner for a half-hour, trying to get a goddamn taxicab. There weren't many people on the street now, anyway, though the activity began to pick up as it came closer to eight and people started going off to work.

There was an underground parking garage across the street from the building, and many of the men who came out went directly across the street and down the ramp to it. Alex counted sixteen women coming out of the building between eight and eight-thirty. All of them were well dressed, and he automatically assumed they were going off to work, since a woman going shopping would not leave the house all dressed up so early in the morning. Your shopping women usually left around ten-thirty, eleven, something like that. Your women who were playing around left near noon. He always knew when a woman was on her way to get laid; there was just something in the way she walked. He made a note to keep this building in mind for future hits. Sixteen working women meant the possibility of sixteen empty apartments from nine to five.

But he wasn't here to case the joint for next July, he was here to look it over for a job that had to be done this Thursday. He'd been standing on the corner too long, he had seen the same man walk by twice with a pair of black poodles on a leash. Also, now that it was getting close to eight-forty, the doorman from the building was running up to Madison Avenue more and more often, blowing his whistle at cruising taxis and then signaling back to the front of the building to this or that person who had asked him to hail a cab. Alex moved off.

There was a coffee shop a block up from the Westbury and he went there and ordered himself a cup of coffee and a toasted English. Then he went to the phone booth and looked up the telephone number for Jerome Rothman on East Sixty-ninth Street, and found a listing for him. He deposited a dime, dialed the number, and listened to the phone ringing on the other end. A woman picked up the receiver.

"Hello?" she said.

"Mr. Rothman, please," he said.

"I'm sorry, he's already left," the woman said. "May I take a message?"

"Do you know if I can reach him at work?" Alex asked.

"Yes, who's this, please?"

"I have the number, I'll try him there," Alex said, and hung up, and went back to the table, where his coffee and toasted English were waiting.

The telephone, of course, was as essential a burglar's tool as was the cylinder jig, and the jimmy, and the various picks and tension bars he would later carry in the expensive leather dispatch case. In the right-hand pocket of his topcoat, he would carry a royal-flush poker hand—the ten, jack, queen, king, and ace of hearts. The cards were plastic coated and could be used to loid any door with a spring latch. But if a cop stopped him for a casual frisk and didn't bother to look inside the dispatch case, Alex could always say he was carrying the royal flush as a remembrance of the one time in his life he had ever drawn such a hand. He realized this was a far-fetched hope—any cop stopping him would naturally look inside the dispatch case, too, and find a potful of burglar's tools. But a plastic-coated playing card made as good a loid as a hotel's DO NOT DISTURB sign, and besides Alex liked to think of himself as a gambler of sorts. Actually, he was a very good poker player, which was not surprising since he'd taken a great deal of time to memorize the odds and never played in crazy wild-card games where the odds got all fucked up. Percentages. It was all percentages.

The percentages on Mrs. Rothman thinking there was anything suspicious about his early morning call were practically nil. The one thing nobody ever suspected was that a burglary was being set up, especially if the caller asked for someone who actually lived in the apartment. He had protected the call by pretending he knew Rothman's office number as well, and had hung up before Mrs. Rothman could ask any more questions. If she ever *mentioned* the call to her husband when he came home that afternoon, Alex would be greatly surprised. On his next call, he would have to be more careful. But that would wait till tomorrow. For today, he wanted to check out the doorman and the elevator operator, and he wanted to find out what time the mailman came. He needed to be dead certain the apartment would be empty when he made it on Thursday. The one thing he never hoped to run across was an occupied apartment. He hadn't so far, not even on those two times he'd been busted, and he hoped he never would.

Alex would no more have dreamed of becoming an armed robber than he would have a lion tamer. Walk into a liquor store and shove a gun in the owner's face? No way. Unless you shot the guy dead, he could identify you later on. And besides, the risk was greater. Armed robbery was a class-B felony, and the maximum rap was twenty-five years, and no one could convince Alex that *any* amount of money was worth twenty-five years behind bars. He never carried a gun on any of his jobs because first of all guns scared him half to death, and secondly, a gun elevated the burglary, even if it was a daytime burglary, to a class-C felony, and for that you could get as much as fifteen years—not to mention what they'd tack on for the gun violation itself. No, thank you. Alex would stick to simple burglary three.

In Sing Sing he'd been leafing through some back magazines in the prison library, and he'd come across a good article about burglary. In it there was a very interesting and comical poem written by a guy who used to be a Manhattan D.A. The poem wasn't about burglary, it was about robbery. But Alex's cellmate at the time was a dumb bastard from Arkansas who'd got in trouble in New York State by sticking up a gas station—with a Civil War pistol, no less. Alex thought he'd get a kick out of the robbery poem, so he'd memorized it, and that night after lights out he recited it to him. The redneck didn't get it, naturally, but Alex still knew it by heart:

> *Most robberies without knife or gun*
> *Are Robbery One or Robbery Two.*
> *If two men rob, it's Robbery One,*
> *If only one, it's Robbery Two.*

> *There's something else called Robbery Three,*
> *Which isn't Robbery One or Two.*
> *I can't define this third degree,*
> *Except to say it's Robbery, too.*

"Whut' choo mean?" the redneck had asked. "How kin robbery *three* be robbery *two*?"

Stupid bastard.

All that week Alex had tried to write a poem on his own about burglary, modeled on the one he'd read in the back-issue magazine. He'd never got past his junior year in high school, but he'd always been good with words, and he figured he'd take a whack at it. What else was there to do in jail? Writing the poem was more difficult than he'd thought at first, but that was primarily because the penal law definitions had changed since he was a kid, and he kept mixing up the new ones with the old ones. But he finally got the poem written according to the new definitions, and he thought it was very good and in fact better than the robbery poem written by the ex-D.A.

A dwelling's the key to Burglary One,
And it has to be nighttime for Burglary One.
In addition to that, you must have a gun,
Or while in the dwelling you must hurt someone,
Or threaten him with the aforementioned gun,
For it to add up to Burglary One.

A dwelling's a building in Burglary Two.
Unless it's at night, like in Burglary One.
But once in this building, if you've got a gun,
Or once in the building you hurt anyone,
Or threaten him with the aforementioned gun,
That's Burglary Two, not Burglary One.

No mention of dwellings in Burglary Three.
No mention of nighttime in Burglary Three.
No mention of guns like in Two or in One.
No mention of threats or of hurting someone.
A building's a building in Burglary Three.
And breaking and entering is Burglary Three.

The key to all this is the dwelling, you see.
The building's a dwelling at all times in one.
The building's a dwelling at nighttime in Two.
The dwelling's a building in daytime in Three.
And none of it makes any damn sense to me.

"What the fuck's *that* supposed to mean?" the cracker asked, and that was the last time Alex tried his hand at poetry, in or out of prison.

He looked at his watch.

It was ten past nine, time to get back on the job.

There was a restaurant on the southwest corner of Sixty-ninth and Madison, but a sign in the window told him they didn't start serving till eleven-thirty. That was too bad because he'd have liked nothing more than to take a table by the window and watch the building from there. He didn't want to hang around on the corner hailing imaginary taxicabs again, nor did he want to walk past the building too often, so he went about a third of the way up the block, sat on the front stoop of the brownstones, and took off his shoe and began massaging his foot. If anyone came out of the brownstone and chased him off the stoop, he would apologize and say he'd had a sudden cramp in his arch. He was well dressed, he was carrying a dispatch case, and he was certain they'd accept his story at face value. In the meantime, he would watch the building across the street at his leisure.

The maids began arriving during the next half-hour. They were black, he assumed they were maids. Almost all of them were carrying shopping bags; he wondered why the hell black maids always carried shopping bags. During that time, the doorman ran up to Madison Avenue a total of four times. On one occasion, it took him ten minutes to get a taxicab. That was good. Alex could count on him being away from the front door more often than he was there. As for the elevator operator, he wasn't at all worried about him. Elevator operators all had their ups and downs, as the saying went, and Alex knew he had to be somewhere between floors at least sometime during the day, hopefully when old Fat Ass was chasing taxis.

The mailman came at nine-forty-five.

This was very important to Alex.

The mailman was inside the building for seven minutes, and then he came out again and went walking up the street. Alex waited another ten minutes, and then put on his shoe and tied the laces. At a little past ten o'clock, he strolled past the front door of the building and left the street. He had learned enough for today. Tomorrow morning, at exactly five minutes past ten, he would call the Rothman apartment again.

It was raining on Tuesday morning, and that annoyed the hell out of him because it meant Mrs. Rothman wouldn't go down for her walk in the park. If she didn't leave the apartment, he couldn't call to find out whether it was true that she normally *did* leave it at ten o'clock each morning—as she was supposed to do on sunny days. He hoped it wouldn't be raining on Thursday. It would do him no good at all to have the maid out of the apartment if rain stopped the old lady from taking her customary walk. Well, if it rained *this* Thursday, the job would just have to wait till *next* Thursday. He was halfway considering a postponement anyway. He still had work to do down there, primarily in the lobby, and he didn't know if he could get it all done by Thursday. One good thing about the rain today, though, was that the doorman would be busier than ever hailing taxicabs, so Alex figured he'd better get down there right away, before it stopped.

He had set the alarm for eight o'clock, knowing he didn't have to get up at the crack of dawn today. He planned to be downtown by ten, shortly after which he'd have called the Rothman apartment and then gone over to check out the mailboxes and the lobby. It wouldn't do him any good to check the mailboxes today though, not if Mrs. Rothman hadn't gone for her walk. Damn it, this rain was a pain in the ass. He was counting on the mailbox for additional insurance, and had planned to check it for two days running before the day of the burglary. But tomorrow was Wednesday already, and that gave him only *one* day to check it.

As he showered, he considered whether he wanted to go ahead with it this Thursday. Trouble was, he needed the damn money. His last hit had been in March, when Vito had set up a job that netted three thousand bucks. But when Alex had money, he spent it, and he was down to almost zilch now, and he didn't like borrowing from any of the shylocks because those bastards charged twenty percent interest a week. You borrowed a grand from a shy, the next thing you knew you owed him two grand, and before long you were working for the company store. Miss too many interest payments, and some gorilla knocked on the door and politely inquired whether you would like to have your legs broken tomorrow night at sunset. No way. His end of this would be a sure $9,000, and the sooner he got it the better. He knew Henry by reputation, and he knew the payoff would be immediate, no waiting till he disposed of the diamonds, nothing like that. Damn it, why did it have to be raining today?

The apartment Alex lived in was on Ninety-eighth and West End, in a building occupied mostly by squares. In fact, he was sometimes tempted to rip off his own apartment building, but he figured that would be playing it too close to home. Anyway, that was crude thinking, he was sorry he'd even thought of it. That was what a junkie would do. A junkie would live on a Hun Twentieth and Fifth, and he'd knock off a building on a Hun Twenty-*first* and Fifth. Cops come around, say Hello, Pancho, you steal something right next door? Junkie burglar looks at them, says Who me? Oh, no, señor, I am clean as the day is long, and meanwhile he's got a stolen radio sticking up his asshole. The building Alex lived in was a pretty good one. The rooms were tremendous, in fact, and Alex had five of them in his apartment, which was very nice when he was living with someone, like when Kitty used to be here. You didn't get in each other's way when you had such a big place.

Kitty was a black girl Archie had introduced him to. He had really liked that girl a lot. He knew she was a peddling cunt, but that didn't matter, who the hell cared if some square john was paying for something *he* was getting free? She had even offered to turn over her earnings, but that would've made Alex a pimp, and he had no respect for pimps. What ended it with Kitty was that he found out she was on dope, hell she'd been on dope even when Archie first introduced them. When Alex found out, he'd gone uptown looking for Archie. He'd said to Archie, "Why'd you introduce me to a junkie?" Archie said he hadn't known about that. *Fuck* he hadn't known.

Anyway, Alex should have known himself. You live with a person, you should realize she's shooting up—unless you're some kind of dimwit. She cried when he told her he wanted her to get out. She said she'd kick the monkey, she'd do anything for him. Sure, kick the monkey. He told her Get the hell out right this minute, I don't want a junkie living here with me, the law comes up here and finds shit stashed around here, I'll be back inside for something I didn't even do. She kept crying, and finally he dragged her to the front door and threw her out in the hall. Then he went through her pocketbook and found the key he'd given her, and threw the bag out in the hall, too. She was sitting on the floor with her skirt pulled way up. He said Go on, get out of here. Up the hall, one of the squares opened a door and looked out. She had her hair in curlers, the square. She said Oh ex*cuse* me, and closed the door again. That was the last time he'd seen Kitty.

He'd thought of moving after he'd kicked her out, not because he thought she'd send someone after him or anything like that, but only because the place seemed so damn *big* without her in it. He'd decided to stay, though, because it was really hard to find anything as good for this price; and besides, the squares all around him were a nice cover. Everytime the cops came around, he said to them, "Look where I live, I'm surrounded by hard-working people, won't you guys *ever* believe I'm out of it?"

"Sure, Alex," the cops always said.

He dressed and left the apartment.

It was still pouring bullets when he got down to the lobby of his building and saw the girl standing just inside the entrance door, staring out dismally at the downpour. The girl was a square who lived in his building. He'd noticed her because she was a very attractive blonde, maybe four or five years older than he was, certainly no older than thirty-one or -two. The first time he'd seen her, she was walking up toward Broadway with her husband, who was pushing a little blonde kid in one of those canvas strollers. That must have been in September. It was still mild outside, and she was wearing a skirt and a blouse without any bra underneath. She had a good set, and her nipples were poking through the fabric. He remembered thinking at the time that if *he* had a wife who ran around advertising her tits that way, he'd have busted her head for her. She and her husband had both recognized him from the building and nodded to him as he went past.

Alex happened to have been carrying sixty-seven hundred dollars in cash that day because he had just ripped off an apartment in the Village and had delivered the goods to Vito, who had paid him on the spot. That had been a good score. He had stumbled upon a coin collection, and there wasn't a fence in the city who discounted a coin collection. You always got face value for stamp collections, too. They were almost as good as credit cards, though nothing but cash beat credit cards. The trouble with credit cards was that you rarely found any during your daytime burglaries; the guy usually had them with him, in his wallet. Your nighttime crib burglar, the stupid bastard who went rummaging around in bedrooms while a man and a woman were asleep across the room, could count on scoring a lot of credit cards. But then, even if he got away without waking anybody up, the man he'd stolen the cards from would report them missing first thing in the morning, so you hardly ever got a chance to *charge* anything with them. The best thing to do if you stumbled across a wallet with credit cards in it was to take only *one* of them, or two at the most. If a guy had a dozen cards in his wallet, he might not miss the one stolen American Express card, and you could charge thousands of dollars of stuff with it before he reported it stolen.

Alex was dressed for the weather, wearing a trench coat and a rain hat, and he was also carrying an umbrella since he figured he might have to spend quite a bit of time standing in the rain on Sixty-ninth Street. The girl had on a black raincoat and one of those clear plastic things on her head, but she wasn't carrying an umbrella, and she'd have drowned in a minute if she stepped outside. As Alex started opening his umbrella, the girl said, "Are you walking up to Broadway?" This surprised him. In New York, people who lived in the same apartment building hardly ever spoke to each other.

"Yes," he said, "I am."

"Would you mind sharing your umbrella with me?" she

said. "I'll never get a taxi here, I've been waiting for fifteen minutes now."

"Sure," he said.

He opened the umbrella and she got under it, and together they began walking up toward Broadway.

"I'm supposed to be downtown by ten o'clock," she said. "I'll never make it."

"You might have trouble getting a cab even up on Broadway," he said.

"I should have allowed myself more time," she said. "I should have told the sitter eight-thirty instead of nine. But I didn't know it'd be raining like this."

"How far down are you going?" he asked.

"All the way to Pine Street."

"That's a good half-hour," he said. "Even if you get a cab right off."

"Yes," she said. "I should have planned better."

They stood on the corner of Broadway and Ninety-eighth for ten minutes and then walked down to Ninety-sixth, hoping they might catch a cab running crosstown on the wider thoroughfare. The girl kept looking at her watch. Alex wondered about her. Ten o'clock was a little early for a matinee, but who the hell knew? Your most respectable-looking ladies sometimes spent the whole damn day fucking their brains out in New Jersey motels while their husbands were breaking their asses at a nine-to-five. He spotted a cab in the distance and whistled for it, and then waved frantically when the cab showed no sign of slowing down. The driver saw him at the last moment, cut across a lane of traffic to get to the curb, and then squealed to a puddle-splashing stop beside them.

"Thank *God*!" the girl said, and reached immediately for the door handle, and then belatedly said, "Can I give you a lift downtown?"

"I don't want to take you out of your way," he said.

"Where are you going?"

"Lincoln Center," he lied.

"I can drop you," she said, "come on," and got into the taxi and slid across the leather seat. He got in beside her, closed the door, and told the cabby where they were going. As the taxi moved away from the curb, she opened her bag, took out a package of cigarettes, and offered him one.

"Thanks," he said. "I don't smoke."

She lit her own cigarette, exhaling a cloud of smoke that seemed a visual sigh of relief. Rain lashed the windshield, the rubber blades of the wipers snicked at it steadily. There was the sound, too, of the tires hissing against the wet asphalt, and the scent in that small contained space of wet and steamy garments, evocative of some other time, a time he could not clearly remember. The girl took the plastic cover from her head and then fluffed out her hair. It was cut close to her head, it looked like a nest of yellow feathers. She had blue eyes that squinched ever so slightly each time she took a drag on the cigarette. Her nose was narrow, with a delicate dusting of freckles on the bridge. She had a wide mouth with a fuller lower lip. A piece of cigarette paper stuck to the lip, and her tongue darted out to free it, and then she picked the paper off her tongue with thumb and forefinger and said, "I just hope he hasn't got another appointment after mine."

"Who's that?" Alex asked.

She crossed her legs. She had good legs, but her nylons were spattered with darkish spots from the rain puddles. "My lawyer," she said, and let out a stream of smoke. "Does this bother you?" she asked, indicating the cigarette.

"No, no. Are you in trouble?"

"Trouble?"

"A lawyer, I mean."

"Oh," she said, and laughed lightly. "Well, yes, I suppose you could call it trouble. My husband and I are getting a divorce."

"Too bad," Alex said.

"*I'm* the one who wants it," she said.

"Still," he said, not knowing really what to say. Only squares got married in the first place. If you could get all you needed without being tied down to anybody, what was the sense?

"We've been separated since just before Christmas," she said, and suddenly shifted her cigarette to her left hand, and extended her right hand to him. "I'm Jessica Knowles," she said, "soon to be the former Mrs. Michael Knowles." She smiled. "I *hope*," she added.

"I'm Alex Hardy," he said, and took her hand. He felt foolish shaking hands with a woman; the handshake was brief and awkward.

"Is that short for Alexander?"

"Yes," he said. "My mother's Greek. Alexander's a big hero to the Greeks."

"He was blond, too," Jessica said. "Alexander."

"Yeah," Alex said, and they were silent till the taxi pulled up in front of Lincoln Center. Alex quickly handed the driver a five-dollar bill, and said, "When you get to Pine Street, take it all out of this."

"No, no," Jessica protested. "Now please, I . . ."

"That's okay," Alex said, and opened the door on the curbside, and said, "Nice meeting you," and stepped out into the rain. He was opening the umbrella as the taxi pulled away from the curb again. In a few minutes, he caught another cab and asked the driver to take him to Sixty-fifth and Madison.

It was still raining heavily when he got out of the cab. He

walked up Madison to Sixty-ninth and saw the building's
doorman standing on the corner whistling for taxis, a big red
and yellow striped umbrella open over his head. With this
kind of weather, he'd be up there all day long; maybe the
rain was a blessing after all. Alex walked toward the building. A black man in coveralls and a clear plastic raincoat was
carrying a garbage can up from the basement, coming out of
a metal doorway that opened onto a narrow ramp on the left-
hand side of the building. Poor bastard needed both hands to
roll the garbage can to the curb, he couldn't have held an
umbrella even if he'd want to; he was drenched before he'd
covered three feet of sidewalk. Alex looked over his shoulder
toward Madison Avenue. The doorman was still up there.
He walked directly to the building and looked in. A man
with a mustache was waiting just inside the glass entrance
doors. He was obviously the one who'd sent the doorman for
a taxi. Toward the rear of the lobby, a lavender-haired
woman in a beige raincoat was standing in front of a pair of
brass doors.

Standing under the awning, Alex took a scrap of paper
from his wallet, consulted it, and then looked up at the address over the entrance doors. Inside, the lavender-haired
lady was just stepping into the elevator. Alex walked directly
past the man with the mustache and into the lobby. He did
not want to be seen today, not by the doorman or the elevator
operator, because they were supposedly paid to notice any
suspicious characters lurking around the building. But the
tenants were another matter. Half the time tenants didn't
know who lived in a building or who didn't. The man with
the mustache didn't even give him a second glance; all *he*
cared about was getting a taxi.

Closing his umbrella, Alex looked quickly to his right. In
many apartment buildings, the mailboxes were just inside the

entrance, but that wasn't the case here. The next usual spot
was somewhere near the elevator bank, so he walked toward
that now, knowing the man with the mustache would expect
him to walk toward the elevator, anyway. He looked up at
the floor indicator over the brass doors. The illuminated bar
had just flashed the number 6, and the car was continuing
upward. Alex did not intend to check the contents of the
mailboxes today, there would be no sense to that; he only
wanted to find out where the boxes were located. He found
them at once, in a recess across from the elevator bank. The
man with the mustache was looking out at the street, his back
to Alex. Alex scanned the lobby for a metal door, found one
diagonally opposite the entrance, and walked quickly to it.

The fire door in any apartment building was normally
locked on the lobby side, in order to keep out burglars and
other such riffraff. Alex tried the knob. The door was indeed
locked. There was a keyway on the lobby side, but Alex
knew there'd be none on the stair side. The whole point of
fire stairs was to give tenants an escape route in case the
building was in flames. You couldn't expect tenants to carry
keys to these doors. They opened from the stair side either
by pushing on a panic bar attached to the door or else by
pressing a thumb latch, either of which operations would pull
the bolt back from the strike plate. The lock on the lobby
side was a flush-mounted, five-pin cylinder lock, and there
was a steel lip on the door frame, protecting the bolt and
strike plate. The lock could not be loided, he would have to
pick it on the day of the burglary.

He heard the elevator whining down the shaft and moved
swiftly to the front of the lobby. He walked past the man
with the mustache again, and again the man scarcely glanced
at him. Coming out of the building, Alex opened his umbrella, and then turned right and began walking toward

Madison Avenue, mainly because he wanted to check out the door leading to the basement ramp. He stopped directly in front of the door and stopped as though to tie his shoelace, the umbrella effectively shielding his face. The lock was a deadbolt, he recognized it at once. It could not be loided, jimmied, or sprung. Given enough time, it could be drilled open. But on Thursday he'd only have the two hours between ten and twelve, and besides who in his right mind would stand on a sidewalk in broad daylight trying to work a deadbolt? So far as entrance through the basement was concerned, he was out of luck. It would have to be the fire door in the lobby. He stood upright just as a taxi splashed past and stopped in front of the building. The doorman got out of the cab, and the man with the mustache got in.

There was nothing more that Alex could do here.

He decided to go uptown to see Archie Fuller.

You could never tell a good burglar from the way he dressed. A pimp you could spot from half a mile away on a foggy day, but a good burglar never—unless you were a cop or another burglar. As the taxi threaded its way through the traffic on Lenox Avenue, Alex looked through the rain-streaked window at the men and women hurrying along the wet sidewalks and made a game of guessing which of them were squares and which of them were in it. Then he made the game more complicated by trying to guess which *part* they were in.

The pimps were the easiest; they should have worn signs around their necks instead of those wide-brimmed hats. There were hardly any hookers on the street at all, too early in the day for any action, even though it was now close to noon. He thought suddenly of Kitty and wondered how she was. He sometimes felt very sorry for that girl. Well, the hell

with her, she should've known better than to get herself
hooked on dope. Still, she was a nice girl. Still, she was a
junkie, the hell with her.

There were plenty of junkies out, in spite of the rain, and
in spite of the hour. Junkies didn't know rain from shine,
they didn't know time, their clocks were internal, the hours
determined by their need for a fix. Junkies congregated.
They liked to stand together discussing the availability or
scarcity of shit. They were always eating candy bars. If you
had the candy-bar concession at a convention of junkies, you
could retire for life. Kitty always used to eat candy bars.
"Sweet for the sweet," she used to say. That was before he
realized she was on dope, how stupid can a guy get?

Your pushers were easy to spot, too. You couldn't tell
Alex that every pusher in the city wasn't known to the fuzz,
and that they could've busted all of them in a minute if it
wasn't for narcotics payoffs. First of all, if you could recognize a *junkie* so easily, then all you had to do was follow him
and sooner or later he'd make contact with the Man. Now the
Man *had* to be carrying dope with him, otherwise he'd have
nothing to sell, right? And depending on how *much* dope he
was carrying, it could be as heavy as an A-I felony, for
which he could get fifteen years to life. Now a pusher, who
is walking around with a minimum of fifteen possible years
in his coat pocket is a man who's looking around all the
time, and he doesn't look around the way a burglar casing a
joint looks around. A burglar setting up a future job isn't carrying any burglar's tools with him, he's got nothing to worry
about; it's not a crime to look around, even if you're looking
for a place to hit that very afternoon. Your pusher has a
furtive appearance, even more furtive than a man with a pistol in his belt. Alex spotted two pushers on the avenue. One
of them was black, and Alex knew him. The other one was

white, and he'd never seen him before in his life, but he knew he was a pusher. There were times when Alex thought he should have become a cop.

He also spotted a burglar, yeah, there he was, a goddamn amateur burglar trying to be very casual about the way he was casing every store on the block. And there, right behind him, was a tail—a bull Alex recognized from the Twenty-sixth Precinct. *He'd* made the burglar, too, and was high-stepping it after him through the rain. Cops were very good at making burglars, though why this one was wasting time following an amateur, especially in the rain, was a mystery to Alex. Big promotion probably involved. Hey, look, Chief, I caught me a nickel-and-dime thief, do I make detective second? Very good, Fosdick, run out and get me some coffee and crullers.

It sometimes seemed to Alex that the only people the cops bothered arresting were the *honest* thieves, the ones who weren't handing out the payola. Look at all those numbers people on the street. Alex spotted at least half a dozen as the taxi moved up Lenox Avenue and could tell you in a minute who was collecting the bets, and where the numbers drops were, and who was picking up the policy slips, and if *he* could do it, then so could the cops. There had to be big pay-offs involved, otherwise all of them would be in jail. Not that Alex gave a shit. As far as he was concerned, if you were going to put *anybody* in jail, then you had to put *everybody* in jail because there was no such thing as an honest man.

There was no answer when Alex knocked on Archie's door, so he figured Archie was still asleep. Archie was a night man, and this fact somewhat diminished Alex's respect for him. He had talked to Archie many times about the greater risks involved in nighttime burglaries, but Archie just laughed and said it was best for him at night because he blended with the air, man. And Alex always replied there was nothing whiter than a black man caught in the glare of a policeman's torch. He knocked on the door again.

"All right, all right," Archie called from inside. Alex heard his footsteps approaching the door; it sounded like a herd of buffalo coming through the apartment. "Who's there?" Archie asked.

"Me. Alex."

Archie opened the door. He was wearing only striped undershorts. He was the kind of black man people crossed the street to avoid. He weighed two hundred and forty pounds, all of it muscle, and he had a jagged knife scar down the right-hand side of his face. Even if he'd been an accountant or a lawyer or a surgeon, if you saw this mother approaching, you knew *knew* he was going to rape you or mug you or hold you upside down by your ankles and bang your head on the pavement just for fun. Which wasn't true. Archie was one of the gentlest men Alex had ever met. And a good burglar besides.

"It's the crack of dawn, man," he said, and turned immediately from the door and walked away. Alex stepped inside and closed the door behind him. He walked familiarly through the apartment, and when he got to the bedroom, Archie was already back in bed.

"Come on, wake up," Alex said.

"Go fuck yourself, man," Archie said genially, and rolled over and pulled the covers up over his head.

It's past twelve already," Alex said.

"Come back later," Archie mumbled from under the bedclothes.

"I'll go make some coffee," Alex said, and went out of the bedroom, across the living room, and into the kitchen. A pile of dirty dishes were in the kitchen sink, the rats and roaches must've had a feast last night. Alex searched around for the coffee pot. He found it in a cabinet near the stove. When he lifted the lid to put water in the pot, he found four hundred-dollar bills in the grounds basket.

"I found your stash," he called through the apartment.

He put the four bills under an ashtray on the counter near the sink, and then filled the pot with water and the basket with coffee. He set the pot on the stove then and turned on the gas under it. There were lipsticked cigarette butts in the ashtray. One of them looked like a marijuana roach. Alex had nothing against marijuana, though he never smoked it himself. He wondered who the girl had been, and thought of Kitty again. Looking through the kitchen window, he saw at least half a dozen apartments with their fire-escape windows partially open. Small-time stuff, true, but easy pickings.

"You boiling my money in that pot?" Archie asked from the kitchen doorway. He was still wearing only undershorts.

"It's under the ashtray there," Alex said.

Archie glanced at the ashtray with the money under it, and then said, "What time is it?"

"I told you."

"What are you doing here so early?"

"Why? Were you working last night?" Alex asked.

"I worked *hard*, man," Archie said. "I had a little fox up here. I had her climbing the walls, man. That was hard work. When you knocked on the door, I thought it was her coming back for more."

"Anybody I know?" Alex asked, half hoping he would say it had been Kitty.

"A Jewgirl from the Bronx. A social worker. She set the alarm for seven-thirty, had to rush out there to assist all those poor social victims," Archie said, and laughed. "There's some bread in the fridge," he said, "whyn't you make us some toast?"

"When did you get crippled?" Alex said.

"Man, *you're* the one woke *me* up," Archie said, and sat at the table, and stretched his arms over his head, and said, "That was *some* festival last night, I got to tell you. That was the Fourth of July in Newark, New Jersey." His arms froze in midair. He rose suddenly, walked swiftly to the ashtray, lifted it, and counted the bills. Rolling his eyes in relief, exhaling his breath noisily, he said, "For a minute there, I thought she might have ripped off a few hundred."

"Would've served you right," Alex said. "Corrupting a social worker."

"Corrupting *her*? Man, she knew things the ancient whore of Babylon didn't know. How's that coffee doing?"

"Coming," Alex said, and took two slices of bread from the refrigerator and put them into the toaster. "I once made an apartment," he said, "the people were away for the summer, they had this stale loaf of bread in the refrigerator, and between the slices there was a thousand dollars in twenty-dollar bills."

"What were you doing in the fridge?" Archie asked, interested.

"I got hungry while I was in there. I don't usually fool around like that, but I knew they were away, so I had plenty of time. I decided to make myself a little sandwich, and I found a thousand bucks in the bread," Alex said, and laughed at the memory.

"Bread inside the bread, huh?" Archie said, and laughed, too. "Man, the places they hide things."

"Like in the coffee pot," Alex said.

"That's a *good* hiding place," Archie said. "Would *you* think of looking in a coffee pot?"

"Kitchen's always the *last* place I look."

"See? You learned something today."

"Live and learn," Alex said.

"You been working?" Archie asked.

"I'm on a job now."

"Vito set it up?"

"No. Guy named Henry Green, he's a jeweler in the Bronx. You know him?"

"Never heard of him."

"Tommy put me onto him."

"How big a score?"

"Pretty big, Arch. I stand to pull down a cool nine grand."

"Nice," Archie said, and whistled. "What are you giving Tommy?"

"Oh, I thought just a few bills. I mean, he only made the contact, you know? That's enough, don't you think? Two or three bills?"

"Yeah, that's enough," Archie said. "What's he doing, Tommy?"

"I don't know *what* he's doing, tell you the truth. Where're your cups?"

"Cabinet over there," Archie said. "If there's any clean ones."

"I hear he's looking to buy a good piece," Alex said, and shrugged. "Maybe he's planning a stickup, who knows?"

"That's dumb," Archie said.

"He just got out last month, he's still wearing prison threads, looks like a panhandler, I mean it." Pouring coffee into the two mugs he'd found in the cabinet, Alex said, "Maybe I ought to give him more than just a few bills, what do you think? Maybe half a grand, huh? Help him get started again, you know?"

"Up to you," Archie said, and shrugged. "You're gonna burn that toast, you don't look after it."

"Shit," Alex said, and went to the smoking toaster, and flipped up the lever. He pulled the two slices of toast out and juggled them in his hands. Dropping them gingerly on the enamel-topped table, he said, "Too well done for you?"

"No, that's okay," Archie said. He rose, went to the refrigerator, looked into it, and then said, "She drank all my orange juice." He took out a container of milk and a wrapped slab of butter and carried them to the table. He went to the counter for the sugar bowl and took a pair of teaspoons and a butter knife from the drawer under the counter. Then both men sat at the table.

"I got to be getting back to work soon," Archie said. "Those four bills are the last of it."

"Yeah," Alex said.

"I'm just like you," Archie said. "I make a score, I get lazy. Won't go back to work till it's all gone."

"Yeah, but I stash *my* money in the *bank*," Alex said, "not in the coffee pot."

"I don't trust banks," Archie said. "Man, this toast is plain *burnt*."

"You said it was okay."

"That was before I tried eating it. How long's it been raining out there?"

"All morning," Alex said.

"What's a man supposed to *do* on a day like today?" Archie asked, and stared glumly at the rain falling steadily outside the kitchen window.

They went to see a mixed-doubles skin flick and then wandered up Amsterdam Avenue. It was still raining but not as heavily. Crowded under the black umbrella, they sloshed along the wet sidewalks until they found a bar serving lunch. It was almost three o'clock. The roast beef was all gone, but there was some good lean pastrami left, and they both ordered that on rye, and a schooner of beer for each of them, and a side of French fries. The place was quiet except for the baseball drone of the television set and the occasional critical comments of a handful of black men lining the bar.

Daisy came into the bar at about ten minutes past three. She was a light-skinned black girl with only one leg, but a good body otherwise, and a narrow Egyptian-looking face with a natural beauty spot just to the left of her wide mouth. Her face was almost unlined, her complexion clear; the years had been good to her, considering she'd been a hooker since she was sixteen.

She spotted them where they were sitting in a red leatherette booth and hobbled over to them on her crutches. She was wearing rain-speckled sunglasses and a yellow rainslicker. She took off the slicker and hung it on a hook on the booth post. Under the slicker, she was dressed for work—a lavender satin sheath cut low over her full breasts, nothing under it. On her one shapely leg, she was wearing a high-heeled patent leather pump with an ankle strap. Sitting, complaining about the weather, she took off the sunglasses and wiped them clean on a paper napkin. Her eyes were narrow and long, slightly tilted, amber colored. She dipped into the platter of French fries and then added salt to them, without asking Archie or Alex if that would be okay. Nibbling on the fries, she told them she was anticipating a busy day because of the rain. Rain always brought the johns out in droves. And wherever there were johns, there was a big demand for Daisy. She couldn't understand her own popularity.

"I ain't a young kid anymore," she said. "Fact is, I'll be thirty-six come Christmas, week before Christmas. There are girls on the street, eighteen, nineteen years old, they just been turned out, they're pretty as pictures. So it ain't my youth or my beauty, that's for sure."

"Then what is it?" Archie asked.

"You know what I think it is?" Daisy asked.

"What?" Alex said. He was really interested. He knew she made more money than half the whores in Harlem, and he'd often wondered why.

"I think it's the leg," Daisy said. "It's got to be the leg. A john sees me hoppin around on my crutches, he right away thinks I'm vulnable. He takes one look at me, he figures when he gets me in the sack he's gonna be in complete control. I don't do what he wants me to do, he'll take away my crutches and throw me out the window. I'm not talking about your freaks now, I'm talking about your everyday johns. Most johns, they're afraid of whores, anyway—well, shit, they're afraid of *women*, period, which is why they *go* to whores in the first place. I ain't got but this one good leg, and that makes them think *I'm* the weak one, and *they're* the big strong studs, and that's what it is. My vulnability."

"Well, maybe so," Archie said.

"I don't think that's the *only* reason men go to whores," Alex said. "Because they're afraid of women, I mean."

"That's what it is, they can't make it nohow with square broads." Daisy said.

"No, some of them just go, I think, because a whore is supposed to be a pro, he can expect like a good blowjob from her, or whatever. That's what I think."

"I got me one john," Daisy said, "all I got to do is lift my skirt and show him the stump, he gets his rocks off."

"Now *that's* a freak, man," Archie said.

"No, that don't happen to be no freak," Daisy said. "I got

lots of them like that, though not all as fast as him. This little ole stump drives them crazy, I don't know what it is."

"They're stump-humpers, that's what it is," Archie said, and laughed.

"I got me another john," Daisy said, "he's a millionaire, he could afford the most expensive call girls, the racehorses. Instead, he phones me from Westchester once a week like clockwork. Every Thursday morning, he phones me. That's when his wife goes in the city shopping. The minute I get his call, I hop in a taxi and go up there to Post Mills."

"May be his wife is out humping a *man* with a stump," Alex said, trying to top Archie's joke, and looking to him for approval.

"You should see the way this cat is hung." Daisy said. "He's sixty-four years old, but I swear to God he's hung like a stallion."

"Well, a man's size has nothing to do with it," Alex said. "I read a book about that."

"The book was full of shit," Daisy said flatly.

"Alex here has just this tiny little pecker," Archie said confidentially, and held up his thumb and forefinger with an inch of space between them.

"Yeah, yeah," Alex said, and laughed.

"Every Thursday," Daisy said, "just like clockwork. He gives me a hundred bucks, plus the round-trip cab fare. You should see this place he's got out there. It's right on a big lake, you should see it."

"Where'd you say it was?" Archie asked.

"Post Mills."

"Where the hell is Post Mills?"

"I told you. Up in Westchester. Near Stamford."

"Stamford's in *Connecticut*," Archie said.

"Yeah, this is right over the border. The New York border.

It's Westchester, Archie, I *know* what the fuck it is, it's Westchester."

"Okay, it's Westchester."

"Two tennis courts, a swimming pool, big black Caddy sittin in the driveway. Another car, too, one of them small foreign jobs. I don't know the name of it."

"A Volkswagen?" Archie asked, and winked at Alex.

"No, what kind of Volkswagen? It's one of those expensive little foreign cars. I figure there must be yet another car, too, otherwise how does his wife get in the city? I asked him once, I said would he like a one-legged live-in maid cause I'd be willing to service him three, four times a week just for the sheer pleasure of *living* in a place like that. He told me No, he didn't think his wife would understand. Man's a millionaire, got five in help as it is, all of them off on Thursdays." In a deep, cotton-picking, watermelon accent, she said. "Tha's cause Thusdee's when he plumbs dee depps oh mah soul," and suddenly burst out laughing.

"What's the inside of the house like?" Archie asked, and Alex turned to look at him because his tone had suddenly become very serious and very professional.

"I never been in the house," Daisy said.

"Well, where do you make it?" Archie asked.

"He's got a studio in the woods behind the house. Way back in the woods. That's where we go. You should see this place. Arch. I'm not kiddin you, the man's a genuine millionaire."

"What's his name?" Archie asked.

"Well, now, I can't go givin you the name of a customer," Daisy said.

"What the hell *are* you, a priest?" Archie asked.

"It ain't professional," Daisy said with dignity.

"Man's a millionaire, huh?" Archie said.

"That he is."

"Pays your round-trip cab fare and hands you a C-note every Thursday," Archie said. The tone of his voice had changed to one of mocking disbelief. Alex suddenly realized he was trying to taunt Daisy into giving him the man's name. "Got tennis courts and a swimming pool, a studio way back in the woods, a yacht . . . you *did* say a yacht, didn't you, Daisy?"

"No, I didn't say no yacht, but he's got a big speedboat, sure enough, sittin right there on the end of a private dock."

"Bet it's a *big* dock, too," Archie said. "How big would you say his dock is?" He extended his arms wide. "*This* big, Daisy? How big *is* the man's dock, Daisy?"

"Bigger'n yours, that's for sure," she said, and reached for her crutches where they were leaning against the side of the booth.

"So what's this big millionaire's name?" Archie asked again.

"His name is none of your business," Daisy said, and raised herself up from the seat, and tucked her crutches under her arms. In stony silence, she put on the rainslicker, dexterously shifting the crutches as she worked her arms into the sleeves. Then she hobbled to the bar, and said to the bartender, "You ought to throw those bums out. They got no fuckin manners."

As she went out the front door, Archie said, "I blew it."

"You leaned too heavy, man. You only got her sore."

"Yeah. A hooker with ethics, would you believe it?"

"You think she was telling the truth?"

"Who knows? The other stuff was straight goods, I know that for sure. They come runnin after her like she was in heat. But a millionaire in Post Mills?" Archie shrugged.

"Whyn't you find out?" Alex said.

"Oh, I intend to, man," Archie said. "Be the goddamnedest score ever, wouldn't it?"

"How do you mean?"

"Ripping off a joint while a sixty-four-year-old man is out in the woods fuckin a one-legged whore?"

They both burst out laughing.

Alex got back to his building on West End Avenue at eight o'clock that night. He had gone to another movie with Archie, and then they'd eaten together in a cafeteria on Broadway. All he wanted to do now was get in bed and watch some television, maybe drift off to sleep by ten o'-clock or so. He planned to go into the lobby again tomorrow, provided it was a good day, and he wanted to be fresh and alert. He hadn't been seen by anyone but a tenant so far, and that was the way he wanted to keep it. If it became absolutely necessary to be seen going in on the day of the burglary, he wanted that to be the one and *only* time he was seen.

Detective Second-Grade Anthony Hawkins was waiting outside the building. He was considerably far uptown, his precinct territory covering the streets from Fourteenth to Thirty-ninth, between Fifth Avenue and the East River. Hawkins was a dark, burly six-footer who enjoyed his nickname "the Hawk," even when it was used derogatorily by thieves. That was because Hawkins thought he looked like Burt Reynolds, which he didn't. But Reynolds had once starred in a short-lived television series called *Hawk*, which happened to be about a New York City detective. The detective in the series was supposed to be an Indian, and Hawkins was half-English, half-Irish ("With a fifth of Scotch thrown in," as he was fond of remarking), but that didn't stop him from enjoying the fact that a television series had been named after a New York cop called Hawk. When Burt Reynolds grew a mustache, Anthony Hawkins grew one, too. When Burt Reynolds shaved it off, Hawkins shaved his off. If Burt Reynolds ever developed an ulcer, Hawkins would probably try to do the same. Hawkins was an asshole. He also happened to have busted Alex the time he got sent to Sing Sing. He was wearing a belted trench coat, which probably made him feel more like a working dick. He was also standing in the rain; leave it to cops not to know when to come in out of the rain.

"Hello there, Alex," he said cheerfully.

"Why, hello, Mr. Hawkins," Alex said.

"How you been?" Hawkins said, but he did not extend his hand. A cop never shook hands with a thief, even though he sometimes knew the thief better than he knew his own brother-in-law. And a cop always used a thief's first name, thought it gave him a psychological advantage somehow. If a cop picked up a thief who had just planned and executed a brilliant burglary of Fort Knox, and the thief's name was Israel Goldberg, the cop would automatically say, "All right, Izzie, you want to tell us about it?" If Izzie was a smart thief, he would mister and sir the cop to death, and tell him nothing at all. It was all part of the game.

"Come on in out of the rain," Alex said cordially. "Were you waiting here for me?"

"I was," Hawkins said.

"Been waiting long?"

"Just a half-hour or so."

"Well, come on inside the building," Alex said. "Long time no see."

They walked into the lobby, and Alex closed his umbrella and shook it out. Hawkins watched him all this time. Detectives liked to believe they could tell what a man was thinking by watching every move he made, even if he was only shaking out his umbrella or picking his nose. Alex took his time shaking out the umbrella, and Hawkins watched every little shake. At last, Alex looked up at him and said, "So what brings you uptown?"

"I have an abiding interest in you and your friends," Hawkins said, and smiled. He thought he looked more like Burt Reynolds when he smiled. Actually, he looked somewhat ghoulish. Hawkins's chilly smile was also part of the game. Alex sometimes thought he'd quit the game altogether if it weren't for the cops. What good was any game, after all, if there weren't players on the other side?

"Well, what's your interest this time?" he asked.

"I'm primarily interest in a burglary that took place on March 21," Hawkins said.

"Um-huh," Alex said.

"I don't suppose you'd know anything about it."

"Nothing at all," Alex said.

"I wouldn't be too interested if it hadn't taken place in my precinct," Hawkins said. "I was away on vacation at the time. Took the wife down to Puerto Rico."

"It's nice down there in Puerto Rico," Alex said.

"I was gone for three weeks," Hawkins said. "Got back yesterday, had a long talk with the detective who caught the squeal. He's new on the squad, just got transferred from the Two-Five up in Spanish Harlem. I also talked to the Burglary Squad."

"Um-huh," Alex said.

"The reason I'm asking *you* about it, Alex, is that it looks a lot like your m.o."

"I didn't know I had a distinctive m.o.," Alex said.

"The broken window, I mean."

"I haven't gone through a window since I was a kid," Alex said.

"That's the point. The window was broken from the *inside*, Alex. Somebody was trying to make it look like an amateur did it."

"Well, I'm clean," Alex said, "you're barking up . . ." and suddenly stopped talking because the elevator doors behind them opened, and a couple stepped out into the lobby. This was where Alex lived, he didn't want any of the tenants to know he was talking to a cop. "Look, would you like to come upstairs?" he asked Hawkins.

"What for?" Hawkins answered.

Alex shrugged and grimaced, hoping Hawkins would get his meaning. But as the couple paused to open an umbrella just inside the entrance doors, Hawkins said, rather loudly, "Oh, don't you want your neighbors to know you're a thief?"

Alex's eyes hardened. He looked toward the entrance alcove. The couple seemed not to have heard Hawkins. As soon as they stepped out into the rain, Alex said, "What's the matter with you? I'm trying to lead a respectable life here."

"Sure, you are. Were you leading a respectable life on March 21, when an apartment on East Thirty-Sixth was burglarized?"

"I don't know anything about that burglary."

"132 East Thirty-sixth," Hawkins said.

"I don't know that address."

"It's a brownstone."

"I don't know anything about it."

"The front door was jimmied, and an inside lock was picked. And then the bedroom window was smashed from the *inside*, to make it look crude. That's exactly what you did the time I busted you, Alex. You smashed a window from the inside."

"Yeah, but I learned my lesson," Alex said. "I've been clean ever since I got out. I won't even go *near* anybody I know is in it."

"No? Not even Tommy Palumbo?"

"What about him? He's clean, too."

"Have you seen him since he got paroled?"

"I've seen him, yeah. He's a friend of mine. Of course, I've seen him."

"I hear he's looking to buy a piece."

"I ain't heard nothing like that."

"When you see him again, tell him we know he's looking for one."

"I'll tell him."

"Tell him that's a parole violation all by itself."

"I'm sure he knows that, he ain't stupid."

"You're *all* stupid," Hawkins said flatly.

"Look, I didn't do your Thirty-sixth Street job, so what else do you want?"

"I want you to know I'm back from vacation, that's all. Sleep tight," Hawkins said, and flashed his Burt Reynolds smile, and walked out into the rain.

You son of a bitch, Alex thought, and stabbed at the elevator call button. What am I, the only burglar in New York who smashes a window from the inside? All right, I *done* the job, it was a job Vito set up, I scored three thousand bucks on that job, but suppose I *hadn't* done it? That's the thing we're talking about here, the fact that you come around whenever *any*body does *any*thing, you son of a bitch. No wonder you ain't been around lately, you've been on vacation. I wish some spic would've put a bullet in your head while you were down in Puerto Rico. Stay out of my way, Hawkins, he thought, or you're gonna be sorry.

But he was frightened.

*   *   *

When he got upstairs to his apartment, he took a bottle of beer from the refrigerator, opened it, and then carried it into the bedroom. His phone was on a night table near the bed. He dialed Tommy's number, and then drank directly from the bottle while he waited for him to answer. He let it ring ten times and was about to hang up, when he heard Tommy's voice say, "Hello?"

"Tommy, this is Alex."

"Hey, hi, Alex, how's it going?" Tommy said.

"Fine. I just got a visit from the Hawk."

"What's he want?"

"Tommy, now listen to me," Alex said.

"Yeah, what's the matter?"

"I been hearing around that you're looking for a piece, and I ain't the only one's heard it. The Hawk know about it, too."

"Yeah," Tommy said.

"Tommy, I think you know what that means. A man doesn't buy a gun unless . . ."

"I haven't bought no gun, Alex."

"But you're looking for one."

"Well."

"*Are* you looking for one, or not?"

"It was just an idea," Tommy said.

"An idea the Hawk already heard about."

"Yeah, but I didn't *buy* no gun, Alex. Just an idea."

"A man has an idea of buying a gun, then he's also got the idea of using it. And if he uses it for what I think, that means he's got to show face, and that also means the Hawk'll be on your doorstep in ten minutes flat."

"Yeah," Tommy said.

"Why don't you take an ad in the newspaper, for Christ's

sake? Is there anybody in this city who *doesn't* know you've
been looking for a piece?"

"Yeah," Tommy said.

"Now listen, Tommy, you put me onto a good thing, and I
think that's worth five bills, but I can't pay you till I deliver,
you understand me? I'm a little short right now, I won't have
the bread till this weekend sometime. What I'm trying to tell
you is not to do anything stupid meanwhile. The five bills
ought to tide you over for a while till you think of something
to do. Something that don't need a piece."

"Yeah," Tommy said.

"You listening to me?"

"Yeah, Alex, I'm listening."

"Okay then, I just wanted you to know you've got five
bills coming if you can hold out till the weekend."

"Oh, yeah, I can hold out. I ain't desperate, Alex."

"Good, I'm glad to hear that. All right then, Tommy?"

"Yeah, fine."

"All right?"

"Yeah."

"Okay then, I'll call you Friday, Saturday the latest."

"Right, Alex. Thanks a lot, huh?"

"So long now."

He put the receiver back onto the cradle, lifted the bottle
of beer, and took a long swallow of it. He didn't know why
the hell he bothered with that dumb kid. Man gets started
with a gun, that's the way it's going to be forever. Tommy
was only twenty-two, but he'd already been busted once for
armed robbery, when he was just eighteen. He'd come up
against a judge who'd let him off with a dime stretch at Sing
Sing, and he'd got out last month on parole, after serving a
third of the sentence. Alex had met him in prison, the kid had
already been there for three, four months when Alex drove

up. Alex was scared. He had never been to prison before; the last time he'd been busted he'd got off with a suspended sentence. But he'd heard about prison, and he knew what could happen to a man inside there. He was younger then, this was three years ago, and he knew he was a good-looking blue-eyed kid with blond hair, and he'd heard all about prison gang-rapes, and he was scared to death something like that might happen to him. He figured later that it didn't happen to him only because of Tommy.

Tommy had been there a little while already, and he was handsome and dark and slight, but nobody had succeeded in turning him out as a penitentiary punk. In prison you had a whole sexual hierarchy, starting with your queens, who were what they called free-world punks, guys who'd been queer even before they got sent up. These guys—or *girls*, as they preferred to call themselves—were usually kept apart from the rest of the prison population, segregated in the punk tank with other queens and guys who'd been sent up for sexual offenses. But you also had your penitentiary punks, who were guys who got turned out while they were in prison. And you had your studs, or your jocks, or your daddies, as they were called, and they looked over every new guy coming into the yard, and before long they'd come over and try to be friendly, offer candy or cigarettes, sound the new man as to the possibility of a relationship. These were guys who considered themselves he-men; if you ever told one of them he was engaging in homosexual acts, he'd slit your throat. That's because he was the one *doing* it to some other guy, fuckin the other guy in the ass or getting sucked off.

But one of the first people Alex met in prison was Tommy, and Tommy told him straight off that there'd be a lot of advances made, him being blond and good-looking and young, but that he didn't have to do nothing he didn't *want* to do; if he once showed these guys he was weak, that was it, mister. He knew one guy, Tommy said, they threw him down on the floor in the gym while somebody was posted as jigger, and they painted the outline of a woman on his back, tits and all, and then a dozen of them fucked him in the ass. That didn't happen too often here, Tommy said, that gang-rape kind of thing. Where that happened mostly was in the county jails or temporary detention centers, where if you happened to be a young kid thrown in with a bunch of hardened criminals, they'd hold a knife on you or burn you all over with cigarettes till you did what they said. It happened here sometimes, of course, but not so you'd have to worry about it day and night. What you had to worry about here were the studs.

The thing to do, Tommy said, was to turn down any kind of offer that was made. Guy offers you a pack of cigarettes till you get some money of your own together, you just tell him Thanks a lot, I'll smoke the Bugler. Guy wants to lend you money, or offer you protection against some of the hard cases in here, you tell him Thanks a lot, I can take care of myself. And, man, you just make sure you *do* take care of yourself. Guy wants to turn you out, you fight him. You may end up in the shitter for a week, but at least that guy'll respect you from then on, and nobody else'll come around trying to get you to suck his dick. And if a *bunch* of them tries to get you, then you have to fight like a son of a bitch till they know you ain't going to let nobody turn you out. Poke them in the eyes, ram your fist in their Adam's apple, they ain't going to risk too much of *that*, man, not when there are other guys who'll go along without a struggle.

He had followed Tommy's advice the first time anybody approached him. The guy was twelve feet tall and a yard wide, and he was a three-time loser who figured if you couldn't have whiskey you might as well have a little taste of the wine. Alex wasn't about to become his bottle of Chianti, though, and when the guy came up to him and very subtly said, "Hey, kid, how'd you like to suck my joint?" Alex replied, "How'd you like to suck mine?" The lifer got rough then, he threw Alex up against the wall, clamped his hand around Alex's throat, and said, "You do what I tell you, punk, or there'll be *fifty* of us on your ass." Alex kneed him in the balls, and when the guy doubled over, he hit him on the back of the neck with both hands clenched together like a mallet. And then, while the guy was writhing around on the floor, Alex kicked him in the side of the head. He got a month in the shitter for assaulting the lifer, and that was what stopped him from getting his parole after having served a third of his three years. But that was the end of anybody sounding him, and when his parole came up later for review, it was granted. The lifer had cost him an extra six months behind the walls, but at least when he got out he was the same as when he'd been driven up.

During his eighteen months in prison, he and Tommy got to be good friends, such good friends in fact that there were prison rumors about them, everybody trying to figure out whether or not they had a little thing going. Alex guessed that maybe forty percent of the guys up there were involved in one kind of sexual activity or another, either giving it or taking it, and the other sixty percent spent half their time talking about who was doing what to whom. But he and Tommy were just good friends, that was all. They weren't even cellmates, though they could have arranged that for a couple of bucks in the right hands. They decided against it because that only would have intensified the rumors and neither one of them wanted to end up in the punk tank with the free-world queers and the short eyes. But in the yard they talked, and in the dining hall they talked, and mostly they talked about what they'd do once they got outside again. Once they got out, what they were going to do was pull out completely, find a nine-to-five, join the world of the worka-day squares, the hell with this prison shit.

Yeah.

He knew now that what you did when you got out was go right back to what you'd *been* doing. He'd gone back to being a burglar, and now Tommy was looking to buy a piece, and probably *would* buy a piece, and then go hold up a liquor store or something. He didn't know what was wrong with Tommy, he didn't seem to be the same guy Alex had known in prison. Maybe one of the jocks had finally succeeded in turning him out, who the hell knew? You spent enough time in prison, maybe you got tired. Maybe you just got tired of trying to be somebody *else* all the time. You could hardly ever be yourself in prison, that was the thing of it. And maybe after Alex had got out, and Tommy was up there all by himself with nobody to talk to honestly and openly, no chance to be *himself* anymore, then maybe one of the studs got to him, maybe that was it. If you ain't going to be *your-self*, then you might just as well be somebody else's boy. Alex didn't know what it was. Tommy just seemed *dead* nowadays . . . no, wait a minute, he seemed more like he was in mourning, yeah, for somebody very close to him who'd died. Damn kid . . .

The telephone rang.

Alex was sitting on the bed right beside the phone, and when it went off he jumped half a mile. Swearing under his breath, he lifted the receiver and said, "Hello?"

"Alex?"

He recognized the voice at once, he didn't think he'd ever forget her voice as long as he lived. He was glad to hear from her, but at the same time he didn't want any part of her anymore.

"What is it, Kitty?" he asked.

"I need help," she said. "Can I come there?"

"No," he said.

"Alex, I really do need help," she said. "Please."

"No, I don't want you here," he said.

"I'm coming, anyway," she said, and hung up.

She rang the bell downstairs in the lobby at nine o'clock, and he didn't answer the ring, but he knew that wouldn't stop her. Five minutes later, she was outside banging on his door. He went to the door and opened it, and said, "I told you not to come here."

"Well, I'm here," she said, and stepped past him into the apartment. It was still raining outside, her coat was soaking wet. She took off the coat and hung it familiarly in the hall closet. Under the coat she was wearing a short, narrow skirt and a white blouse. She took off her pumps, left them in the foyer, and then walked directly into the living room and to the bar, where she poured herself two fingers of his Scotch.

"Make yourself at home," he said.

She didn't answer. He watched her as she drank the whiskey neat and poured herself another shot. She didn't seem at all strung out, he wondered what she wanted from him, if not money for a fix. But she looked as if she'd been taking very good care of herself, looked in fact a great deal prettier than she had when they'd been living together. She had let her hair grow out in an Afro, and somehow the style emphasized the good bones of her face, the thin, flaring nose, the high, padded cheekbones, the generous mouth. She was wearing no makeup except for a greenish-blue eye shadow over her eyes. Her complexion was smooth, the color of walnut, warm and rich and glowing in the light of the floor lamp near the bar. She carried the second drink to the couch, sat, and crossed her legs.

"So," she said, smiling, "how are you?"

"Fine."

"Man of few words," she said.

"What do you want, Kitty?"

"Money," she said.

"Forget it."

"Not for what you think. Not for dope."

"Whatever you need it for, I haven't got it."

"You don't believe me, do you?" she asked.

"Should I? Six months ago you were shooting a hundred dollars a day."

"I've kicked it," she said flatly.

"Good. I still haven't got any money to give you."

"All I want is a loan."

"Go to the shys."

"That'll only get me in deeper. You *know* that, Alex."

"Kitty, I don't *care* how deep you're in, or how deep you're gonna *get* in. That's *your* business."

"You want me to get hurt, man?"

"I don't care what happens to you."

"That's not true," she said.

"It's true."

"What are *you* so sore about?" she asked. "You're the one kicked *me* out, remember?"

"Only because you lied to me."

"I didn't lie to you. You never asked me was I doing smack, and I never told you. Anyway, what's that got to do with here and now? I'm off it, I just told you that."

"Sure," he said.

"I need two thousand dollars, Alex. I need it right away, or there's somebody going to hurt me very bad. Now that's the story, Alex. If we ever meant anything to each other . . ."

"Kitty, you are hot stuff," he said, and shook his head. "You are really the cat's ass."

"I'm in very heavy trouble," she said. "I took two thousand dollars from a john's wallet, and it turns out I shouldn't have done that. He's not the kind of man anybody should take two thousand dollars from his wallet. He wants it back."

"So give it to him."

"I can't. It's gone."

"Who's got it? Your pimp?"

"I'm not working with a pimp."

"Then where's the money?"

"I spent it."

"Who's the man?"

"His name is Jerry Di Santis. He runs a numbers bank in East Harlem."

"Smart. Very smart, Kitty."

"I didn't know *what* he was, he seemed like a square john. I was working the Algonquin, he picked me up in the bar. This was Saturday night. I waited till he was asleep, and then I . . ."

"Saturday night? You mean to tell me you've spent two thousand bucks since Saturday?"

"Sure," Kitty said simply. "Alex, please, huh? This man isn't kidding around, he's been searching for me ever since I ran out with his money. He had a pair of gorillas with him today, they both looked like Sonny Liston, only white."

"I don't have two thousand dollars to give you," Alex said.

"You scored last month," she said. "Vito told me you scored for three grand just last month."

"Vito ought to learn to keep his mouth shut."

"He thought we were still living together, don't blame it on Vito. He mentioned it casual, asked how I liked that three-grand score you made."

"That's gone already," Alex said. "I've got a hundred and fifty bucks in my wallet, and that's it."

"Alex, don't lie to me. This man is going to do terrible things if I don't come up with his money."

"I told you. Go to the shys."

"If I once get into them for money, the next thing you know they'll have me in a Hoboken whorehouse turning five-dollar tricks."

"Tough," Alex said.

"When will you be working again?" she asked suddenly.

"That's none of your business."

"It's got to be soon. If you're down to only a hundred and fifty bucks, it's got to be soon. I know you, Alex, I lived with you too long. When are you going out again?"

He did not answer her.

"Alex," she said, "is there at least a *chance* you can help me before Saturday?"

Again he did not answer.

"Okay," she said, and rose from the couch. "You told me what I want to know, I'll be back tomorrow, Alex."

"I won't be here."

"I'll come, anyway. And if I don't catch you tomorrow, I'll be back on Thursday. And again on Friday."

"I'll be out of town," he said.

"Alex," she said, "we used to love each other."

"We don't anymore," he said.

"Don't we? The man said he'd throw acid in my face, Alex. You want the man to do that?"

"Kitty . . ."

"I'll be back tomorrow," she said.

"Tomorrow won't do you any good," he told her.

"Then when?"

He wanted to say Never. He wanted to say Kitty, leave me alone, it's over and done with, I don't owe you anything, least of all two thousand dollars.

"When, Alex?" she asked.

"I must be out of my fuckin mind," he said.

"When will you have the money, Alex? Will you have it by Friday?"

"Maybe," he said.

"Alex, tell me yes or no. Please. If I can't count on you, I've got to start running. I've got to run to China, if that's far enough."

"I'll have the money for you Friday," he said.

"Thank you," she said softly, and went to him, and put her arms around his neck, and gently pressed her body against his.

"Now get out of here," he said.

"You don't want to?" she said.

"No."

"It doesn't feel that way," she said.

"That's my wallet."

"You afraid of me?" she asked.

"Yes."

"Why? You didn't used to be afraid of me."

"I am now. Get out of here, Kitty. I'll have the money for you Friday. I want it back in a week, I don't care if you have to roll drunken sailors to get it."

She lowered her arms, smiled, and then went out to the foyer, where she put on her shoes and her coat. "You sure?" she asked.

"Just go," he said.

*   *   *

In the morning, he was sorry he'd told Kitty she could have the money. All the while he shaved, he worried about it. It only made sense that if she didn't have the money to pay the numbers racketeer, then she wouldn't have it to pay *him*, either. In fact, she'd probably spent the two grand on junk, probably rounded up all her junkie friends and had a gay old time shooting up round the clock. So now he was about to hand her *another* two grand, which she'd probably spend the same way, and the numbers racketeer *still* wouldn't get his money back, and she'd *still* be in trouble, only now Alex would be out two grand as well. He'd been out of his mind, he should have kicked her out the way he'd done six months ago.

The day was sunny and bright, at least that much was going for him. He was on the corner of Sixty-ninth and Madison by nine-thirty. The mailman arrived at nine-forty-five, and as soon as he was gone, Alex walked up to the coffee shop on Seventieth. He ordered a grapefruit juice and a cup of coffee, drank both, and then went to the phone booth and called the Rothman apartment. It was five past ten. The maid answered the telephone.

"Hello, may I speak to Mrs. Rothman, please?" he asked.

"She just went down," the maid said.

"Do you know when she'll be back?"

"A little past twelve."

"I'll call her then. Thank you," he said, and hung up.

He paid for the juice and coffee, and then walked down to Sixty-ninth again. The doorman was standing under the awning, his hands on his hips, watching a woman trying to park a Benz across the street. It was twelve minutes past ten, and Alex wanted to check the mailboxes, but he didn't want to be seen by either the doorman or the elevator operator. He walked to the building, and knelt to tie his shoelace just out-side the entrance doors. Inside the lobby, he could see women coming out of the elevators and going directly to the mailboxes. They knew what time the mailman came, rain or shine, hail or sleet, and they wanted to get down there as soon as possible to see what he had brought.

Alex was interested only in finding out what Mrs. Roth-man's habit was. Did she pick up the mail when she *left* the apartment at ten, or did she pick it up when she *returned* at noon? It wasn't imperative that he know this, but it could be helpful tomorrow morning, especially if she normally picked it up at ten. It never hurt to double-check. Suppose he called the apartment tomorrow and got no answer only because Mrs. Rothman was in the shower and couldn't hear the phone? So he'd go upstairs and find a sixty-one-year-old lady with a towel wrapped around her. On the other hand, if he called and got no answer, and *then* checked the lobby mailbox and found she'd already picked up her mail, then he could be relatively certain she was out of the apartment as she was supposed to be. Percentages. You tried to weigh them in your favor. He moved away from the building, walked halfway down the street, and then looked back. Old Fat Ass was still at the curb. Alex sighed, walked all the way to Park Avenue, and then started back toward the building again, wondering how he could get the doorman away from those entrance doors.

He didn't like this.

On Monday morning, the doorman had been pretty active running after taxicabs, and that had been a sunny day like today. Alex discounted yesterday's activity because it had been raining. But it occurred to him that on Monday most of the cab chasing had taken place between nine and nine-thirty. He should have stuck around longer, instead of running off shortly after the mailman arrived. Because if this was *normal*, if all the doorman had to do between ten and twelve was hang around outside watching the street, Alex would be in trouble tomorrow morning.

He walked past the building again, behind the doorman, who was standing at the curb. The lobby phone was ringing as he went by, and the doorman hurried into the building to answer it. Alex stationed himself on Madison Avenue and watched the entrance doors. The doorman came out a moment later, crossed directly to a parking garage across the street, and then hurried down the ramp. Alex debated making his move, and decided it had better be now or never. He did not know how long the doorman would be over there, but he had to chance getting into the lobby. He looked at his watch. It was ten-twenty.

He walked immediately to the building and into the lobby. At the elevator bank, he paused to look up at the floor indicator. The elevator was on the twelfth floor and, as he watched the illuminated bar, the numeral 11 flashed, and then the numeral 10 . The elevator was on the way down and would be in the lobby within seconds. Alex stepped quickly into the alcove containing the mailboxes. He knew the Rothmans were in Apartment 16A, and he quickly found the box. There was no mail in it.

He was starting out of the lobby when the elevator doors opened. He did not break his stride, he continued walking toward the entrance doors, but he could feel the elevator operator's eyes on him, and he knew he would be challenged.

"Help you, sir?" the elevator operator said behind him.

Alex turned with a look of surprise on his face. The elevator operator was a redheaded man with shaving nicks on his chin and cheeks. He was short and squat and ugly and suspicious. His right hand kept twitching at his side as he walked toward Alex, almost as if he were longing to draw a nonexistent six-shooter from a holster.

"Where's the doorman?" he asked Alex.

"I have no idea," Alex said.

The elevator operator peered out into the street, as though suspecting Alex had done something to the doorman. Turning back to Alex, he said, "Were you looking for someone, sir?" The "sir" was his insurance. If Alex had legitimate business in the building, the elevator operator could then apologize all to hell, explaining that one couldn't be too careful these days, sir.

"Yes, as a matter of fact I am," Alex said. "I checked the mailboxes, but maybe you can help me." He reached into his coat pocket and took out a scrap of paper upon which he had scrawled a name and address before leaving his apartment this morning. He had chosen the name at random from the telephone book. The address was the address of this building—except that it was on East Sixty-*eighth*, a block further downtown. He showed the scrap of paper to the elevator operator.

"No Ralph Peabody in this building," the elevator operator said, and then saw the address. "Anyway, you're too far uptown. That's Sixty-*eighth* you're looking for."

"Isn't this Sixty-eighth?" Alex asked.

"This is Sixty-ninth."

"Thank you," Alex said, and took back the scrap of paper. Shaking his head, he walked out of the building. Across the street, the doorman was driving a '73 Cadillac up from the garage. Alex looked at his watch. The time was ten-twenty-four. As Alex walked up the street to Madison Avenue, the doorman parked the Caddy in front of the building. Not two minutes later, an elderly man in a dark topcoat and a gray homburg came out of the building, followed by the doorman, who went around to the driver's side of the car and held the door open. The time was ten-twenty-six. Between then and eleven-fifty, the doorman did not move away from the entrance doors. Not once. At noon sharp, Alex was in the coffee-shop phone booth again, dialing the Rothman apartment. The maid answered the phone.

"Rothman residence," she said.

"Mrs. Rothman, please."

"She's not home. Who's calling, please?"

"I called a little while ago," Alex said. "You told me she'd be back by twelve."

"I said a little *past* twelve," the maid said.

"All right, I'll try again in a few minutes," Alex said, and hung up. At twelve-oh-three, he dialed the number again, and again the maid answered.

"Rothman residence," she said.

"Is Mrs. Rothman back yet?" he asked.

"Is this *you* again?" the maid said, and giggled.

"I'm anxious to talk to her," Alex said, "I'm sorry to keep bothering you this way."

"She should be back any minute," the maid said. "You want to leave your number, I'll ask her to call you. "

"No, I'll try again," Alex said. "Thank you."

At twelve-oh-seven, he dialed the apartment again. The maid recognized his voice this time. "Just a moment," she said, "I'll get her for you."

Alex waited.

"Hello?" a woman's voice said.

"Mrs. Rothman?"

"Yes?"

"This is Arthur Platt calling for the Association of Handi-

capped Workers. We're soliciting telephone orders for light
bulbs made by the handicapped . . ."

"No, I'm sorry." Mrs. Rothman said. "We have all the
light bulbs we need, thank you."

"You may order as few as you . . ."

"No, I'm sorry," she said, and hung up.

He knew all he had to know about the Rothmans now, but
he was still worried about that damn lobby. This didn't look
too simple anymore. In fact, it was beginning to look like a
bigger risk than he was ready to take. In fact, he began considering calling it off.

He had a lot of thinking to do.

Troubled, he headed uptown.

He caught a hot dog and a bottle of soda pop from a stand
on Broadway and then walked up to the park on Riverside
Drive. Sitting on a bench in the sunshine, he tried to work
out the percentages.

He was reasonably certain now that Mr. Rothman left the
apartment at nine each morning, and that Mrs. Rothman left
it at ten. The gambler had reported that Thursday was the
maid's day off, and Alex had no cause to doubt this; Thursday was the usual day off for maids everywhere. He would
have to make only one call tomorrow morning, to check on
whether the Rothmans had both left the apartment. Once he
got into the lobby, he would double-check at the mailbox. If
there was no mail in it, then he would go upstairs and make
the apartment, certain that it was empty.

The trouble, as he saw it, was getting into the damn lobby.
The lobby door was a cinch, and he didn't expect anything
tougher upstairs. But getting *into* the lobby, and *through* it to
the fire door—that was the problem. If the doorman stayed
glued to the entrance between ten and twelve . . .

Now, wait a minute, Alex thought.

At ten-twenty, the doorman had taken a call in the lobby and then rushed across the street to the garage. He'd come out of the garage driving a Caddy about five minutes later, and a few minutes after that a guy in a homburg had come downstairs and driven off. Now if this was a regular thing, if the guy in the homburg called the lobby *every* morning at twenty after, and told the doorman he was coming down in five minutes, to have his car ready for him, well that meant the doorman would be away from the front of the building for at least five minutes tomorrow morning, and that was plenty of time for Alex to get in and pick the lobby door. *If* this was a regular thing. But even if it was a regular thing, that meant Alex couldn't get into the building till ten-twenty, which cut the working time from two hours to only an hour and forty minutes, and that was cutting it *real* close.

He didn't know what to do.

If it turned out to be a Mickey Mouse box, hell, he could be in and out of the apartment in five minutes flat. But suppose it was something impossible? Damn it, if only he didn't need the money so bad, he'd . . .well, *what?* What else *could* he do? The maid didn't know what kind of box it was, Henry's gambler had pumped her about it, and all she could say was that it was a wall safe. Getting into the lobby was going to be tough as hell, anyway; there'd be no chance for a dry run on this job. Do your dry run, check out the box. If it was a ball-breaker, forget it, man. He wondered now if the job was worth it. He kept stacking a possible seven years against the nine grand he'd be getting. He just didn't know whether it was worth the risk.

An hour and forty minutes. To get in the lobby, pick the lobby door, climb sixteen flights of stairs to the Rothman apartment, open the door to the apartment—and who the hell knew what kind of lock he'd run into *there*—get inside, open the box, and get out before Mrs. Rothman came back at noon. Well, wait a minute, she didn't get back till about five *after* twelve this morning, that gave him an extra few minutes. But he wasn't planning on waiting till she was right outside the front door of the apartment. In fact, to play it perfectly safe, he'd like to be out of there by ten *to* twelve, five to at the very latest, just in case she decided to cut her walk short. So figure he got in the lobby at twenty past ten and out of the apartment at ten to twelve, that gave him only ninety minutes—it was getting better and better all the time. The hell with this job, he'd call Henry Green and tell him to shove his fuckin job. Let *Henry* go in there and make the place in ninety minutes. Still, he needed the money. If only he didn't need the money so bad . . .

"Hello there," a woman's voice said.

He looked up. The sun was behind her, he squinted up into it. It was Jessica Knowles, the blonde who lived in his building.

"Hi," he said.

"Taking the sunshine?" she asked.

"Yeah, it's too nice to waste," he said.

She was wearing white slacks and a green T-shirt, no bra under it. You couldn't tell Alex that anybody who walked around without a bra wasn't asking for something. Her kid was in the same canvas stroller he'd seen her pushing around in September, eating a sticky piece of chocolate. Alex couldn't tell whether it was a girl or a boy. Jessica sat beside him on the bench.

"How'd it go yesterday?" he asked.

"Who knows?" she said, and shrugged. "Getting a divorce is just like having a tooth pulled. Without anesthesia."

"Yeah," he said.

"How'd *your* day go?"

"Fine," he said.

"I've been wondering," she said. "Are you an actor?"

"What makes you think I'm an actor?"

"Well, you went to Lincoln Center."

"Oh."

"Of course, you could have been going there to buy tickets. But I see you around a lot during the day, so I naturally assumed . . .well, if you worked in an office . . . Are you an actor?"

"No," he said. He knew what she was going to ask next. With squares, the conversation always reached a point where you had to lie about what you did. He had once, with a girl in Miami, just for the hell of it said he was a burglar. The girl had laughed and said, "Sure."

"What *do* you do?" Jessica asked.

"You're pretty close," he said. "I'm not an actor, but I do theater work." He had never used this particular lie before, but she had helped him with it, in a way. Besides, it was only a half-lie; up at Sing Sing, he had helped hang the lights for one of the shows.

"I *knew* you were in the theater," she said, delighted with her perception, and inadvertently helping him with the lie by providing the proper terminology.

"Yes, I'm in the theater," he said, immediately picking up on the expression. "I'm an electrician."

"Do you work at Lincoln Center?"

"No. I was going there to see about a job."

"What shows *have* you worked on?" she asked.

"Oh, lots of them," he said.

"Any I might have seen?"

"Well, what have you seen?"

"My husband and I used to go to the theater at least once a week," she said. "When we were together."

"Then you must've seen at least one or two I worked on," he said, and wished to hell they could get off the subject.

"That must be interesting work," she said.

"Well, it's like any other job," he said.

"What I mean is, you get involved with a lot of creative people, I imagine."

"Oh, yes," he said.

"When you say you're an electrician . . ."

"I just hang the lights, that's all. And I have to be there, of course. When the show's on. See everything's all right, you know."

"Do you run the switchboard?"

"No. What there is, there's usually another man running the switchboard," he said, and thought Let's get the hell *off* this, okay? "What do *you* do?" he asked.

"Right now, nothing. Well, I shouldn't say that. Taking care of Peter and the house is a full-time job."

"How old is he?" Alex asked, looking at the boy, whose face and hands were smeared with chocolate.

"He's two."

"He looks a lot like you."

"Actually, he looks more like his father. He has his father's mouth."

"But he's got your eyes," Alex said.

"Well, his father's eyes are blue, too."

"So that's what you do," Alex said. "Take care of your son and the house."

"Yes, and run around trying to get a decent settlement from that cheap bastard I married. I'm a copyeditor, actually. That's what I *used* to do, anyway, before I got married. Prob-

ably what I'll go back to as soon as all this legal business is
out of the way."

"What is that, a copyeditor?" Alex asked. "Is that in advertising?"

"No, publishing. I check over an author's manuscript for
errors or contradictions, inconsistencies in spelling
or . . . well, that's simplifying it a lot. I also help in styling
the book, I don't mean typographically—a stylist does that—
though I will indicate where a poem in the text, for example,
should be centered on the longest line, and set in italics
rather than roman, or where a different typeface should be
used, though I won't pick the actual type, the stylist will do
that."

Alex didn't know what the hell she was talking about.
"Mm," he said.

"You'd be surprised how often a writer says that someone's eyes are blue on page four, and then on page six the
character will miraculously have green eyes. I'm supposed to
flag that for him—call it to his attention."

"That must be interesting work," Alex said, thinking it
sounded dull as shit.

"Yes, it is. I've worked with some very big writers. With
their manuscripts, I should say. I rarely got to meet the au-
thors personally."

"Mm," Alex said.

"So we're both sort of on the fringes." she said. "Of creative work, I mean."

"Yeah," he said.

"Offstage, so to speak," she said, and smiled.

"Yeah, offstage," he said, and returned the smile.

"No, Peter," she said, "don't eat that," and rose immediately from the bench. Taking her son's fist in her hand, she
pried loose the chocolate's foil wrapper. "He's at the age

where he tries to put everything in his mouth," she said. As she moved back to the bench, Alex glanced at her breasts. Seeming not to notice his gaze, she sat beside him again, and said, "Now *I'm* all covered with chocolate," and reached into her bag for a tissue.

"He must be a handful," Alex said.

"That he is," Jessica said. "I used to have a full-time housekeeper, but I had to get rid of her when Michael and I separated. He's been so damn *chintzy* about this divorce . . .Well, I won't bore you," she said.

"You're not boring me."

"It's just that he is absolutely a cheap penny-pinching bastard," she said. "He's supposed to send me five hundred a month until we iron this out, but he never sends the money when he's supposed to, I've always got to call him and practically beg for it. I'm trying to be decent about this whole thing, you know. I told my lawyers I don't want alimony, all I want is some kind of support money for my son. I can't work and take care of a child at the same time, I figured I'd use the support money to hire a sleep-in. That's reasonable, isn't it?"

"Sure it is," Alex said.

"But he's resisting every inch of the way. I don't think he can quite get it through his head that I just don't love him anymore. That's very hard for a man to understand. Especially a man like Michael."

"What kind of man is he?" Alex said.

"To be blunt, he's a prick," Jessica said.

Her language startled Alex. He did not expect square girls to talk like whores. Again, he glanced at her breasts, more openly this time. Maybe she wasn't quite as square as he thought she was. A square is a square, he reminded himself. Be careful.

"There," she said, crumpling the tissue and putting it back into her bag. "Every time Peter eats anything, *I'm* the one who has to take a bath afterward. Remarkable," she said, and smiled again. "Are *you* married?"

"No," he said.

"Ever been married?"

"Never."

"How old are you?" she asked.

"Twenty-five," he said.

"I'm twenty-nine," she said.

"I figured that's about how old you were."

"I sometimes feel like a hundred and two," she said.

"Come on," he said.

"I mean it. This whole business has been very debilitating. I haven't even been to a movie in the past three months, would you believe it?"

"Can't you get a sitter or something?" he asked.

"Oh, sure I can."

"Then why don't you?"

"I hate to go alone," she said, and he figured this was it, this was where he was supposed to say Well, how'd you like to go with *me* sometime?

"Yeah," he said. "It's rough for a woman going anyplace alone."

"Meals are especially difficult," she said. "Eating alone."

"Yeah, that can be rough," he said.

He really did feel some sympathy for her situation, but at the same time he was figuring what might be in it for *him*. Percentages; it always got down to percentages. The percentages looked attractive here, but he was nonetheless wary of making the move she was seemingly hoping he'd make. On the plus side was the fact that she was a good-looking woman, obviously lonely, and conveniently located. He had no doubt something could be developed here, if he wanted it to develop, but he wasn't sure it would be the same kind of thing *she* was looking for. That was the trouble with squares, they always seemed to be looking for things Alex didn't want or need. Another trouble was that if he got to know her better, go to know her in the only way he really *cared* to know her, which was in the sack, she would then begin to ask all sorts of questions about him, and the story he'd given her about being a theater electrician wouldn't hold water for a minute. Still, there were days when he missed having a woman around, not that this one would be around the way Kitty had been when she was living with him. Which was maybe an advantage, her being close enough to drop in on whenever he felt like it, but not so close that she'd get under-foot.

She took a cigarette from her bag and lit it. She was giving him plenty of time, she wasn't pushing him at all, he kind of liked her and respected her for that. The thing to do, he supposed, if he really wanted to move on the opening she'd given him, was ask her out for tonight. The trouble was that tomorrow was Thursday, and tomorrow was the day he had to make the Rothman apartment. He wanted to get a good night's sleep and be on his toes when he went into that lobby. There was no sense spending money on her if all it netted was a handshake outside her door. Hell with that noise. That was for high-school kids. Still, she was a damn good-looking woman, and she'd been on the wagon for a long time, hadn't even been to a *movie* in three months. This could be very choice goods.

"What are you doing Saturday night?" he asked.

She didn't hem or haw around, she didn't say, "Saturday, well let me see"; he respected her for that, too. "Nothing," she said, and smiled. "As usual."

"Maybe we could do something together," he said. He figured he'd have the money from Henry by tomorrow afternoon, Friday morning at the latest. Saturday would be a good night to go partying.

"Sure," she said.

"Okay?"

"Mm-huh," she said, and nodded.

"Well, good. You think you'll be able to get a sitter?"

"Yes, I'm sure I can."

"Okay then, maybe we can . . . You like Chinese food?"

"Mm-huh."

"Good," he said. "Let's say seven, seven-thirty, we'll eat and maybe go to a movie afterwards. Or else go back and listen to some records, if that's what we feel like doing. I've got a pretty good record collection. You like jazz?"

"Yes," she said.

"So we'll see what we feel like doing," he said.

"Okay," she said.

She was blushing. The goddamn girl was blushing.

The alarm went off at eight on Thursday morning, but he'd already been up since dawn, had in fact watched the sun coming up over the rooftops. It was going to be a good day. Mrs. Rothman would go down for her walk, and when she came back her precious ring, and maybe a few other things besides, would be gone. Looking forward to the job, he felt the first faint twinges of expectation. By noon today he would be richer by at least nine thousand dollars. The Rothmans would be poorer by a lot more than that, or course, but the Rothmans meant absolutely nothing to him. He conveniently thought of burglary as a victimless crime, thought of the ring and whatever other jewels might be in the box as things to be stolen, but not things to be stolen from *people*.

The jewels themselves were the victims in Alex's mind, not the Rothmans. He didn't know the Rothmans, and he didn't care about them. The jewels were probably insured, anyway, and only the insurance company would suffer a loss. Insurance companies were big business, and bigger thieves than Alex could ever hope to become.

As he showered and shaved, he didn't think about the job at all. That was a trick he'd learned when he was in high school and a test was coming up. He'd study for the test all afternoon, and then go to a movie that night, putting the test completely out of his mind. He thought of Jessica instead of the job, and wondered if he'd been smart asking her out for Saturday night. Kitty would be here tomorrow asking for the two grand he'd promised her, and then she'd probably run over to pay the man, and come back later full of gratitude— if he knew Kitty at all. Her gratitude might be so overwhelming, in fact, that she'd maybe decide to spend the entire weekend with him, expressing it all over the place. So why had he asked Jessica out, when Kitty was a sure thing and Jessica was a question mark and a square besides? He had not played the percentages properly, he had bet against the goddamn odds. A party with Kitty was something to remember, especially when she was feeling grateful about something. Once, when she was still living with him, he had ripped off an apartment and come back with a very good haul, including a pair of ruby earrings which he'd decided not to fence but had given to Kitty instead. She later sold them to get dope money, of course, but her gratitude that night had reached spectacular heights; there was nothing like a grateful whore.

Still, being balled by Kitty was something close to pulling off a job that had been set up. No surprises. She was a pro, she had her bag of tricks all put together, and the tricks were guaranteed to satisfy. But there never was any hope of accidentally stumbling upon that once-in-a-lifetime score, not with Kitty there wasn't. Well, maybe in the beginning there had been. Maybe, when he'd found himself *liking* this girl a lot . . .well . . . *loving* her, he supposed, yes, he'd loved her, he supposed he'd loved her, well then it had been a different story. And then the surprises hadn't been in the sexual exploration, but in something much deeper—he had cried one time, he had actually, for Christ's sake, cried. And that had been afterward, they'd been lying side by side on the pillow and he'd suddenly clutched Kitty to him fiercely, and he'd begun crying, and she'd cradled his head on her breasts, and stroked his hair, and said Hey, baby, come on, baby, hey, baby, and he'd nodded against her breasts wet with his own tears, and wondered why he was crying, and could not understand why. Yes, he supposed he had loved her once. He supposed that was why he was lending her the two grand. Because once he had loved her so much he had cried.

He dressed in a lightweight gabardine; the radio had said the temperature would be in the high seventies today, and he didn't want to be sweating while he worked. He still didn't know what he'd do if he came up against a really tough box. Maybe give it the old college try, and then say the hell with it. He didn't want to think about that now. He put on a nice blue and gold silk rep his mother had given him last Christmas, when he went down to see her in Miami. His mother was living with a square john who worked as a tennis pro at one of the chintzier hotels. The guy was sixty-three years old, but still in pretty good shape, told Alex he was ranked twelfth in the United States, which Alex didn't believe. Alex had hit a few balls with him, feeling like a goddamn fool with everybody watching him. The guy had told Alex he could become a very good tennis player with a little practice, and Alex had wondered why anyone in his right mind would want to get good at hitting a fuckin ball over a net. His mother had seemed happy enough, though he'd noticed lots of bruise marks on her arms. The ones on her legs he knew came from banging into furniture when she was drunk, but the ones on her arms he suspected came from Mr. Tennis Pro.

"Are you happy, Alex?" she asked him just before he left for New York again.

"Yes, Mom, I'm happy," he said.

"I am, too," she replied, but there was something in her eyes, something he could not fathom. She had told Mr. Tennis Pro that her son was a salesman for the Gillette Company. Alex's father had been a salesman for the Gillette Company, but he hadn't seen his father since he was eight, when the old man went off on one of his road trips and never came back. His mother had cried for a month, alternately proclaiming her love and her hatred for the old man. Finally, she told Alex his father had never been anything but a no-good son of a bitch. Still, when he'd gone down to see her at Christmas, she'd told Mr. Tennis Pro that Alex worked for the Gillette Company. "Are you happy, Alex?" and something in her eyes. He'd been glad to get the hell out of Miami.

Her took his leather dispatch case from the top shelf of his bedroom closet and unclasped it. The case was a foot wide, eighteen inches long, and four inches deep—big enough for the tools he needed to carry, but not so big that it would attract attention. The jimmy and the power drill were the bulkiest tools he'd be carrying, anyway, and the jimmy was a sectional that unscrewed into three parts, and the power drill just cleared the space inside the case when the lid was closed. He put those in first because he'd be using them last, when he attacked the box. He also put in an extension cord, a flashlight, a set of punches and driftpins, a small sledgeham-mer, and a cold chisel. He would either punch the box or peel it, and those were all the tools he would need for either of the jobs. If the box looked like one that could neither be punched or peeled, he would leave it alone, take whatever stuff was around, and get the hell out.

His picks and tension bars were inside a folding, cloth tool kit he had bought in an automobile accessory store. He un-folded the kit, took out the tools he knew he would need for the lobby door, and laid them out on the dresser top. Then he put a dish towel into the case on top of the bulkier tools and placed the cloth kit on top of that. He knew some burglars who preferred a pick gun to your standard pick because all you had to do with the gun was pull the trigger and the pick moved up and down very fast, bouncing all the tumbler pins at once. There was also a little knob on top of the gun, which you could twist to adjust the spring tension, increasing or de-creasing the bouncing action of the pick. He preferred feeling around for the pins himself, shoving them up one at a time as he worked his way into the lock. The way a cylinder lock worked, you shoved a key into the keyway and the notches in the key moved the tumbler pins up one by one, shoving them back up against the springs that were holding them down. Once these pins were up, you twisted the key, and that turned the cylinder and pulled back the bolt. Alex could du-plicate the action of a key with his picks and tension bars, all of which he'd owned for a long time. He knew he could pick the lobby door, but he didn't know what he'd find on the door to the Rothman apartment, so he packed into the case a small cylinder drill jig and bit for drilling through the pins, and also a pair of vise grip pliers, if he had to yank out the cylinder itself to expose the lock.

He doubted he'd find a tubular lock on the door to the

Rothman apartment, but he packed his three tubular-lock picks just in case. The pick with the red handle was for right-of-center locks; the one with the blue handle was for left-of-center locks; the one with the white handle was for regular center-spaced pins. The picks had come directly from the manufacturer that way, the handles color-coded for the convenience of the locksmith—or the burglar, as the case might be. He had only run across a tubular lock once in all the time he'd been a burglar, but it paid to be prepared for anything he might come up against. He closed the lid on the case, snapped the clasps shut, and then went to his dresser drawer and took from it an aluminum strip he had cut from a Venetian blind slat. The strip was an inch and a half wide and twelve inches long; he would use it to loid the lock on the Rothman door, if he was lucky enough to find a Mickey Mouse up there. He left his royal-flush shim in the drawer, though he was tempted to take it along for luck.

He slipped the aluminum strip into his inside jacket pocket, and from the same drawer took a pair of thin, black leather gloves, which he put into the right-hand waist pocket of his jacket. On top of the gloves, in the same pocket, he put his hand picks and tension bars. From the top of the dresser, he picked up a new, unsharpened yellow pencil to which he'd fastened a rubber band by pulling one end of it through the other, leaving him with a wide loop just below the eraser tip. He put this into his inside jacket pocket, too, and then picked up a three-by-five index card upon which he had hand-lettered the words OUT OF ORDER the night before. He put this into his left-hand waist pocket, together with a roll of Scotch tape and a slip of paper onto which he'd scrawled another name he'd taken from the telephone book—for an address on Sixty-ninth this time, but further up the block. He could not expect to pull the same ploy on the elevator operator again, but it might work if he ran into trouble with the doorman. Into that same left-hand pocket, he put a box of wooden toothpicks.

He picked up the dispatch case, looked at himself in the mirror over the dresser, tried to think of anything he might have forgotten, decided he was all set—and left the apartment.

At five minutes past ten, he dialed the Rothmans' phone number. He counted the rings. One, two, three . . .

Don't be home, he thought.

Four, five, six . . .

Don't answer.

Seven . . . eight . . . nine . . . ten.

Relaxing, he let the phone ring another ten times, just to make certain. Then, instead of hanging up, he lowered the receiver, allowing it to dangle on the end of its cord. He glanced over his shoulder toward the counter, and then he took the Scotch tape and the three-by-five index card from his pocket. Tearing off a sliver of tape, he fastened the OUT OF ORDER sign to the phone, covering the coin slots. The receiver was still dangling on the end of the cord when he left the booth and the shop and began walking swiftly down Madison Avenue. On the corner of Madison and Sixty-ninth, he checked his watch. It was ten minutes past ten, and the doorman was standing in front of the building. In ten minutes, if Alex had figured correctly, the lobby phone would ring, and the man in the homburg would tell the doorman to go fetch his '73 Caddy.

Alex waited.

He could not hear the lobby phone when it rang, but he was certain it *had* rung because he saw the doorman rush inside and then come out again not a moment later, heading for the garage across the street. Alex immediately walked toward the building. He hesitated only briefly outside the glass entrance doors, looking into the lobby toward the elevator bank. The brass doors were closed, the elevator operator was nowhere in sight. He moved swiftly into the lobby and walked directly to the mailboxes, glancing up at the floor indicator as he passed the closed brass doors. The elevator was on the eighteenth floor . . . the nineteenth . . . it was still heading upward as Alex turned away into the alcove.

There was no mail in the Rothman box. Good. She'd come down already, the apartment was empty. His heart was pounding. He came out of the alcove and did not even glance up at the floor indicator over the brass doors. There was no time to waste now, no time for superfluous action; he had to pick the lock on that fuckin fire door and be out of the lobby before either the elevator came down or the doorman returned or some tenant walked in from the street. He hated going in, going in was the worst fuckin time, especially in a lobby like this one. Couldn't wear your fuckin gloves, ran the risk of leaving prints all over the goddamn lock, he should've told Henry to go to hell with his fuckin job.

His hand was shaking as he took his tools from his pocket and selected a pick thin enough to slide into the keyway. In the movies, you saw a man picking a lock, he stuck a pick into the hole, jiggled it twice, and whammo the door was open. Bullshit. You could use your pick to raise each of the spring-loaded pins to their proper position, but they'd spring right back and the fuckin door would *stay* locked if you didn't hold them in the raised position. There were five pins inside that fuckin lock, and Alex had to get them all up, one at a time, *hold* the first one up with the tension bar while he moved on to the next one, and then tension that one, too, working his way down the line till he had all of them up, the

tension bar offset so he could hold it in a way that didn't in-
terfere with the manipulation of the pick. He got the first pin
up and tensioned it, and he thought Now come on, baby,
open for me, and he felt for the second pin, guiding the pick,
working the pin up and then holding it up with the tension
bar, Come on, sweetheart, open for me, come *on*, you cunt!
He heard the elevator whining down the shaft, his upper lip
was beaded with sweat as he jiggled the pick, attacking the
third pin, Come on, feeling it yield. Yes, come on, the pin
was up, he tensioned it, he was almost there now, the fourth
pin went up, and then the fifth, and he used the tension bar to
rotate the cylinder, and the bolt sprang back. He twisted the
knob and opened the door. Holding it open, he wiped the
knob clean with his handkerchief and then stepped inside.
Quickly, he closed the door behind him and leaned against it,
breathing heavily.

He looked at his watch. The time was ten twenty-three. He
had opened the door in less than two minutes, it had seemed
like a fuckin year. He started up the metal steps, counting the
floors, just in case they weren't numbered on this side of the
fire door on each landing. But they *were* numbered, in red.
Thank you very much, he thought, taking the steps two at a
time as he went up to the sixteenth floor. He paused outside
the fire door there, to catch his breath and to listen for sounds
in the hallway. Then he took the thin leather gloves from his
jacket pocket, and put them on. Opening the door, he stepped
into the service alcove. The alcove was perhaps eight feet
square. There was a door on his left, and it was marked 16B.
The door on his right was marked 16A. The door directly opposite him was unmarked, and undoubtedly led to the corridor that ran past the elevator bank and the front doors of the
two apartments. There was no question in his mind about
whether he should try the front door or the service door. The

service door, for some reason, usually had a crappier lock on it than the front door. Besides, the front door could be seen by the elevator operator if he dropped anyone off on this floor, whereas the only danger Alex might run into in the service alcove was somebody in 16B deciding to put out the garbage. There were three small garbage pails in the hallway, one outside 16B and two outside 16A. The alcove stank to high heaven.

Alex put his ear to the door of the Rothman apartment. Inside, he could still hear the phone ringing. He had dialed the apartment at ten-oh-five, and it was now almost ten thirty, and the phone was still ringing, which was good enough insurance for him. He put down the dispatch case and looked at the lock. He almost couldn't believe his eyes. It was the cheapest fuckin lock you could buy. People had a thirty thousand dollar diamond in there, they put a ten-cent lock on the back door. This one he *could* have opened with a playing card. He slid the shim in above the bolt, working it around the wooden door frame and into the crack where door met jamb. That's it, he thought, nice and easy, working the shim down, feeling for the bolt, feeling the resistance when aluminum met steel, and then twisting the shim, working it against the bolt. Celluloid was more flexible, you could do things with celluloid you couldn't do with a fuckin piece of aluminum, but there we go, that's the way, you could loid a cheap lock in ten seconds flat, Come on, sweetheart, edging it into the narrow slit now, feeling it, That's the way, he was almost in there, he shoved the shim all the way down, and the bolt sprang back.

He twisted the knob and shoved the door inward. It opened three or four inches, and then stopped. A chain lock. No problem. He reached into his inside jacket pocket, took from it the pencil with the rubber band fastened below the

eraser, and then eased the pencil into the open crack between
the door and the jamb. Fishing with the wide loop of the rubber band, it took him less than a minute to snare the knob on
the chain. Easing the door slightly closed, he kept the pressure tight on rubber band and knob, and the knob snapped all
the way back to the entrance hole at the opposite end. He jiggled the pencil, and the chain fell free.

He was in.

Picking up the dispatch case, he stepped into the apartment, closed the door behind him, and then turned the latch
so that the door was now unlocked. If anybody came home
while he was in here, he wanted to be able to get out fast,
and he didn't want to be fooling around with any latches.
The phone was still ringing, he knew it would drive him out
of his gourd if he let it ring like that while he was working
on the box. He walked to the wall extension on the wall near
the refrigerator, lifted the receiver from the hook, and just let
it dangle. Then he went out of the kitchen, through the dining
room, and into the living room, where he went directly to the
front door. The front door had a better lock on it, but not
much better than the one on the service door. He unlocked
this one as well, took a toothpick from the box in his pocket,
opened the door a crack and stuck the toothpick into the
lock's keyway. He broke it off flush with the cylinder, closed
the door, and then locked it again. If either of the Rothmans
came home unexpectedly, they would undoubtedly try to
enter through the front door, because that's where the elevator would leave them off. They would try to put a key into
the lock, but they'd meet the resistance of the toothpick, and
while they fumbled around out there trying to push the key
in, they'd make enough racket to wake the dead. Satisfied
that he now had his own personal burglar alarm system, plus
a safe escape route, Alex went into the bedroom. A clock on

the dresser told him it was already twenty minutes to eleven. He had an hour and ten minutes to get the hell out of here.

The maid had said the safe was on the back wall of the double-door closet opposite the windows. He went to the doors immediately, slid one of them open, and then shoved aside a dozen or so dresses hanging on the clothes bar. Your boxes came with square doors or round doors, and you also had what was called a cannonball, which was just what it sounded like, a big black ball with a screw door. Your cannonball was obsolete, you never ran into one of them these days. The Rothman box wasn't a cannonball, he hadn't expected it to be, nor was it even a round-door box. But neither was it an old box. You could punch one of your old boxes in twenty seconds flat, if you were experienced, but this one was a bright, new square-door job, and he knew he'd have trouble with it. It probably had a lead spindle shaft and lock nuts that were away from the shaft, so that he wouldn't be able to pound the shaft through the gut box and break the lock nuts that way. He'd try punching it, because maybe he'd get lucky, but he doubted punching it would work.

Before he started any manual labor, though, he automatically checked the safe to see if it was on day combination. A lot of people, especially if they went into a box five, six times a day, would give the combination dial just a partial turn each time they closed the box. This made it impossible for anyone to turn the handle and open the door, and it also made it easier for the guy going into his own box; all he had to do was twist the dial slowly back to the last number in the combination while applying pressure on the handle. Saved him the time of going through the whole combination whenever he wanted to open the box. Trouble was, if you left the box on day comb, it wasn't really locked, and *anybody* could do what the owner of the box had done—just twist the dial slowly, and keep the pressure on the handle, and the door would open.

Alex tried that now. The box didn't open, it was not on day comb. He then tried the five-ten method of opening a box without forcing it. Lots of people had difficulty remembering combinations, and when they ordered a box, they asked that the three digits in the combination be multiples of five. Or four. Eight-twelve-sixteen, like that. Or three, or seven, or any multiplication table that was easy to remember. Most people steered away from the nine table; nine was a hard one to remember, for some reason. Sometimes they asked that the digits be their birthdate. Like if he'd known, for example, that Mrs. Rothman had been born on September 15, 1913, he'd have tried nine left, fifteen right, and thirteen left again. He didn't know her birthday, though, so he tried some simple multiplication table combinations, and then he tried the first six digits of the Rothman telephone number. But the Rothman box wasn't keyed to their phone number, and he gave up trying to manipulate the dial after four minutes of playing around with it. This was going to be work, after all.

He opened his dispatch case and dug down under the dish towel for his sledgehammer and one of his punches. With one sharp blow of the hammer, he broke off the combination dial, revealing the spindle shaft beneath it. It looked like lead to him; he'd find out in a minute. Holding the punch in his left hand, and the hammer in his right, he centered the punch on the spindle and began pounding on it. He was aware of the noise he was making, but he was counting on two factors that had always worked in his favor. First, your average apartment house tenant got used to hearing all kinds of construction or repair noises during the daytime, and second, even if anybody *did* hear the pounding and wonder about it, they'd feel stupid investigating it. In New York City, people tended to mind their own business. A junkie burglar had once told Alex he'd spent fifteen minutes on a fire escape trying to get in a window, while in a building across the way a guy sat on his *own* fire escape watching him all the time. Guy never moved from the fire escape. Sat there fascinated. Probably thought he was watching a big caper movie.

The fuckin spindle wasn't budging, it had to be lead, it was mushrooming with each successive blow of the hammer, the hell with it. He'd have to peel the box. Which meant he could be into it in either five minutes or five hours, depending on how strong the box turned out to be. He looked at his watch. It was ten to eleven, he had to be out of here in an hour. Getting a start on the door would be the tough part. Basically, you had your two kinds of boxes—the record box and the money box. Your record box usually had a square door, and your money box had a round one. The round door locked with a mechanism that engaged lugs all around the door frame, and it was originally designed to stop your burglar who was using explosives. Alex hardly knew any burglars nowadays who used explosives, but the stronger door style was still common. Your money box was usually constructed entirely of heavy steel layers, and it was advertised by safe manufacturers as being "burglar-resistant." There wasn't a safe company in the world who'd ever claim its produce was "burglar-proof," it was always "burglar-resistant." Your money box always had a punch-resistant spindle and sometimes a boltwork relock device, and sometimes even a copper sheet in the door to resist an acetylene torch attack.

The Rothmans had a standard record box, and Alex knew exactly what to expect in its construction. The door and all the sides of a record box were made like a sandwich, with several layers of thin steel on either side of an insulating material. Your money box was burglar-resistant, but your record box was only fire-resistant, designed to protect the contents from destruction in case the place went up in flames. This didn't mean it would be a cinch to get into. It just meant it would be a little easier. Why the Rothmans would want to keep a $30,000 piece of jewelry in a *fire*-resistant box was a mystery to Alex—unless Rothman had some stocks and bonds in there, too. He was, after all, a stockbroker, so maybe he had some valuable papers in there.

In any case, with either a money box *or* a record box, you had to peel back the steel until you had a hole big enough to get in with a jimmy. Once you exposed the locking mechanism, you could pry it loose and open the door. That took time. And hard work. And the hardest part was getting it started, getting a grip on the thing so you could peel it back. He dug in his dispatch case for his drill and extension cord and was carrying the cord to a socket where he could plug it in when he heard a noise that startled him.

Everything stopped.

The forward motion of his body stopped, his breathing stopped, he felt for a second that even his heart had stopped. He listened. The noise was coming from somewhere in the direction of the living room. He stepped quietly to the bedroom door, stood just to one side of it, and listened again. The noise sounded like . . . what the hell? Somebody bouncing a rubber ball? He moved swiftly into the living room and walked directly to the front door of the apartment. The noise was coming from outside in the hall, and, yes, it *was* a kid bouncing a rubber ball on the floor, he was sure of that now. The bouncing stopped, there were footsteps approaching the door.

The bell sounded.

He leaped back from the door in sudden panic. The doorbell rang again. There was another silence. Then Alex heard the sound of the rubber ball bouncing down the corridor, and then the sound of a door slamming shut. Did the kid live in 16B? Had he come to visit with dear old Mrs. Rothman, not realizing she was out for her morning stroll? Or had someone in 16B heard Alex pounding on the box spindle and sent the kid to investigate? He waited. He was half-tempted to get the hell out now, but he waited, standing just inside the front door, listening. He heard nothing more. Usually, when you were in one of these new apartment buildings, you could hear noise all over the place, toilets flushing, pipes rattling, sometimes even people arguing upstairs or next door. He heard nothing now, and the silence was reassuring; it told him the walls were well-insulated, and he could risk making at least some noise working on the box.

He went back into the bedroom, plugged in his extension cord, carried the drill to the box, and began working on the upper left-hand corner of it. He did not know of any burglars who peeled a safe from the right-hand side. That's where the hinges were, and hinges could stop you dead. All he wanted to do now was get a hole started in the outer layer of steel so he could get his chisel under it and begin bending it back. That outer layer would be maybe just a quarter of an inch thick, and if he could peel that one back and then get in there with his jimmy, he could pry along the edge of the door plating to break the rivets or the spot welds that were holding it in place, and keep peeling back layers of steel till he got to the insulation material. He was using a high-speed bit, but the work was slow, and it took him close to ten minutes to get a hole he thought he could use. He picked up his hammer and his cold chisel, and began working the hole, the tempered cutting edge of the chisel seeking purchase on the smooth steel of the door. There was another way to get a peel job started, but it made too much noise for a fuckin apartment house. Your nighttime men who didn't have to worry about waking anybody up in a store or an office building would sometimes pound on a corner of the door till the plating was bent out enough to get a jimmy behind it. Sure, that was all he had to do here, pound on a corner of the door—the little ball-bouncer next door would come running down the hall again wanting to know who was breaking things in the Rothman apartment.

The chisel kept slipping, it refused to get under the steel, the damn corner of the door simply would not get going. He was breathing hard now, and his face was beaded with sweat. The clock on the bedroom dresser was an electric one, but he could hear its hum in the silence of the bedroom, a steady drone behind the sound of the sledge against the head of the chisel. His ears were alerted to any alien sounds; the only sounds that *belonged* now were those of his own breathing, the hum of the electric clock, and the steady metallic ring of steel against steel. He paused, wiped sweat from his upper lip with the back of one gloved hand, and then looked at his watch.

It was eleven-fifteen.

Ten minutes later he got the box started. He let out his breath in relief because from here on in it was duck soup. He took the sectional jimmy out of his dispatch case, screwed the three parts together, and slid the hooked end under the corner he'd bent back with the chisel. Clutching the jimmy with both hands, he put all the strength of his arms into pushing on it, and the corner of the door bent back further. Working alternately with the chisel and the jimmy, he ripped rivets and welds, pried loose a second layer of steel, and then a third—and suddenly a puff of something resembling smoke came up out of the hole. He had hit the asbestos fireproofing

material, he was home free. A grin broke on his face. It took
him another five minutes to chip out the concrete and the asbestos and pry open the locking bar inside the box. The door
opened. It was exactly twenty minutes to twelve.

He dumped all his tools on the floor, emptying the dispatch case. He had never left his tools behind on a job before, but the Hawk had given him a good tip the other
day—even though he hadn't meant to—and Alex now realized that another way to throw the opposition off the trail
was to vary his m.o. each time out. This had never occurred
to him, and he suspected it hadn't occurred to any of the
thieves he'd met in prison or out. A man got used to doing
things one way, he generally did them the same way each
and every time. He knew the risk of taking his tools with
him—if he got caught coming out with burglar's tools on
him, this would automatically add a year or a thousand-dol-
lar fine to the rap, and besides, would be incontrovertible evidence that he'd been in there intending to commit a crime.
A man didn't go inside an apartment with a sectional jimmy
unless he intended using it, and Alex didn't know what the
hell anyone could use one for except to pry open a door or a
box. But he was really fond of his tools—they fit his hand,
he knew each ball, hook, diamond, and rake pick by its feel,
they somehow added to his peace of mind while he was
working. The tools were easy enough to replace since they
were the same tools used by legitimate locksmiths, that
wasn't the point. They were *his* tools, and he simply didn't
like the idea of leaving them behind, the way lots of burglars
did because they were afraid of the possession rap and also
of paint scrapings or scratches that might link them to the
burglary. So Alex had never left his tools behind, and he had
almost invariably smashed a window before he went out, to
make it look as though the job had been done by a junkie or

any other kind of crude burglar. The Hawk had wised him up. Today, he would leave his tools behind, and he wouldn't bother smashing a window, either. Let the Hawk figure it out, the cocksucker.

He reached into the safe.

The papers in there weren't stocks or bonds, they were things like a marriage certificate and a deed to a house some-place and also a Xerox copy of a Haitian divorce decree—apparently this was a second marriage for Mr. Rothman. Alex threw the various documents on the floor and began digging into the safe for the good stuff. He'd been told he would find the ring in a small black box with "Henry Green, Jeweler" stamped onto its lid. He lifted the lid of the box to make sure the ring was inside it, and then he closed the lid and put the box into the dispatch case. There was a long, vel-vet-covered box inside the safe, too, and he opened that and found a diamond bracelet inside it, and quickly put that into the dispatch case. He didn't bother opening any of the other boxes that were inside there. He knew what he had already, and this wasn't the kind of job where there was plenty of time to separate the crap from the real goods. He figured if something was in the safe to begin with, it *had* to be valu-able, so he just reached in, and put whatever he found into the dispatch case. When the safe was empty, he looked at his watch. It was almost a quarter to twelve, he still had five minutes.

He didn't want this to look like a crude burglar had been in here, but neither did he want it to look like an inside job. Somebody comes in, goes straight to the safe, and doesn't bother anything else in the room, you've got to figure he was tipped off. So he went to the dresser now, and began pulling out the drawers, dumping the contents onto the bed, and then tossing the empty drawers on the floor. He found a Hamilton wristwatch, which he put into the dispatch case, and he also found a pair of gold earrings with diamond chips, mixed in with a lot of costume jewelry. He left the costume jewelry where he had dumped it on the bed, but he put the gold earrings into the dispatch case. He threw some panties, slips, and blouses around the room to make it look as if the burglar had been in haste, and he went back to the closet and threw a few suits and dresses on the floor, and then he knocked over one of the lamps on purpose, and looked at his watch again, and figured it was time to call it a day. Lots of burglars he knew, or rather burglars he'd *heard* about—he hadn't yet met one who was willing to admit it—would take a shit in the middle of the floor before they went out of a place, or else piss on the bed or in somebody's shoes, let the people know they'd been there, and also let them know what the burglar thought of them. Alex didn't think *anything* about the Rothmans or any people he burglarized, and he also happened to feel that the place to go to the toilet wasn't in the middle of somebody's bedroom or in his shoes. That was sick.

He went out of the place the same way he'd come in, through the service door. He listened at the door before he stepped out into the alcove, and then he opened the door quickly and crossed the several feet to the fire door and started down the steps. He felt almost giddy. There were burglars who dreaded coming out of a place, but for Alex the going-in was tough and the coming-out was always joyous. His juices always ran high when he was inside an apartment, but he never felt nervous unless he heard an unexpected noise, and thank God he'd never run into a human being while he was burglarizing a place. He wasn't sure what he'd do if ever he did. He knew he'd never go back to jail again, *never*, and if that meant hurting somebody, or even killing somebody to avoid getting busted, then he supposed that was what he'd do. Still, he hoped he'd never have to do it.

He came down the sixteen flights of stairs to the ground-floor lobby and then continued down another flight to the basement. He didn't think he'd run into the black handyman down there, but if he did he'd just tell him he lived in the building and thought his wife might be down there doing the wash. If there weren't any washing machines in the basement, he'd make up another story. He was good at that sort of thing, talking his way out of situations, especially when the guy he was talking to was a machine. Alex considered anyone who did manual labor a machine. Nine-to-five office workers were something slightly higher than machines, but people who lugged garbage cans or dug ditches or brushed your coat in the men's room were nothing *but* machines, and he had no respect at all for them.

The black man wasn't in the basement. Alex looked over the room quickly, orienting himself. He spotted the exit door almost immediately, went to it, opened it, and started up the ramp to the street. The door at the top of the ramp was the one he'd stopped to examine on Tuesday morning, when he'd bent to tie his shoelace in the rain. It was no damn good for getting *into* the place, but it was just fine and dandy for getting *out*.

He opened it, stepped onto the sidewalk, and began walking immediately toward Madison Avenue. If the doorman was behind him standing at the curb, he either didn't notice Alex or didn't care to challenge him. No one called to Alex, no one came running after him, no one did a damn thing but let him get away with the dispatch case full of goods.

He was smiling broadly when he hailed a taxi on Madison and told the driver to take him to Yankee Stadium. He got out there, hailed another taxi, and gave the driver Henry Green's address on Fordham Road.

TWO

As Kitty took off her clothes, she started telling Alex what had happened when she'd delivered the two grand to the numbers racketeer. Lying on the bed naked, he watched as she peeled off her dress and her half-slip. She had never shot dope into her arms, preferring the inside of her thighs, and there were scars on them still, marring the smooth dark flesh, but he could not detect any fresh punctures, so maybe she'd been telling the truth after all. She folded the slip over the back of a chair, and then carried her dress to the bedroom closet and put in on a hanger. She was a very neat person, always had been, cleaned up after herself like a cat. She had not yet removed her shoes, and as she stood at the closet wearing only panties and bra and the high-heeled pumps, he studied her, and began to want her, and became suddenly bored with the story she was telling.

" . . . is in Harlem, but *he* lives in a very fancy neighborhood. Doorman stopped me, wanted to know what I was doing there. Told him I had a package for Mr. Di Santis. He asks me my name and then calls upstairs. Send her up, Di Santis says, and I take the elevator to the twelfth floor and ring the doorbell. You got any cigarettes in the house, Alex?"

"You know I don't smoke," he said. "Hurry it up there, okay?"

"Patience, sweetie," she said, and smiled at him, and then went out of the bedroom. He heard her crossing the living room to where she'd left her handbag, heard the click of the clasp as she opened the bag, heard her striking a match. When she came back into the bedroom again, a lighted ciga- rette was in her hand. She walked to the foot of the bed, took a long drag on the cigarette, and then stood there like a model, hip jutting forward, right elbow cupped in left hand, cigarette trailing smoke in her relaxed right hand.

"One of his gorillas opened the door," she said, and dragged on the cigarette again. "He asked me did I have the money, and I told him yes, and he took me in to see Di San- tis. This was maybe ten o'clock, it took me about a half-hour to get there from here. Di Santis is wearing a robe, he's smil- ing, he says to me You're a woman of your word."

"This is the longest fuckin story I ever heard in my life," Alex said.

"Patience, sweetie," she said.

"This is a fuckin *opera*," Alex said.

"I hand him the envelope," Kitty said, "and he takes the rubber band off it and begins counting the bills. He takes his good sweet time counting them. Then he counts them again, and then he asks me are they counterfeit. They better not be counterfeit, he says. I tell him the money is good, and he counts it yet a third time, and then he says It's not all here. His gorilla is standing behind me, Di Santis is sitting at this desk with a leather top, the money is spread out on the desk in front of him. I tell him What do you mean it ain't all there? There's two thousand dollars there, you just counted it three fuckin times. He says That's the principal. I'm talking about the *interest* on the principal. Behind me the gorilla laughs, and Di Santis is smiling now, and he tells me You know something? I was hoping you wouldn't be able to come up with the money. I was hoping I could fix your face. I can still do it, you know. If you don't come up with the interest."

"So what are you saying?" Alex asked. "Does he want more money, is that it? I can't give you no more money."

"No, no," Kitty said, and went to the dresser and looked for an ashtray, and then said. "Where can I put this out?" and without waiting for an answer, went out of the bedroom again. He heard her searching for an ashtray out there, and then she said, "Never *were* any fuckin ashtrays in this place," and he heard her going into the bathroom just off the entrance foyer, and then he heard the toilet flushing. When she came back into the bedroom, she took off her bra and carried it to the chair where her slip was folded over the back, and put the bra on top of the slip, and came to the bed and sat on the edge of it. He reached out to touch her breast, and she said, "I ain't finished with the story."

"So finish it," he said.

"He made me blow him," she said. "He told me that was the interest on the two grand, unless I wanted him to fix my face. The gorilla stood there all the while I did it, and then Di Santis said I think my boy here would like a little something, too, and I had to go down on the gorilla, too. Then they let me leave."

"You shouldn't have done it," Alex said.

"I *had* to do it. I'd have done anything to get out of there. He wasn't kidding, Alex. He opened the top drawer of the desk and took out this little bottle, and he said This could blind you, I decide to throw it in your face."

"It coulda been water," Alex said.

"Yeah, it coulda been, that's right. Only way to find out was to have him throw it in my face."

"You still shouldn't have done it."

"You'd have done the same thing."

"I wouldn't go down on nobody, he could have a whole fuckin *gallon* of acid, I still wouldn't go down on him."

"Took him a half-hour to come, the cocksucker. I think he was holding back. Just to make me work harder. The gorilla got off right away, but not Di Santis."

"What are you telling me this fuckin story for?" Alex asked.

"I think it's an interesting story."

"I think it's a fuckin disgusting story."

"Hey, come on," she said, and reached down for him. "Come on, sweetie, it didn't mean nothing."

"So what's this supposed to be now?" Alex asked. "Is this paying back the principal or the interest or what?"

"This is different. Come on, what's the matter with you?"

She rose suddenly, eased her panties over her hips, and then stepped out of them. Sitting on the edge of the bed again, sl took off her shoes and then swung her legs up onto the bed. Her hand immediately found him again.

"Why didn't you blow the doorman on the way out?" Alex said.

"Why don't I blow *you* right this minute?" she said, and grinned. "I think that's a much better idea."

"What you done was disgusting," Alex said.

"You're something," she said.

"Yeah, I'm something, And you're a cheap fuckin whore, is what you are."

"Anyway, what's this concern with johns all of a sudden? You never used to worry about johns."

"This wasn't johns. This was two guys strong-arming you, that's an entirely different thing."

"Come on, it didn't mean nothing. I was just glad to get out of there, that's all."

"Yeah, and suppose they come around again tomorrow, with *another* little bottle of water, and this time they got two *dozen* guys with them? You gonna do the same thing all over again?"

"I don't know what I'll do tomorrow, let's concentrate on today, all right?"

"You *already* concentrated on today."

"How about a little concentration from *you,* huh?"

"Go wash your mouth," he said.

She looked into his face. Her eyes seemed suddenly injured.

"You hear me?" he said.

"Yes, Alex."

"Then go do it."

Wordlessly, she got off the bed and went out of the room. He heard her padding across the living room to the hall toilet. He heard the water running. He heard her gargling. Fuckin cheap whore, he thought. By the time she came back into the bedroom, his mind was a million miles away. As she worked on him with her hands and her mouth, he thought of the ease with which he had picked the lobby-door lock, and then loided the lock on the Rothman back door, and slipped the chain lock. And he thought of the box, thought of how difficult it had been to get a start on the door, but he'd worked it, he'd stayed with it till he got the thing going, and that puff of smoke at last, Christ, that always *was* a kick in the ass, that smoke from the insulation puffing out of the hole.

Well now, Henry had said, what do we have here?, and had put his jeweler's loupe to his eye, and looked over the ring first to make sure it was the same thing he'd sold the Rothmans back before Christmas. Then he checked out the diamond bracelet, which he told Alex was worth six thousand dollars retail, it being an antique set with a hundred and two diamonds totaling eight carats—That gives you another eighteen hundred dollars, Alex. And there was a pair of platinum earclips with twenty-eight round diamonds totaling three carats; and an eighteen-carat, white-gold, diamond and opal pendant; and a double strand of cultured pearls, seventy-seven in all, with a fourteen-carat yellow-gold clasp; and also an eighteen-carat gold Piaget lady's watch with fourteen marquise diamonds set in the band. Mr. Rothman also kept some of his own stuff in the safe together with his wife's jewels—a fourteen-carat, yellow-gold ring with a seven-carat star ruby, and a pair of eighteen-carat white-gold and jade cuff links, and a pair of plain, round gold links which Alex kept for himself. He also kept the gold earrings he had found in the dresser, the ones with the diamond chips. For the complete haul, he got the nine thousand Henry had promised him for the ring, and he also got an additional eighty-four hundred dollars as his thirty percent of the other stuff in the safe. It was a very nice score. Not your once-in-a-lifetime score, and in fact not even as good as his best score had been, but nothing to sneeze at for a few hours' work.

He turned his head away when she tried to kiss him on the lips.

Afterward, she got out of bed and went out to the kitchen, and he heard her opening the refrigerator door. He put on his shorts and went out after her, and she was standing by the window, drinking beer from a bottle, just staring out the window and drinking the beer. Without turning to look at him, she said, "You gonna be wantin anything else?"

"Yeah," he said. "I'm gonna be wantin my two grand back."

"You'll get it, don't worry," she said.

"I want it by next week."

"Okay," she said.

"Next Friday," he said.

"Okay."

She lifted the bottle to her mouth, drank some more beer, and then stared out the window again. He didn't know what she was looking at out there. There were only rooftops out there.

"My brother used to fly pigeons," she said. Her voice was very low.

"No pigeons out there," Alex said.

"I know. I'm just sayin. Used to be up on the roof all day long, his fuckin pigeons. Somebody got in the coop one night, put poison or somethin in their feed. He went up next morning, found them all dead. Each and every one of them dead. Came downstairs and said Kitty, somebody killed the pigeons. I said Well, you get yourself some new pigeons, Oz. He said Yeah, and he went in the toilet, I heard him cryin behind the door. I knocked on the door, I said Hey, Oz, and he said That's okay. Never *did* learn who killed his fuckin pigeons." She put the beer bottle down on the counter top near the sink, then turned from the window and sighed heavily. "Well, got to move my ass," she said, "I expect to make two grand by next Friday."

"I'm not kidding about wanting it back," Alex said.

"I know you ain't."

"Just so you understand."

"Yeah, I understand," she said, and then walked past him out of the kitchen. He went into the living room and turned on the television set, and sat watching a quiz show while she dressed in the bedroom. She came out a few minutes later and stood by his chair watching the quiz show with him, neither of them speaking. When the commercial came on, she said, "Well, see you next week, Alex."

"I'll be here," he said.

At the front door, she paused, and turned to him, and said, "They were only like any two johns," and opened the door and went out.

When the doorbell rang a half-hour later, he thought it was Kitty coming back. He almost hoped it was. Now that she was gone, he missed her, was in fact kicking himself for not having made the most of her visit. The girl meant nothing to him anymore, why should he care what she did with anybody else? Still, what she'd done wasn't right, it just wasn't right. She should have fought them, she should have told them *What* interest, what the hell are you talking about, interest? Acid or no, she shouldn't have knuckled under that way. Besides, it was probably water in that bottle. You show them you're weak, that's it, man. He'd learned that from Tommy up at Sing Sing, you just never showed them you were weak, or they'd get to you. Well, what the hell, she was just a whore. Still, he hoped it was her ringing the doorbell.

He threw back the peephole flap.

It was Anthony Hawkins standing outside there in the hall. Alex was still in his undershorts. He said, "Just a second, Mr. Hawkins," and went into the bedroom to put on a pair of pants and a shirt. When he came back to the door and opened it, Hawkins said, "Did you stash the loot, Alex?"

"What loot?" Alex said. "Come on in, Mr. Hawkins, I was just about to make some coffee."

"I could use a cup of coffee," Hawkins said.

"Come on in the kitchen."

Hawkins looked around the living room. "Nice place you've got," he said.

"That's right, you've never been up here," Alex said, and walked toward the kitchen, Hawkins following.

"Very nice," Hawkins said. "Maybe I'm on the wrong side, huh? Place I live in, you could fit in your living room here."

"Well, it's big, yeah," Alex said, "but the rent's very cheap."

"How many rooms have you got?"

"Five. That's counting the kitchen," Alex said. "Sit down, Mr. Hawkins."

"I didn't wake you, did I?" Hawkins asked, pulling a chair out from the table.

"No, I've been up a while. You mind instant?"

"Instant's fine," Hawkins said. "Alex, what were you doing yesterday morning between ten o'clock and twelve noon?"

"Yesterday?" Alex asked, and went to the sink and began filling the pot with water. "Was it raining yesterday?"

"No, it was a nice day," Hawkins said.

"Oh, yes, I remember now. I slept late yesterday. I didn't get up till maybe one o'clock. Why do you ask?"

"I got a call from the Nineteenth. I don't know why the hell they always call me. They must think I'm some kind of burglary expert," Hawkins said.

"Well, you are."

"Sure. Then let them promote me to first grade and put me on the Burglary Squad, I'm such a hotshot. Anyway, this man named Gregoriano, Gregoriani, I can never tell with those wop names what they end in. He's a detective third up there at the Nineteenth, he had himself a burglary yesterday morning. Woman got back to her apartment a little after twelve, place was a mess."

"Gee, that's too bad," Alex said, and put the pot of water on the stove.

"Woman named Rothman."

"That's too bad," Alex said again.

"So Gregoriano, Gregoriani, what*ever* the hell, calls to ask does it sound like anybody I'm familiar with."

"Did it?" Alex asked.

"The description sounded like you, yes."

"What description?" Alex asked immediately.

"Well, what do you care? You were here asleep yesterday morning."

"That's right," Alex said. He was spooning instant coffee into the cups, and he looked up now and said, "Do you take sugar?"

"Black," Hawkins said. "The man did a very nice job on a wall safe they had there."

"Must've been a pro, huh?" Alex said.

"Oh, no question."

"How'd he get in?"

"Loided the back door, we figure. Mickey Mouse lock on it."

"You think these people would invest in good locks, huh?" Alex said, and shook his head.

"Put you out of business," Hawkins said.

"Well, I ain't *in* that business anymore, Mr. Hawkins."

"Oh, I *know* you're not. What business *are* you in these days, Alex?"

"I've been thinking of getting involved in the theater," Alex said. "I helped out on a couple of shows when I was in the joint, I was thinking of doing something along those lines now."

"Yes, but what *are* you doing?"

"That's what I'm doing."

"No, that's what you're *thinking* of doing. In the meantime, how do you pay the rent?"

"Well, I had a little put aside."

"So you're thinking of becoming an actor, huh?"

"No, no, an electrician."

"Oh, an electrician. That's too bad, Alex, because you're a very good actor. You're one of the best actors I know, and I've seen some pretty good actors in my time."

"Mr. Hawkins," Alex said, "you certainly don't think *I* had anything to do with that burglary, do you?"

"Well, the m.o. wasn't yours," Hawkins said. "But then again, it wasn't exactly *not* yours, either."

"How could it be mine and not mine at the same time?"

"Fellow loided the door. That sounds like you, Alex. Celluloid strip, plastic card, Venetian blind—sounds a lot like you."

"And also a hundred *other* burglars in this city."

"True. Fellow called the apartment a few times, though. Risked talking to the maid and *also* the victim. That sounds a lot like you, Alex. Most of your cheap thieves, they'll call and hang up. Not you. You've got balls, Alex."

"Well, thanks," Alex said, "but . . . "

"I didn't mean it as a compliment," Hawkins said flatly. "Fellow broke off a toothpick in the front door, that's you, too, Alex. But he left his tools behind, and that *isn't* you."

"That's right. Besides, I don't *own* any tools, Mr. Hawkins."

"Sure, sure. And he didn't do anything dumb like smashing a window from the inside. You learn very fast, Alex."

"I don't know what you mean," Alex said, and took the

pot from the stove and filled the cups. He added milk to his own cup and then carried both cups to the table.

"Thanks," Hawkins said. "Also, we think the job was set up, Alex. Fellow went straight to the safe, though he tried to cover up afterwards, threw a few things around, swiped some crap from the dresser, like that. Still, the safe was the prime target, he must've spent most of his time on the safe because the lady was only out of the apartment for two hours, and it wasn't an easy box to open. So it was a setup job, and we know you've had jobs set up for you in the past."

"No, that's not true."

"We know people who've set up jobs for you, Alex."

"Like who?"

"Like Vito Baloney."

"Vito Bolognese? You've got to be kidding? Vito runs a body repair shop."

"He's also a fence."

"I didn't know that. Why don't you bust him?"

"We'd bust him in a minute, if we could find his drop. Anyway, that's not the point. I'm trying to tell you this was a setup job, which means a fellow like you—with such good connections—could've done it, and also could've peeled the safe, which took a little skill. It could've been you, Alex."

"But it wasn't."

"The description *was*."

"What description?" Alex asked again.

"Gregoriano talked to both the doorman and the elevator operator, asked them if they'd seen any suspicious characters lurking around the building."

"Did they?"

"Doorman didn't see anybody," Hawkins said, and lifted his cup and sipped at the coffee. "Elevator operator saw somebody, though."

"He did, huh?"

"Yeah. Saw somebody who sounds a lot like you. That's how come Gregoriano called me, actually. He got to looking through the files at the I.S., finds a guy fits the description the elevator operator gave him, guy named Alex Hardy. Sees I made the bust, calls to find out what I know about you these days. Of course, there are lots of blond, blue-eyed people in this city, about your height and weight . . . "

"Yeah."

"Who get lost looking for an address, and who go in checking the mailboxes."

"Must be millions of them," Alex said.

"Yeah, but not all of them are burglars."

"Are you trying to say I was at that building yesterday morning? The elevator operator saw me there yesterday morning?"

"No. He saw you there *Wednesday* morning. Or somebody who looked an awful lot like you."

"Tell you what," Alex said. "Whyn't you have a lineup, ask the elevator operator to pick me out of it?"

"Well, let's say it *was* you. What could we prove?"

"Nothing."

"Right. It's no crime to be in the lobby of a building."

"Anyway, it wasn't me, Mr. Hawkins."

"Who set it up, Alex?"

"I don't know anything about it."

"Alex," Hawkins said, "I am going to get your ass."

"*No* one's gonna get *my* ass, Mr. Hawkins. Mr. Hawkins, it's always nice seeing you, but if you came all the way uptown to tell me about a crime I didn't commit, you just wasted your time, Mr. Hawkins."

"I've got plenty of time," Hawkins said.

"So have I."

"I'll bet you have. There was a ring in there worth thirty thousand. Your piece of that should last you a while, huh?"

"I wish it was true, Mr. Hawkins. As it is, I'm struggling to make ends meet."

"Aren't we all?" Hawkins said, and smiled like Burt Reynolds. "I don't suppose the ring is still here, is it?"

"Tell you what," Alex said. "Whyn't you go get a search warrant and come back and look for it?"

"I may do just that."

"No, you won't do that cause you know you won't find a fuckin thing here. You know why, Mr. Hawkins? Cause you know I didn't do that job, and you're just hassling me all the time, anyway. Now why do you do that, Mr. Hawkins? Why don't you just give me a break, huh?"

"Thanks for the coffee," Hawkins said, and rose, and shoved his chair back under the table.

"I'm sorry it was instant," Alex said.

"Well, it's better than what you get in jail, huh?" Hawkins said, and grinned again, and then went to the front door and let himself out.

At the mailboxes downstairs, Alex checked out Jessica Knowles's apartment. 5C. That was just two floors down from him, very convenient. He debated going upstairs, drop in on her unexpectedly, Hello there, just thought I'd stop by, see how you were doing. Maybe catch her in a nightgown or something, what time was it, anyway? He looked at his watch. Twenty after twelve, maybe it was worth a shot. Kitty had left him feeling crummy. He didn't know why, hell, she could do whatever she wanted to do, that was her business, he just didn't give a damn. But why'd she have to tell him that story? Knock on the door, Hi there, Jessica, anything you need at the store? No, he'd better wait till tomorrow night. He didn't want to rush her. Cool and easy. Patience, sweetie. That fuckin Kitty.

He was carrying in his pocket seventeen thousand dollars in cash, and he went first to the Chemical Bank on Broadway and Ninety-first, where he deposited five thousand of it into his savings account there. Then he taxied down to Seventy-third and Broadway and deposited another five thousand into his checking account with Chase Manhattan. His third bank was on Fifty-ninth and Lex, the Dry Dock. He put fifty-five hundred into his second savings account, leaving himself with fifteen hundred in cash. He had to give Tommy five hundred of that, which would still leave him one thousand for spending money.

Making the deposits almost wiped out the lousy feeling Kitty had left him with. He just couldn't understand that girl. Getting herself in trouble that way to begin with, and then going down on those two wops when she should have picked up a letter opener from the desk, stuck it in somebody's eye, fought her way out of it the way he'd done that one time at Sing Sing when the lifer got rough with him. You had to show them. You didn't, why then they walked all over you. Hell with her. All he wanted from her now was his two thousand bucks back. And she'd be one sorry whore if she didn't deliver.

Tommy Palumbo lived downtown on Mulberry Street, in Little Italy. He lived with his mother and father, but neither of them was home during the day because they ran a grocery store on Mott Street. Tommy was on the front stoop with a couple of other guys when Alex drove up in the taxi. They all turned to see who this was, pulling up in a taxi.

Tommy recognized him right away and came bounding off the stoop. He was twenty-two years old, but he was small and slight, and he looked more like seventeen. He was wearing dungaree pants, a white T-shirt, and a light blue poplin windbreaker. He was also wearing high-topped sneakers; looked like a teenager about to play some stickball.

"Hey, man," he said, and stuck out his hand. Alex shook hands with him, and then paid and tipped the cabby.

"Your people home?" he asked.

"No," Tommy said, "they're at the store."

"Then let's go upstairs, huh?"

"Sure," Tommy said. "Something I want to show you, anyway."

They moved past the guys on the stoop, who looked Alex over as though he were fuzz. The hallway was clean, it smelled of antiseptic; your tenements down here in Little Italy never stunk of piss the way they did in Harlem. They walked up to the third floor, and Tommy let them into the apartment with his key. They sat in the living room. On the wall opposite the sofa, there was a picture of Jesus Christ on the cross. Over his head, it said INRI.

"What does that mean, anyway?" Alex asked. "Inri."

"Iron Nails Ran In," Tommy said.

"Come on, it's Latin or something."

"No, it's Iron Nails Ran In. From when the Jews nailed him on the cross."

"I never heard that before," Alex said.

"Yeah, it's true. My grandmother told me."

"I got something for you," Alex said, and grinned and took out his wallet. Henry had paid him in twenties, and he counted off twenty-five of them now and handed the bills to Tommy. "Five hundred," he said. "Okay?"

"That's too much," Tommy said.

"You were the one put me in touch with Henry."

"Still, that's a lot."

"Be my guest," Alex said. "How do you know him, any-how?"

"Henry? I met him through this Jew used to be my fall partner. Before I got busted that time. A guy named Jerry Stein, you know him?"

"No."

"Yeah, we done two jobs together. He went out as a single afterwards, but there was no hard feelings, we got along fine together. Yeah, we hit two liquor stores up in the Bronx. Jerry goes in, he don't fuck around. He sticks the gun right in the guy's ear, he says Empty the cash register or you have a tunnel through your head. He's the one introduced me to Henry, right after I got out. He knew I was looking for some-thing, he figured maybe Henry could think of something for me. He's into a lot of things, Henry. But Henry told me what he needed right now was a good burglar, so I told him I knew the *best* burglar in New York . . . "

"Yeah, yeah."

"That's no shit, Alex." Tommy shrugged. "So that's how it happened. It was a good job, huh?"

"Oh, yeah."

"Easy?"

"Medium. I would say medium."

"No trouble, huh?"

"None at all."

"Good," Tommy said. "Wait'll you see what *I* got."

"What is it?"

"Just sit right there, I'll get it."

"It ain't a gun, is it?"

Tommy did not answer. Smiling, he went out of the living room and into the rear of the apartment. Alex waited. He knew fuckin-A well it was a gun.

"Close your eyes," Tommy said from the other room.

"Come on, I don't have to close my eyes," Alex said.

Tommy came back into the room with his hands behind his back.

"It's a gun, ain't it?" Alex said.

"Yeah, but what *kind* of gun you think it is?" Tommy said. His eyes were glowing, there was a broad smile on his face.

"I'll tell you what kind," Alex said. "It's the kind that'll get you in trouble, what*ever* the fuck kind it is."

"Look," Tommy said, and pulled his right hand from behind his back and thrust the pistol almost into Alex's face. The gun was huge, the biggest pistol Alex had ever seen in his life.

"What *is* that thing?" he asked. "Get that thing out of my face, will you? Is that thing loaded?"

"No, it ain't loaded," Tommy said. "You know what it is?"

"No, what is it? How do you know it ain't loaded?"

"Cause it ain't loaded, look," he said, and rolled out the cylinder to show Alex there were no cartridges in it.

"How do I know there ain't one in the chamber?" Alex said.

"I'm telling you it ain't loaded. What do you think of it?"

"It looks like a cannon," Alex said.

"It *is* a cannon. It's a .357 Magnum, that's what it is. You know who's using this gun now?"

"Who?"

"The troopers upstate, and also the Connecticut troopers."

"Whyn't you go put it away?" Alex said. "You make me nervous, waving it around like that."

"You can blow off a man's leg with this gun. One shot, you can blow off his leg."

"I believe it," Alex said.

"You know how long this barrel is?"

"How long?"

"Almost a foot long. Eleven and one-quarter inches, that's how long it is."

"Yeah," Alex said, and looked at the barrel. "Put it away, all right?"

"There're cases," Tommy said, "a guy shot somebody with a .357, the bullet went right through him and also killed a *second* guy. This is one fuckin powerful gun. The Connecticut troopers are using hollow-point bullets in it, they tumble through the air and flatten out when they hit somebody. That's so if they shoot in a crowd, the bullet'll rip into the body and go off at angles inside there, and it won't pass through and hit no innocent bystander. Cause this thing is so powerful, it could put a hole in an engine block, would you believe it?"

"I told you I believe it. Now put it away."

"You know how much I paid for this thing? On the street, I mean."

"How much?"

"Two hundred and forty bucks. You could stop a buffalo with this fuckin piece."

"Too bad there ain't no buffalos in New York," Alex said.

"I got me a very big buffalo in mind," Tommy said, and grinned conspiratorially, and then said, "I better put this back in my drawer. My old lady walks in here, she'll take a fit."

"You got a drawer big enough to *put* it in?" Alex said, and Tommy laughed and went out of the room. "You're crazy, you know that?" Alex called after him.

"Yeah, yeah," Tommy said.

"You must want to go back up real bad."

"Anybody tries to send me back up," Tommy said, "I'll blow his fuckin head off. This piece can blow a man's head off."

"I *thought* you said his leg."

"His head, too," Tommy said, and came back into the room. "You want to hear my idea?"

"No. Not if it involves that thing you just showed me."

"Of *course* it does, why you think I bought it?"

"'Cause you're crazy."

"You want to hear this, or not?"

"Tommy, you want my advice? Throw that gun in the garbage."

"It cost me two hundred and forty bucks," Tommy said.

"Throw it in the garbage. Here," Alex said, and took out his wallet and opened it. "Here's the two-forty, go throw the gun away."

"I *need* that gun," Tommy said.

"What for?"

"I been feelin like shit ever since I got out. Didn't know what was the matter with me, my mother kept askin was I sick. You should be glad you're home, she said, why you goin around with a long face all the time? Okay. This morning, I bought the piece. You see a long face on me now? What you see now is a happy person."

"Who's heading right back to Sing Sing."

"Not me," Tommy said. "I got a good plan for that piece."

"I don't want to hear it."

"You're the one give me the idea," Tommy said.

"Me?"

"You. I wouldn't have thought of it, it wasn't **for** you."

"Tommy, are you crazy? Are you *really* crazy, or what?"

"Just listen a minute, and you'll see how crazy I am. You want a beer? There's Heineken and Schlitz in the fridge, which you want?"

"The Heineken."

"That's what my old man drinks," Tommy said, and went

out to the kitchen. "He used to make wine, you know? In the basement? No more. All he does now is drink Heineken beer. He brings home *three* six-packs every day, drinks them at night while he's watching TV. He counts them, makes sure nobody else in the house is drinking them. For me, he brings home the Schlitz. I touch the Heineken, he whacks me in the head."

"Okay, I'll have a Schlitz," Alex said.

"No, I'll tell him a friend stopped by. My old man's a real ginzo, hospitality's a big thing with him." Tommy came back into the room with a bottle of Schlitz, a bottle of Heineken, and an opener. He uncapped both bottles, and handed the Heineken to Alex. "Here's looking up your whole family," he said, and tilted the bottle of Schlitz to his mouth. "Good," he said, wiping his lips. "Just as good as that Dutch shit. You want to hear my plan?"

"I got no choice," Alex said. "I'm drinking your old man's beer."

"Don't worry about it," Tommy said and laughed. "I'll tell him a very good friend drank it. You could even drink another one if you like. I'll tell him I knew you from Sing Sing. He just *loves* my old pals from Sing Sing."

"I'll bet he's gonna love that Magnum, too, he ever gets a look at it."

"Only one person gonna see that piece," Tommy said, "and then it goes down the sewer."

"Who's that?"

"The person who's gonna see it? Guess."

"Who?"

"Henry Green."

Alex put down his beer bottle, and then turned on the sofa to look at Tommy.

"Yeah," Tommy said, and grinned. "I'm gonna stick up Henry's shop. Whattya think of *that*?"

"I think it's the stupidest fuckin idea I ever heard in my life."

"You think so, huh? Well, I don't think so. I think it's a very good idea, in fact. You want to know why? Here's why."

"I don't want to know why."

"Henry set up a job for you, am I right? Okay, I got to figure a jeweler don't go settin up a job there's nothing in it for him, am I right? He doesn't go sendin you in after a two-dollar watch, he's got to have something bigger in mind, no? Okay. So yesterday you done the job, I know that cause you're here now to pay me off, so you musta done it yesterday, that's maid's day off. Okay, so where's the haul now? I got to figure if Henry already paid you for it, then it's in Henry's shop. I can't believe he could've got rid of it so fast, so it's still got to be there, am I right? Okay. It *ain't* gonna be there after six tonight."

Tommy was grinning. Alex was staring at him.

"Good, huh?" Tommy said.

"Very good," Alex said. "I'll send you cigarettes and spending money."

"What's wrong with it?"

"What's *wrong* with it? Henry *knows* you, you stupid fuck!"

"That don't matter."

"Oh, it don't. I see, it don't. It don't matter he'll call the cops the minute you go out of there, tell them Tommy Palumbo just held up his store."

"He won't call the cops."

"What're you gonna do? Put a bullet in his head before you leave? Add a little homicide to the rap?"

"I don't have to put no bullet in his head."

"Tommy . . ."

"The stuff is *hot,* don't you see? He *can't* report the fuckin holdup. Because if he tells them it was me, and the cops come after me, what they're gonna find is all the stuff you stole yesterday. Henry can't risk that because then they'll know he fenced the job and maybe set it up besides. You understand, Alex? I got him by the balls."

"Unless he already got rid of the stuff," Alex said.

"What do you mean?"

"Suppose he already got rid of it? Suppose it ain't there in his shop?"

"No," Tommy said, "he wouldn't have got rid of it so fast. You think he might have got rid of it?"

"Sure," Alex said.

"So fast?"

"Sure."

"Yeah," Tommy said.

"So if you hold him up for just the legitimate stuff he's got in the shop there, he'll call the cops the minute you go out."

"Yeah," Tommy said.

"Unless you kill him, of course."

"Yeah."

"Now you don't want to *kill* the man, do you, Tommy?"

"No, I don't want to kill him. But . . ."

"That's very heavy shit, killing a man."

"Yeah. I know, but . . . Jesus, it was such a good idea."

"It was, Tommy. I'll give you that. It was a good idea. But only if the stuff would still be in the shop. If he already got rid of it, then it wouldn't work. Cause he'd blow the whistle, you see."

"Yeah, that's what he'd do, all right."

"So you better forget it."

"Yeah," Tommy said. "Jesus, it was such a good idea."

On Saturday night, while he was dressing for his date with Jessica, the telephone rang. Archie was on the other end of the line.

"What are you doing tonight?" Archie asked.

"I'm busy. Why, what's up?"

"I been talking to Daisy," he said. "I want to fill you in on this."

"How does it look?"

"Not bad. You think you can get up here tomorrow morning?"

"That depends on how tonight goes," Alex said. "I don't want to leave nothing good here in the sack."

"Man, you mixin business with pleasure," Archie said.

"Let me call you in the morning, okay?"

"I hope you can get up here," Archie said. "This looks kind of interesting."

"I'll let you know," Alex said.

He hung up, and went back to the dresser, and began knotting his tie. Archie wouldn't have called if he hadn't done some preliminary work and figured there was a chance for a shot. He was almost tempted to call Jessica and tell her something important had come up, he'd have to take a rain check. No, Archie could wait till tomorrow. If what he had was so hot, it would hold till tomorrow. Anyway, Archie had only said it looked *kind* of interesting, and that was no reason to go running uptown, not for something that looked only *kind* of interesting. Still, Archie had a way of making things sound small and unimportant, that was *his* particular superstition. Never make the thing sound big, because then you'd only be disappointed if it turned out to be small potatoes. He wanted very much to hear what Archie had come up with, but it could wait. He realized as he put on his jacket that he was pretty excited about seeing Jessica.

The last time he'd dated a square girl was that time in Miami, when he'd told her he was a burglar. He had struck out completely that night because it turned out the girl thought he was being what she called "flippant." Even after he told her he wasn't *really* a burglar but just an insurance salesman, she insisted he was being "flippant," and said she didn't know *what* to believe from him anymore. He had taken her to dinner at an expensive restaurant and then had driven the rented car all the way to Lauderdale, but the minute he pulled into the motel courtyard, she said, "Hey, what's this?"

"I thought we'd go in and watch some television," he said.

"You said we were just going for a drive."

"Yeah, but now the drive is over."

"What kind of girl do you think I am?" she said.

"I don't know," he said. "Are you a burglar?"

"Very funny. Just turn this thing around and let's get out of here, okay?"

"You don't want to watch some television? The sign says they've got color television."

"I've got television in my own room," she said. "If I want to watch television, I can go back to the hotel."

"Okay, let's do that," Alex suggested.

"I don't want to watch television."

"What do you want to do?"

"I thought this was going to be a big night," she said.

"It could be a very big night."

"Not *that* kind of night."

"I've got a good idea," Alex said.

"Yeah, I'll bet."

"Get the fuck out of the car."

"What?"

"Get out." He leaned over her and opened the door on her side, and then said, "Out."

He still wondered how she had got back to Miami that night. The last time he'd seen her, she was standing under the motel sign with her hands on her hips. That was in the rearview mirror, as he drove off. He supposed he had played it wrong. Maybe he should have taken her to the fronton after dinner, or maybe the track, show her a good time, play it slow and easy.

Tonight, he'd play it slow and easy. He took one last look at himself in the mirror, and then went out of the apartment and downstairs to 5C. The girl who answered the door looked sixteen. She was wearing eyeglasses, and she had pimples all over her face. She looked him up and down the way young kids did nowadays.

"Hi," he said.

"Hi," she answered.

"Is that you, Alex?" Jessica called from someplace in the apartment.

"That's me," he said.

"Be with you in a minute," she called. "Sit down, will you? Felice, show him where the bar is. Fix yourself a drink if you like, Alex."

"Thanks," he said, and followed Felice into the living room.

"The bar's there," she said, and pointed to a corner of the room. He walked to it, and checked out the liquor supply. Jessica had some nice stuff. Her husband was maybe a chintzy bastard, like she'd said, but she sure wasn't scrimping on the booze.

"How long you gonna be?" he called through the apartment.

"Oh, just a minute," she said. "But fix yourself a drink."

He figured that meant she'd be at least ten minutes, so he poured himself some Scotch over ice, and then went to sit on the sofa. Felice sat in a chair opposite him, watching him like an owl from behind her glasses. The living room was nicely furnished, though not to his taste, with a lot of ornate-looking stuff with inlaid wood and curlicues, Louis XV, he supposed it was, or XVI, who the hell knew? Or cared. There was a piano in one corner of the room, he wondered if Jessica played the piano. He also wondered what her husband did for a living; the place must have cost a penny or two to put together.

"Felice, huh?" he said to the babysitter. "Is that your name?"

"Yes," she said.

"What do you do, Felice? Do you go to school?"

"Yes," she said.

"Where?"

"Fieldston, Riverdale."

"What's that, a private school?"

"Yes," she said. "Is that Scotch you're drinking?"

"That's Scotch," he said, "yeah," and looked at the glass in his hand.

"I hate Scotch," she said. "I like rye and ginger."

"Well, that's a nice drink, too," he said. "How old are you, anyway?"

"Fifteen," she said.

"That's a little young to be drinking, isn't it?"

"My parents know about it," she said flatly.

"Well, fine then," he said, and thought Fuck you, kid.

He had finished the drink and was about to pour himself another, when Jessica came into the room. She was wearing a green dress that was cut low in the bodice, with a pleated flaring skirt and a hemline that ended about three inches above the knee. She had on green earrings and a green pendant that hung just between her breasts; he didn't know whether they were real emeralds, he couldn't tell from this distance, but he guessed they weren't. There was green eye shadow over her eyes, and she was wearing a pale orange lipstick and green high-heeled pumps. Her legs looked spectacular, and he could tell from one quick glance at the front of her dress that she wasn't wearing a bra. She came striding into the room like an actress or a model, knowing she looked terriffic and waiting for his response, waiting for the approval on his face, but at the same time seeming embarrassed about wanting the approval and lowering her eyes somewhat shyly as she came toward him.

"You look beautiful," he said, and suddenly felt very foolish. She was dressed to kill, and all he had in mind was the Harbin Inn up on a Hundredth and Broadway. He was wearing gray slacks and a blue blazer, with a simple gold tie, and he felt too casually dressed now, and realized he should have worn a suit. "Really beautiful," he said.

"Well, you look beautiful, too," she said, and glanced at the empty glass in his hand, and said, "Shall we go? Or did you want another one?"

"I'm ready when you are," he said.

"Felice," she said, turning away from him, the pleated skirt of the dress flaring, "Peter's in his crib, but he's not asleep yet, so please check on him in ten minutes or so."

"Sure," Felice said. "How late will you be?"

"Well, I'm not sure. Do you have a curfew?"

"No, I just wanted to know."

"I have no idea. Felice, don't let anyone in. Lock the door after we go out, and then don't open it for anyone. I'll let myself in with my key."

"Okay," Felice said. "Did you want to leave a number where you'll be?"

"I don't know where we'll be. I'll call later, anyway," Jessica said.

"Fine," Felice said.

"Okay?" she said, and started toward the entrance foyer. "Do I need a coat, Alex?"

"Well, I don't know. I haven't been outside. It might be a little chilly, with just the dress."

She took a light topcoat from the hall closet, and they went out of the apartment. Behind him, he heard Felice locking the door. A lot of good it would do if anybody wanted to get in there. The lock was a cheap piece of crap.

He had secrets.

He had secrets from her, and secrets from the world.

His biggest secret was that he was a burglar. He lived outside the law, and took pride in this; he was *not* like her or any of the squares surrounding them in the restaurant. He lived by his wits and his skill and his daring; he was like an adventurer, who looked for challenge after challenge, beating each one in turn. He kept his secret as tight as if it were locked inside a cannonball keyster. Neither she nor any of the restaurant patrons or waiters could pry the secret from him. It was his alone, locked tight behind layers of impenetrable steel that couldn't be punched, drilled, peeled, or torched. His secret could look out through the one-way mirrors of his eyes, but no one could see through those eyes and into his secret; all they got was a mirror image of themselves. He was a burglar; that was his *biggest* secret. And though it was securely hidden, he felt it gave him a touch of swagger, style, and danger—the way you looked at a sword in its sheath and all you saw was the handle, but you knew there was a razor-edged blade inside there.

There were other secrets, too.

Secretly, he was pleased by the way she looked, the way heads had turned when they walked together into the restaurant, the way even now men sneaked glances at her. And by extension, the radiance her beauty emanated seemed to include him as well, and made him feel better looking, and stronger, and smarter than the square johns who didn't have Jessica sitting opposite them at *their* tables, Jessica leaning forward to accept a light for her cigarette, Jessica laughing, Jessica studying the menu seriously and then suggesting that he order for both of them since he probably knew more about Chinese food than she did. He knew that every man in the place was envying him—that was *their* secret, though a transparent one—but he suspected that *everyone,* men *and* women alike, were envying them, a beautiful, blue-eyed, golden-haired pair having a great time together.

They were special, that was it. They gave off an aura of something special. And this added to the secret of his occupation: He was Alex Hardy, burglar, and he had the most beautiful girl in the room, and she was hanging on his every word, her eyes sparkling and attentive, her hand darting out every so often to touch his. Secretly, he glowed with the pleasure of simply being there with a woman so extraordinarily beautiful, though she had not seemed quite this beautiful that first day in the taxi.

And secretly, he took pride in understanding Chinese food, and in being able to order knowledgeably and extravagantly from the menu, his expertise as unchallengeable as his skill at burglary. He knew Chinese food, and he knew burglary, and he knew jazz, and he led the conversation around to jazz because jazz was what he wanted her to listen to after they'd finished eating, and this led him to his final secret, which he also chose not to share with her, but which he suspected she already knew, and the secret was that he was going to lay her tonight. Not only was she beautiful, not only did every man in the place acknowledge her beauty and envy him for it, but inside they were probably aching as well because they also knew Alex was going to lay her before the night was through. He never doubted it for a moment, and he suspected she'd already accepted it as fact, and he hoped every man in the place knew it, and this made him feel more important than all the other secrets combined.

"I've been collecting jazz a long time," he said, "started when I was just a kid."

"Do you mean Dixieland?" she asked.

"Well, some Dixieland," he said, "but mostly other stuff. I have a lot of Charlie Parker records, he's the king, he's the one I really dig."

"Mm," she said.

"Do you know Charlie Parker?"

"No, I don't," she admitted.

"Oh, then you've got a real treat coming," he said. "If that's what you want to do afterwards, go back and listen to some records."

"I'm starved," she said. "Are you starved?"

"Yeah, we'll be eating in just a bit," he said. "He'll bring the appetizers with our drinks, and then he'll bring the rest of the stuff. This is a really good Chinese restaurant, you know, this is really good Northern cooking. You can get your usual spareribs and egg rolls here, too, but I thought you might want to try something a little different."

"Yes," she said.

"The sea bass is terrific, I hope you like fish."

"Yes, I do. I love fish."

"Ah, here's the drinks. Thanks," he said to the waiter, "the lady gets the whiskey sour, I get the Scotch. They cook it in this paper bag," he said, and lifted his glass. "Cheers."

"Cheers," she said, and clinked her glass against his.

"I'm really enjoying this," he said.

"So am I."

"You're beautiful," he said, "you look just terrific."

"Thank you. I *feel* terrific," she said, and shrugged her shoulders slightly and giggled. "I haven't been out in such a long time. This is something very new for me."

"What is?"

"Going out with a man," she said. "I mean with a man who's not my husband. I've been married for six years. I haven't been out with anyone else in all that time."

"Well, there's always a first time," he said.

"I'm learning that. Tell me more about your jazz collection."

"Well, it's very difficult to explain jazz," he said. "When I've got the records on, later, I'll tell you what I know about the artists, the performers. That's if you want to go back later and hear the records."

"We'll see," she said. "Is there anything good playing around?"

"I didn't check the papers. We'll see, okay? If you want to go to a movie, we can do that. Whatever you want to do. Here's the appetizers."

"Mm, they smell delicious," she said.

"They are delicious. Waiter, bring us some sweet-and-sour sauce, huh? And some mustard. You want another drink, Jessica? Make it another round, waiter."

"How'd you happen to become a theater electrician?" she asked.

"Well, my father was an electrician," he said. "Try some of these. They're water chestnuts wrapped in bacon."

"A theater electrician?"

"Yes. That's how I got into it. It's a very tight union, you see. A father-and-son union, actually."

"I didn't realize that," she said.

"Oh, yes."

"Then you must have been interested in the theater even when you were a child."

"Well, my father didn't get into it till I was a teenager."

"What did he do before then?"

"He was an electrician, but not a theater electrician."

"In New York, was this?"

"Yes."

"Are you originally from New York?"

"Yes. The Bronx. Can't you tell?"

"Well . . . "

"That's all right, I know I don't sound like a Harvard graduate. I never even finished high school," he said. "I only got through my junior year, and then I quit." He looked directly into her eyes and then said, "I always regretted not having gone to college," which was a deliberate lie since he'd never given a single thought to going to college.

"That doesn't matter to me," she said. "Whether or not a man's been to college. My husband's got a master's, but that doesn't make him the kind of man I particularly respect and admire."

"What kind of man *do* you respect and admire?" Alex asked.

"Well . . . I like honesty in a man. It's very honest of you to recognize, for example, that there's a . . . well . . . a trace of New York accent in your speech, and to . . . "

"The Bronx," he said.

"Yes, and to admit it freely, and not get all uptight about it."

"Well, I *do* sometimes get uptight about it," he said. "Sometimes, when I'm with people who are . . . well . . . who sound more refined than I do, I guess I get uptight about it. Last year about this time, I was down in Puerto Rico, for example, and I was staying at the Conquistador down there, El Conquistador, and I had a conversation with a doctor and his wife, this was around the pool, and he made me feel like two cents. He was a surgeon. From Detroit, I think, or Chicago, I forget which. I got home, I remember, I started looking up words in the dictionary, and doing crossword puzzles, you know, lots of crossword puzzles, trying to build a vocabulary. So I *do* get uptight sometimes."

"Even that's an honest admission," Jessica said.

"Well, thank you," he said. "What else do you look for in a man?"

"Why do you want to know?"

Alex shrugged. "I'm a man, and I'm sitting here with you, so naturally I want to see how I shape up."

"Well," she said, and smiled, and then struck a thoughtful pose, and said, "I like men who are appreciative."

"Yeah, how?"

"Who tell me I'm beautiful," she said. "When I've gone to a lot of trouble to make myself *look* beautiful."

"You *are* beautiful," Alex said.

"Thank you," she said, and lowered her eyes. "And I like men who have . . . I suppose you'd call it an air of certainty, yes. Men who seem to know what they're doing."

"That lets me out, I guess. I sometimes don't know which side is up."

"I don't believe that about you," she said, and raised her eyes and looked full into his face. "I think you're a man who's very much in command of a situation, whatever the situation might be."

"What do you think the situation is here and now?" he asked, and reached across the table and covered her hand with his own.

"I'm not quite sure," she said.

"But you think I'm in command of it, huh?"

"Yes. Very much so."

"That could be dangerous," he said. "For you, I mean."

"I don't think so," she said.

"Well, we'll see," he said.

There was no thought of going to a movie after dinner; neither of them even raised the question again. Instead, they walked back to the building and then went upstairs to Alex's apartment. He asked her if she wanted some Courvoisier or Grand Marnier, and she said she'd like the Grand Marnier, please, and then asked him where the telephone was. He told her it was in his bedroom, and she went in there and he heard her dialing as he poured the drinks into brandy snifters. She was sitting on the edge of the bed, the telephone to her ear, when he came in.

"Yes," she said, "in a box on the floor of the linen closet. Be sure you get the *overnight* Pampers. And, Felice, it would be a good idea to put him on the potty first." She listened for a moment, and then said, "Yes, I'm sure he'll go back to sleep after you change him. But I'll give you the number here, if there are any problems," and read Alex's number from the telephone dial. She listened again, and said, "I don't know what time. If there are any problems, just call me." She hung up, took the snifter from Alex, said, "Ahh, thank you," sipped at it, and then said, "I hope she can handle it. She seemed responsible, didn't you think?"

"Yes," Alex said, remembering that old Felice had told him she liked to drink rye and ginger, but not willing to divulge this; that's all he had to do, tell Jessica her darling baby boy was downstairs with a teenage boozer, she'd rush right out of here. Anyway, Felice had probably been trying to sound like a big shot, probably never drank anything stronger than a Pepsi. "So you want to hear some records?" he asked.

"That's why we're here," she said and smiled, and stood up and followed him out into the living room.

"You ought to sit on the couch," he said. "The way the speakers are positioned, you'll get the best sound there."

"Okay," she said.

"Some of these are kind of scratchy. I've had them a long time, and I play them a lot. The thing I missed most when I was in . . . " He stopped short. He'd been about to tell her he'd missed his records while he was in prison.

She had just sat on the couch and was putting her drink on the coffee table when he stopped speaking. She looked at up at him and said, "Yes?"

"The records," he said.

"What about them?"

"When I was down with my mother in Miami," he said, "I missed them a lot. I was only there for a week, but I missed the records."

"I can understand that," she said.

"You get used to things, you know. I play them all the time, so I missed them while I was down there."

"Yes," she said. "I hope that damn kid knows how to change a diaper."

"Oh yeah, she seemed very bright. She goes to a private school, you know."

"Yes, I know that."

"Well," he said, "this is Charlie Parker," and he held up the album to show it to her. "Now what I've done, I've picked a record that'll give you an example of what his different styles were like. I've got records here, for example, some of his early records, that would just tell you what he was playing at *one* time in his career, you understand? But this was, this is a reissue that covers a lot of the different bands he had, and it'll give you some idea. Okay?"

"Okay," she said. "I'm ready."

Smiling, he put the record on the turntable. As the first sounds came from the speakers, he adjusted the treble and brass, and then asked, "Is that loud enough?"

"Yes, that's fine."

"Okay," he said, and sat opposite her in a chair near the bookshelves, where the record albums were stacked on edge.

"But can you hear it all right from there?" Jessica asked.

"Yeah, this is fine." He thought she might have been inviting him to join her on the couch, but he wasn't going to make the same mistake he'd made with the square in Miami. Slow and easy tonight. "This first cut he did with the Neal Hefti Orchestra, it's called 'Repetition.' There are some very good people on this cut, some of them maybe you're familiar with. Shelly Manne is on drums, for instance, do you know Shelly Manne?"

"No," she said.

"Or Flip Phillips? He plays tenor sax."

"No," she said.

"Here's Parker now," he said, "listen. He's about to come in on the alto."

"Um-huh," she said, and nodded and closed her eyes and then leaned her head back against the couch and crossed her legs. The flared skirt moved higher on her thigh for just an instant. Automatically, she lowered it with one hand and then began jiggling her foot in time to the music. "That's very nice," she said.

"Yeah," he said. "None of this is arranged, you know. He's making it up as he goes along. What they do is there's chords in a song, and they just take the chords and make up their own melodies. That's the beauty of it. This is all being made up as they go along. They could play this same song two nights in a row, and it'd be different each time out."

"Improvisation," Jessica said.

"Right, improvisation, that's the word. Listen to what he does here."

"Yes," Jessica said. "My husband plays the piano, you know. But not jazz piano."

"I didn't know he was a musician," Alex said.

"It's just for his own amusement. He's not a professional."

He was not too pleased that they were talking while the record was on, you weren't supposed to *talk* when you were listening to jazz, you were just supposed to *listen* to it. She opened her eyes now, and uncrossed her legs, and leaned forward to take a cigarette from her bag. Lighting it, she blew out a stream of smoke and then cocked her head to one side, as though paying strict attention to what was coming from the speakers, but he knew she wasn't digging it at all. When she said, "This must be difficult to dance to," he wanted to say You're not *supposed* to dance to it, you're supposed to *listen* to it, and you're also not supposed to *talk*, but he didn't say anything.

She finished the Grand Marnier, and then said, "I haven't danced in ages. My husband didn't know how to dance. Do you mind if I help myself to a little more of this?"

"I'll get it for you," he said, and started out of the chair, but she was already up and walking toward the bar. As she poured from the bottle, she said, "It's funny how little you know about a man before you marry him. We lived together for a year before we got married, and I never knew he couldn't dance." She put the stopper back on the bottle and then instead of going back to the couch, she did several pirouettes across the room, almost spilling her drink, and laughed, and said, "This is *very* difficult to dance to," and then went to sit in a chair near the speaker on the left.

"Now *this* cut,"he said, "is the Charlie Parker Quartet he had in 1948, the fall of 1948. This is called 'The Bird,' that's his nickname, Parker's nickname."

"Um-huh," she said. "I didn't have a record player when I was growing up. I used to listen to the radio a lot. I listened to Country Western, that's what we had out there. I lived on a dairy farm in Wisconsin, my father still has it out there. I had a cow when I was a little girl. My *own* cow. I'll bet you didn't have a cow of your own when you were growing up."

"No, I didn't," he said.

"Daisy. I named her Daisy."

He almost said he knew a one-legged whore named Daisy, but he caught himself in time.

"Used to feed her, milk her, I took very good care of her. When I went off to college, my father just put her out to pasture. She was too old to give milk anymore, but he didn't want to sell her for slaughter because he knew how much I loved that old cow."

Alex figured there was no sense trying to get her to listen to the record. If she wanted to talk, he'd let her talk. Slow and easy, give her enough fuckin rope. "Where'd you go to college?" he asked.

"UCLA. In Los Angeles. I was an English major. My husband was there at the time, my then *future* husband, that's where I met him. He was going for his master's in educational psychology. We dated a few times, but nothing came of it, we went our separate ways. I met him again after I came to New York. I was doing some work for Random House, and they had this huge cocktail party for a writer whose manuscript I'd copyedited, and there was Michael. My husband. He'd written a book Random House was supposed to publish. They asked for a lot of revisions later on, and he told them to go to hell, but at the time he thought he was going to be on their list, and there he was, there *I* was, and we met all over again. We started seeing each other a lot, neither of us were kids at the time, this was seven years ago, I was twenty-two and he was twenty-six, so we figured we might as well move into the same apartment."

She was toying with the hem of her skirt as she spoke. She held the brandy snifter in her right hand, and with her left hand she plucked at the hem of the skirt, almost rhythmically, though not in time with the music that was still coming from the speakers. "We lived together for a year," she said, "and then decided to get married. We were happy at first, I suppose. I think we were. In fact, I guess we were happy until our son was born, and then Michael began playing around with other women, one that I knew about for sure, an older woman who was a physics instructor at Columbia, where he was going for his doctorate nights. In the daytime he was teaching at CCNY, and between lessons plans for his ed psych classes there and the assignments he had to do for his classes at Columbia, not to mention his playing around with the physics instructor and Christ knew how many other women, I hardly ever got to *see* him anymore. Even *before* we were separated." She drained the snifter, and said, "I love this stuff, I could drink it all night long."

"There's plenty there," Alex said.

"The only good thing about Michael," she said, somewhat wistfully it seemed to Alex, "was that he was good in bed."

She laughed, and then said, "Of course, I never had any basis for comparison."

"Do you miss him?" Alex asked.

"*Miss* him? I hope the bastard gets hit by a bus," she said, and laughed again.

"Listen," Alex said, "if you want to dance, I can put on . . ."

"No, that's all right," she said. "I like what you've got on."

"Well, I saw you twirling around the room there . . ."

"Oh, that was just . . . Do *you* want to dance?" she asked.

"I'm not a very good dancer," he said. "But if you want to dance, I can put on the flip side. There's a lot of stuff there he did with the strings. If you want to dance."

"I'm probably very rusty," she said.

"Should I turn the record over?"

"Yes, I'd like to hear it," she said, "but we don't have to dance if you don't want to. Would you mind if I called downstairs again? I just want to make sure he went back to sleep all right."

"Go right ahead," he said. "Did you want me to fill your glass again, Jess?"

She was already on her way to the bedroom, and she stopped and turned to look at him, and very softly said, "Why'd you call me that?"

"Huh?" he said. He didn't know what she meant. Called her *what?*

"Jess," she said. "My father used to call me Jess."

"I don't know, it just came out," he said, and shrugged.

She smiled, and nodded, and then went into the bedroom. He heard her dialing as he turned the record over. He moved the arm to the second cut, because the first cut on this side was "Passport No. 2," and he knew she wouldn't dig any of the small-group stuff, and probably wouldn't recognize that the tune was based on the "I Got Rhythm" chords. He went to the bar to refill her glass, and when she came out of the bedroom again, he said, "Everything okay?"

"Yep," she said. "Got him changed and tucked him back in. All quiet on the western front."

"Good," he said. "Now this is Charlie with string," he said. "He's got Mitch Miller on oboe in there. You know Mitch Miller, don't you?"

"Oh, sure," she said. "I used to watch him on television."

"And also Buddy Rich, he's a drummer."

"I'm not sure I recognize the song they're playing," she said.

"That's 'Just Friends,' it's almost over. You'll know this next one, it's 'Everything Happens to Me,' that was a very popular song."

"Oh, it's *nice* with the strings," she said, and began swaying and lazily tossing her head. "Mmm, I like that."

"Do you want to try to dance to it?" Alex asked.

"Let's just listen for a while, okay?"

"Sure," he said. "Here's your drink, if you want it."

"Thank you," she said, and took the snifter and sat on the couch and crossed her legs. Her skirt rode up again, but this time she did not move to lower it. "I think I like the strings much better," she said.

"Well, jazz experts don't think too much of this band he had with the strings. But I suppose it's easier to dance to."

"Mm," she said. "It's very lush. And sensuous."

"Yeah," he said.

They listened in silence to the next two cuts, and when "Summertime" came on, she said, "Ahhh, 'Summertime,' I love this song. *This* I want to dance to. Shall we try it, Alex?"

"Sure," he said.

She got off the couch, and he moved to meet her in the center of the room.

"I'm probably very rusty," she said again.

"I won't be able to tell the difference," he said. "I'm really a lousy dancer."

He took her into his arms, but he did not pull her in tight against him. The dress she had on was made of nylon jersey that felt smoothly electric to his spread fingers, where his hand rested on the small of her back. As they circled the floor, he kept a circumspect distance between them, telling himself that the only way to play this was slow and easy. He felt that things were going along nicely, but he didn't want her to spook. He kept the distance between them, the only points of contact being her right hand in his left hand, his other hand on the small of her back.

"You're a nice dancer," she said.

"Oh, sure."

"Honestly."

"Well, thank you," he said. "But I know I'm not."

"Mmm," she said, "that's beautiful, I love that song," and suddenly eased in closer to him. Just the top of her body. Just pressed her breasts, naked under the clinging fabric, against his chest, leaning into him, but keeping the lower part of her body away from him. He responded to this at once, automatically and involuntarily, a sudden aching twinge in his groin. But he did not pull her in closer, kept his hand just where it was in the small of her back, did not in any way reveal to her that he knew what she'd done and was already responding to it.

"Mmm," she said.

"You're not rusty at all," he said.

"I haven't done this in a long time," she said, and then

moved in gently against his thigh and put her cheek against his. But still he did not tighten his arm around her, waiting instead for her to make the next move, waiting for her to slide off his thigh and around front, just to the left of where she was rhythmically pressing against him.

The song ended, and she moved abruptly out of his arms, and said, "That was nice," and went immediately to where she had put her drink down on the coffee table. He turned away at once, not wanting her to see how excited he was, and went for his own drink, forgetting for a moment where he had put it down, and then finding it, and shifting his jacket slightly in an attempt to cover himself. When he turned back to her, she had taken off her shoes and was sitting on the couch with her legs tucked under her, the green dress pulled back over her knees. Her knees were smooth and shiny, he wanted to touch them, wanted in fact to thrust his hands up under the pleated skirt, but instead he sat on the opposite end of the couch and she turned slightly to face him, the knees pointing toward him.

"Where'd you learn to dance?" she asked. There was a slight tremor in her voice and her cheeks were flushed. He saw, too, that she could not seem to sit still on her end of the couch and kept shifting her knees in an apparent effort to make herself comfortable.

"At church socials," he said. "When I used to live in the Bronx."

"Where's your bathroom?" she asked abruptly, and smiled.

"Just off the foyer there."

"Same as mine," she said, still smiling, and started to get off the couch, unfolding first one leg and then the other from where they'd been tucked under her. There was the briefest flash of nylon, she was wearing only panties under the green dress. She rose from the couch and walked swiftly across the room. He watched the deliberate sway of her hips—she knew his eyes were on the tight jiggle of her ass under the clinging jersey.

He was encouraged by the fact that she had to pee. It was only a matter of time now. When a girl had to pee, she was excited. This one was excited, this one was in heat, in just a little while she'd be spread under him on the bed in the other room. He tried not to think of this because he wanted to get control of himself before she came back, wanted to hold her off as long as he could till she built a real fine head of steam that either had to explode or be taken care of. He was going to take care of her real fine. He was going to hump her clear through the bed, and down through the floor, and also the ceiling of the apartment downstairs and through that floor and also the ceiling till they ended up humping in her *own* apartment two flights down, came crashing through the plaster ceiling and kept right on humping while Felice's eyes bugged out of her head.

When Jessica came out of the bathroom, the first thing she said was, "I didn't realize how late it was, Alex."

"It *is* getting kind of late," he said, and smiled knowingly.

She sat on the couch again, and he expected her to tuck her legs up under her again, expected her to point those smooth knees toward him, maybe open her legs just a trifle so he could see her panties again, maybe she'd even taken them off in the john. Instead, she put on her shoes, and then stood up, and picked up her handbag, and very matter-of-factly said, "I have to go."

"Go?" he said.

"Mmm," she said, and smiled. "I've had a lovely time, Alex, but really it's getting very late."

He looked swiftly at his watch. Panic was rising in his

throat, he did not want her to get away, not now when he was so close. "It isn't even midnight," he said.

"I know, but Peter wakes up at six. I really have to go. And Felice is only fifteen, you know, I don't want to keep her up too late."

"But it isn't even midnight," he said again.

"Cinderella," she said, and smiled, and kissed the tips of her fingers and pressed them to his cheek. "Thank you, Alex, I've had a wonderful time, really." He started to get up, and she said, "No, please don't, it's only two flights down," and smiled again.

He followed her to the front door anyway, and took her topcoat from the closet. She draped the coat over her arm, looked around as though she had forgotten something, and then said, "Good night, Alex."

"Good night, Jess," he said.

"Jess," she repeated, and looked tenderly into his face, and then turned away, and opened the door and went out. He closed the door behind her and double-locked it, and then went into the living room and stood staring down at her lip-sticked cigarette ends in the ashtray on the coffee table. Behind him, the Charlie Parker record clicked emptily in the retaining grooves near the center of the disc. Impulsively, he picked up the ashtray and hurled it at the wall in the entrance foyer.

"So how'd you make out last night?" Archie asked.

"Great," Alex said.

They were in Archie's car, a '72 Oldsmobile, and they were driving toward Stamford on the Merritt Parkway. The day was sunny and bright, the road thronged with Sunday drivers. Archie kept the speedometer needle at a steady fifty miles per; if there was one thing he didn't need, it was a bull-shit traffic violation.

"Who *is* this chick, anyway?" he asked.

"She lives in my building," Alex said. "She's separated from her husband. I think last night was the first time she's been fucked in six months. She was really something, Arch. Couldn't get enough of it. I woke up this morning, she had my cock in her mouth again, I thought she was going to swallow the fuckin thing she had it in so deep. I finally got rid of her about twelve o'clock, just before I called you."

"She white or black?" Archie asked.

"White. Why?"

"White chicks dig suckin, that's a fact. That's cause suckin's sophisticated. You get your down-home girls, they don't know suckin from callin in the hogs. Unless they're hookers, you know, that's a different story."

"Yeah, well this one dug it all right."

"Where do we get off?" Archie said. "You got the map there? I marked it on the map. What does it say there?"

"Exit 35. Is this it?"

"Yeah, where I marked it."

"That's right, exit 35."

"Daisy never takes the Merritt up, they don't allow taxis on the Merritt. But she says this is the quickest way."

"What do you think of this thing, Arch?"

"I don't know. What do you think?"

"Well, from what you told me, Daisy doesn't know too much about the setup. We liable to go in there and find only a piano and a floor lamp. She's never been inside the house itself, ain't that right?"

"That's right."

"Also, I don't believe this business about there being five

in help, and *all* of them being off on Thursdays. That don't sound right to me, Arch."

"I talked to her about an hour yesterday, Alex. She says the guy wouldn't chance bringing her out there if everybody wasn't off. That's what she says."

"What's the guy's name again?"

"Harold Reed. The *Third*."

"Shit," Alex said, and began laughing.

"Ain't that something?" Archie said, and laughed, too.

"Harold Reed the Third, and he brings a one-legged whore out there to fuck in his barn."

"His studio," Archie said.

"What's he do out there in his studio," Alex asked, "besides fuck one-legged whores?"

"He's an artist. He paints out there."

"And he's a millionaire?"

"He made his money in supermarkets or something. The painting's just a hobby."

"Did Daisy say what this five in help was?"

"He's got a chauffeur, a gardener, a cook, and two maids."

"And all of them are off on Thursdays, huh?"

"That's what she says."

"If *I* had five in help, I'd keep some of them on. Case I needed my back washed. Who drives his wife into the city? Does she drive in by herself?"

"Why?"

"I'm thinking if maybe the chauffeur *isn't* off on Thursdays, then maybe *he's* the one drives the wife in. And be just our luck she'll say James, you may pick me up at six in front of Bonwit's, and he'll drive back out to the country early and find the two of us in the house there working the box. If there *is* a box."

"I thought three guys," Archie said.

"Three? Why three?"

"Well, Daisy don't want any of this to rub off on her, you dig?"

"No, I don't. What do you mean?"

"She doesn't want this to look like an inside job. She says her twenty-five percent ain't worth . . . "

"Twenty-five per*cent*! Forget it."

"She'll earn it, man. She's gonna try getting in the house next Thursday, check it out for us."

"Still, time we fence the stuff . . . and what do you mean *three* guys? We got to give *her* twenty-five, and then split the rest three ways? After the fence skims seventy off the top? No way, Arch."

"This could be a big score, Alex."

"It could be shit, too. We got to split thirty percent four ways, that comes to . . . What does it come to, anyway?"

"Little more than seven percent each. Seven and a half, actually."

"What do we need a third guy for?"

"I told you. To give Daisy an out."

"Fuck Daisy. Tell her to . . . "

"Without Daisy, there's no job."

"*With* her, there's only seven percent of a job."

"Seven and a half," Archie said.

"I still don't know what the third guy is for."

"To put a gun on Daisy and the old man. Go in the studio there and put a gun on them. To make it look like Daisy had nothing to do with it. Maybe smack her around a little.'

"Forget it, we don't need a gun. And all Daisy's worth is ten percent."

"I already told her twenty-five."

"So go back and tell her ten. She don't like it, that's too fuckin bad. I don't know what's the matter with you, Arch, tellin a whore twenty-five percent. There's your exit, comin up there."

"Yeah, I see it."

"You ever give anybody twenty-five percent before? For just fingering a job?"

"No, but she's the only one can get in there and look it over. What do I do when I get off, Alex? I wrote it on the edge of the map."

"You make a left when you get off the parkway. There's a sign says Stamford and North Stamford, you head toward North Stamford. When you cross over into New York State ... "

"All right, give me the rest when I get to it," Archie said.

"*We* go in, *we* take all the risk, and you're ready to hand Daisy twenty-five percent. Ten is enough, Arch. We give *her* ten, and we split the rest. Let's say this is a really big score here, okay? Let's say we go in there, we find maybe half a million bucks' worth of goods, okay? Tremendous score. The fence takes ... Who you got in mind for swagman, anyway?"

"I thought maybe Vito."

"We don't even know what's in there yet. If this is lots of jewels in there, Vito's no good for it. Maybe we go to Henry Green. Anyway, whoever we go to, he gives us thirty percent, which on a five-hundred-grand haul is ... What? A hundred and fifty grand, right?"

"Right," Archie said.

"Okay, we give fifteen grand to Daisy, that leaves a hun thirty-five to split between just the two of us. So let's sweeten it just a little for her; let's say we give her twenty grand, round it out. That's sixty-five grand left for each of us, Arch. That makes it worthwhile."

"What about the gun?"

"No way. We bring a gun in on this, put a gun on the old
man and Daisy, that makes it armed robbery. No way, Arch."

"How's it armed robbery if it's two separate buildings?
There's two buildings, Alex, the studio and the house. We
got a man with a gun in one of the buildings . . . "

"No fuckin gun, I said."

" . . . and we're doing the burglary in the other building,
how's that armed robbery?"

"It's armed robbery even if we put a gun on him and sent
another guy to a fuckin bank to pick up money he made a
phone call for, we forced him to make a phone call. Now
that's armed robbery, Arch, and I happen to know it, and I'm
telling you no gun."

"Okay, okay."

"And, anyway, Arch, this whole thing sounds shitty to
me."

"Well, let's look over the house, okay? We come all the
way out here, let's at least look it over."

They drove up and down Pembrook Road a dozen times
before they even located a marker for the house. The marker
was a round brass escutcheon engraved with the name Reed,
set high up on one of the huge stone pillars flanking the entrance drive, partially obscured by a branch from a pine tree.

"There it is," Archie whispered.

He stopped the car and then backed it up so they could
look into the driveway.

"You see anything?" Alex whispered.

"Nothing. House must be all the way back in there. Daisy
says it's right on a lake."

"So what do you want to do?"

"You want to drive in there?"

"If you weren't black, Archie, I'd say yes. I'd drive in
there and tell them I'm looking for my cousin Ralph Hen-

nings the Fourth. But you being black, and you being such a *mean*-looking motherfucker, we'd have six German shepherds on us in a minute."

"There's no dogs in there," Archie said, laughing. "Daisy says there's no dogs. Whyn't you get in the back seat," he said, still laughing, "and make like I'm your chauffeur? We'll drive up there, and you can tell them your man here seems to have lost his way. Let's see how far this stone wall runs, now we know which house it is."

They followed the stone wall down the road in one direction for about three hundred feet, where it ended in a clump of pines. Then Archie backed the car around in the next driveway up the road and followed the wall to its end on the other side of the property. The wall ran a good six hundred feet on that side.

"Old Reed the Third has a nice chunk of land in there," Archie said.

"Come on, let's go home," Alex said.

They talked about it all the way back to Harlem. They didn't know much about it yet, and were skeptical even about what they *did* know, but they talked about it nonetheless. It seemed to them both that the next step was for Daisy to give them a report on the house itself. If she couldn't get in there and look around, then the hell with the job, they weren't about to go in blind. They debated her percentage again, and Alex admitted he had once paid fifteen percent to a finger, but the guy had really done a lot of preliminary work for him, and fifteen percent had seemed fair in that particular case. He agreed to go to fifteen now, but only if Daisy *really* set the thing up for them, which meant reporting on the alarm system and giving them the exact layout of the house, and how much they could expect to get in there, and where the Reeds stashed their valuables and cash if there *wasn't* a box.

He also wanted a full report on the live-in help, because he needed to make certain they were all off on Thursdays—he still couldn't believe this was possible. He hoped to do a dry run on the house, and he wouldn't appreciate running into any two-hundred-pound chauffeur who used to be a heavy-weight prizefighter. And he wanted to know when Daisy usually got out to Post Mills, and when she and Reed the Third were busiest out there in the studio, because that's when he planned to do the dry run, while they were out there banging away. He figured the dry run was necessary so they could study the alarm system themselves, see if it was some-thing they could knock out, or maybe find a point of entry that wasn't tied in to the alarm, if there *was* an alarm. He knew one guy, for example, who'd gone down the chimney in a place that was otherwise wired like Fort Knox. He thought they should try the dry run Thursday after next, by which time Daisy would have already been inside the house and given them her report. Daisy was going to try to get in next Thursday, and they'd do the dry run the following Thursday, and maybe pull the job the Thursday after that—May the second.

"Does that sound all right to you, Arch?" he asked.

"I was hoping it could be sooner," Archie said, "I'm really running low."

"Yeah, but we need the dry run, don't you think?"

"Oh, sure. And I don't see how we can do one less all the help is away, and that's only on Thursdays."

"Right."

"So I guess we'll have to wait till May second to pull the job, though I sure wish it could be sooner."

"You think this guy is really a millionaire?" Alex asked.

"That's what Daisy says."

"We ought to go in there with a truck," Alex said, and laughed. "Really wipe the fuckin place out, load up the fur coats and the paintings and the jewelry and the cash and everything that ain't nailed down."

"I don't want nothing to do with paintings," Archie said. "They're too hard to get rid of. Only way to realize any cash on paintings is to hold them for ransom, give them back when the owners cough up. But that's more like kidnapping."

"I don't much care for paintings, either," Alex said. "But if we roll in there with a truck, we could really cart off everything but the fuckin speedboat."

"Maybe we could get a truck big enough to put the speedboat on, too," Archie said, and they both laughed. They fell silent then, and Archie seemed very thoughtful for the longest time. At last he said, "I *still* think a gun would be very valuable on this job. Not only to protect Daisy, but to make sure Reed the Third stays put out there in the studio while we're loading the goods. Daisy won't be able to keep him out there all by herself, she's got only the one leg, he'll knock her over and come barreling out of there if he hears any noise in the driveway."

"No, absolutely not," Alex said. "No fuckin gun."

"Well," Archie said, and shrugged.

"But I'm glad you brought up this matter of noise because it's important to know just how far the studio is from the main house. So we'll know whether noise'll carry out there if we have to peel a box."

"Yeah, I'll ask Daisy to check on that," Archie said.

There wasn't much else they could do until they had a full report from Daisy; wasn't even much else to talk about. So they had something to eat at a Spanish restaurant, and then they went to a movie. They left each other at ten that night, promising to meet again on Friday, after Daisy had got in the house.

Alex went home, watched Johnny Carson till he signed off, and then went to sleep.

When he had it, he spent it.

The first thing he did on Monday morning was get out there and shop for some new threads. Summertime was coming, and his stuff from last year, though still practically new, was beginning to bore him. He had maybe thirty tailor-made suits and sports jackets in his closet, a dozen of them summerweight stuff, but he got tired of clothes fast, wore a suit six or seven times and then let it hang there gathering dust. It was the same way with ties. He'd spend twenty-five bucks for a tie, wear it once, and then never look at it again.

Shoes were a different story. He loved shoes, *good* shoes. You could tell by the kind of shoes a man was wearing whether he was flush or not. Alex usually bought his shoes from an English bootmaker on Madison Avenue, and he took very good care of them—worked the leather with expensive creams and polishes, had them resoled or heeled whenever they needed it, kept shoe trees in them when he wasn't wearing them. He never threw away shoes he'd grown tired of. There was always somebody could use a good pair of shoes, and when he gave them away it wasn't with rundown heels or holes in the soles. He gave them away in mint condition, and usually polished besides. He liked polishing shoes. He liked the smell of the leather and the smell of the polish, and it gave him a great feeling of satisfaction to work a pair of shoes till the leather glowed under his hands. It made him feel good to give them away, too, when he'd grown tired of them. Put a pair of expensive shoes in a man's hands, shoes he could see you'd taken good care of, his eyes lit up like diamonds. Man had a good pair of shoes on his feet, he walked taller. You're standing in something cost a hundred and ten dollars, you've *got* to feel there's a solid base under you, a foundation.

He went to his tailor first. He was a regular customer there, and though his usual salesman was busy fitting another customer, he excused himself and walked right over and shook Alex's hand, told him he'd just be a minute, why didn't Alex look over some tropical-weight materials meanwhile—he *was* interested in a new wardrobe, wasn't he?

Alex told him that's why he was here, and to take his time, there was no rush. He went to the end of the room, where the big windows faced out on Forty-fourth Street below, and began looking through swatches and bolts of material. His taste in clothes was somewhat conservative, he knew burglars who dressed like getaway cars. He picked out a tan worsted with a faint windowpane pattern, and even though he wasn't looking for any winter clothes, he found a beautiful gray cloth he thought would make a nice suit. He also picked out a tropical-weight blue hopsack weave, and was looking over a possibility for a sports jacket when the salesman came over.

"No, Mr. Hardy," he said, "you don't want that."

"Too flashy, huh?" Alex asked.

"Not your style. No, no," the salesman said. "Definitely not. No. Ah, you found the windowpane. Isn't that beautiful? That's an English tropical, a Rangoon cloth. It's cool, and it'll hold a press nicely. That'll make up beautifully. I've seen it made up. Good with your hair coloring, too. Perfect for you. What else did you see?"

"I thought this one," Alex said, indicating the gray cloth.

"Not for the summer, but I can use a good dressy suit this fall."

"Elegant," the salesman said. "You're right, it's elegant. That's an English hard-finish worsted. Very dressy, and elegant, too. The bird's eye design, elegant. And because it's so subdued, we can afford to be more colorful in the lining. A Thai silk? No, I don't think so. But a red wouldn't hurt for the lining. Open the jacket, we see a flash of red. Or at the back vents. You have it made with two back vents, don't you?"

"Yes," Alex said.

"I remember. I have your card here, but I remember."

"Red may be too much," Alex said. "For the lining."

"Not if we use the dull side. I'm not talking about fire-engine red now, this is too elegant for that. Let me show you the lining," he said, and reached under the counter and pulled out a bolt of cloth. "This is the bright side, but look at the reverse."

"It's more like maroon," Alex said.

"Maroon, that's right. It isn't red, it isn't fire-engine red, it's more like maroon, you're right. Look at that against the bird's-eye," he said. "Is that elegant?"

"Yeah, that would be nice, I think," Alex said. "You don't feel it too much, huh?"

"I know how you dress," the salesman said, "I wouldn't suggest anything too flamboyant. Unless you *choose* to go that way. I mean deliberately. I have a fabric we got in yesterday, it's flamboyant, yes, that's the word, flamboyant. It's flamboyant. But it makes up beautifully as a sports jacket, if that's the way you choose to go. It's flamboyant, it has flair, and it makes up beautifully. But the maroon lining with the bird's-eye, yes, definitely. And a simple button, a very dark gray button . . . You take *three* buttons on the sleeve, don't you?"

"Yes," Alex said.

"I remember. I have your card here, but I remember. Open buttonholes on the sleeve, am I right?"

"Yes."

"I remember. Were you looking at the hopsack, too?"

"What do *you* think?" Alex said.

"If you want a blue, I have one here with a faint shadow stripe . . . "

"I have that in the standard weight," Alex said.

"Yes, I remember. Then you don't want it in the tropical, no. Well, let's see, have you decided on the windowpane? If you're taking the windowpane, that's in the beige area, you don't want another in beige, do you? No, that wouldn't, no, *blue* is what we want to concentrate on. The bird's-eye is for the fall, but for the summer you've got the windowpane, and a blue is what we're looking for. Or, if you'd like another gray, gray's a very good color for you. I have a pearl-gray worsted flannel you can wear both summer *and* fall, a beautiful fabric, unfinished worsted flannel. Would you like to see *that*?"

"I'd also like to see the flamboyant one," Alex said.

"For a sports jacket, mind you. It would be too much for a suit, *too* flamboyant."

"Yes, for a sports jacket. I also had in mind, for a sports jacket, something like a camel's hair—that color, but in a tropical weight."

"That's beautiful on you, camel's hair. We made up a camel's hair for you, didn't we?"

"Yes, but it's a winter jacket."

"I remember, yes. With the bone buttons?"

"That's right."

"I remember. I have your card here, but I remember. Would you go for a cashmere? It's the same color as the camel's hair, but it has the lightness we're looking for, and it makes up beautifully. Well, let's see what we have here, we'll find something perfect, I'm sure."

Alex bought three suits and two sports jackets, one of which he picked from the rack, but which he knew they would alter to his measurements. The suits cost him $510 apiece; the cashmere jacket cost him $450, and he paid $360 for the Shetland he had picked from the rack.

He left his tailor at about one o'clock and walked crosstown to a French restaurant he knew on Fiftieth and First, where he had a Beefeater martini, and then ordered the escargots and the sole meunière, with a half bottle of Pouilly Fumé. After lunch he walked over to Battaglia's on Park Avenue and bought himself half a dozen T-shirts in different muted pastel colors, and a long-sleeved pale blue polyester sports shirt. The T-shirts cost him $37 each, but they were made of fine wool jersey and the one he tried on fit him beautifully. The polyester shirt cost $22.

It was almost three o'clock when he got to Gucci's on Fifth Avenue. He wasn't in the market for shoes, not really, though he supposed he was *always* in the market for a good pair of shoes. He went in there to buy an enameled belt he had seen in the window a few weeks back, but after he'd made the purchase—he chose the navy blue enamel—he wandered back to the shoe department and picked out two pairs of patent leather shoes, one in white and the other in brown with the Gucci red and green fabric trim. He walked uptown to the Doubleday's on Fifty-seventh then and looked through the record albums there, finding a Monk album that wasn't in his collection and also picking up the new Miles Davis, though he didn't much care for what Miles was doing these days, trying to mix jazz with rock, what kind of combination was that?

At four o'clock he wandered into the Sherry-Netherland's bar, ordered another Beefeater martini, and struck up a conversation with a Chinese girl at the table next to his. The girl was wearing a wide-brimmed red hat that looked like a pimp hat. She was also wearing a Jewish star that showed in the V-slash of her blouse, nestled between tiny cupcake breasts. She explained the star was just for decoration, she was really a Catholic. He steered the conversation around to Chinese food, telling her he ate Chinese three, four times a week, and that as far as he was concerned it was the best cuisine in the world. Did she know Bo-Bo's down in Chinatown? Or Hong Fat's? Or Wah Kee's? Things were going along very well until a Chinese guy, wearing glasses and dressed in a dark gray ready-to-wear, came into the bar, waved at her from the door, and then took the chair opposite her at the table. Alex finished his drink and took a taxi home. It was a little past five when he got upstairs to his apartment.

He didn't know what he planned to do tonight—maybe go down to Broadway or up to Harlem, see if anybody was around. He felt very good about the purchases he had made, and he took out the shirts and tried on each and every one of them, looking at himself in the mirror, sucking in his stomach and expanding his chest. He looked like a fuckin weight lifter, he thought, or maybe a fag, one of your beach fags, well, more like a weight lifter; were the goddamn T-shirts too faggoty? He debated returning them to the store, and then decided he'd keep them and wear them. Anybody called him a fag, he'd hit them with his fuckin purse. Grinning, he put the shirts in the second drawer of his dresser, and then tried on first the belt and then the shoes he had bought, opening the closet and looking at himself in the full-length mirror hanging on the door. He liked both pairs, they were real stud shoes. He put trees into them and then put them on the floor together with his other shoes. The clock on his dresser read twenty to six.

He went out into the living room, mixed himself another martini and then sipped at it leisurely while he changed his clothes. He put on a tan sports shirt and a pair of brown tailored Italian slacks and tan socks and the new brown patent-leather shoes with the red and green trim. He debated whether he would need a sports jacket, decided to put one on because you never knew what might come up, what kind of place you might want to go to, and then left the apartment.

He didn't see anybody he knew down on Broadway, so he had some pizza at a sidewalk stand on Forty-second, then went to a massage parlor on Eighth Avenue and asked for a girl named Pearl, but they gave him a girl who looked a lot like the Chinese girl he'd talked to at the Sherry-Netherland. When she finally got down to business, he asked her would she like to make an extra twenty, and she told him thirty was more like it, and they settled on twenty-five for a blowjob. He got home about midnight, and went straight to bed.

In the middle of the night, he woke up, turned on the light, went to the dresser, and opened the second drawer. Taking out one of the wool jersey T-shirts, he tried it on over just his jockey shorts and then looked at himself in the mirror. He decided to bring them all back to the store tomorrow because they made him look fruity.

On Tuesday morning, before he returned the shirts, he walked over to the park. Jessica wasn't there. He didn't know why he was looking for her, anyway. He sat on a bench in the sunshine for close to half hour, and then said the hell with it and taxied downtown. At Battaglia's he told the salesman he thought the wool shirts might be too hot for the summer, and the salesman told him they had the same style in cotton. He said no, he didn't think so, and they gave him his money back without any static; he was, after all, a steady customer there. It was 11:00 in the morning; he didn't know what he wanted to do next. He didn't normally feel restless after a score, especially a nice one like the Rothman job, but he felt restless this morning and didn't know what the hell it was.

He didn't realize he was going to commit another burglary until he found himself in a store on Madison Avenue, buying a deck of playing cards. When he got outside the store, he separated the ten, jack, queen, king, and ace of hearts from the deck, and then threw the rest of the cards into a sidewalk trash container. He had no other tools with him, he still hadn't replaced the tools he'd left behind on the Rothman job. But he wasn't looking for anything difficult, just a nice easy score, and that royal-flush shim would be good enough for what he had in mind. He told himself he was keeping his hand in, staying in shape, even though he had done his last job only five days ago. He also told himself the Rothman job had been something of a disappointment because he'd known exactly what he was going to find in there, and even though he'd picked up an additional eighty-four hundred, it still had been a setup job without any real excitement to it. Maybe today would be his lucky day. Maybe he'd stumble upon that once-in-a-lifetime score, net himself enough to get out of the business completely.

He didn't know where he'd go, he knew only that he was looking for an easy score, a door he could loid open with the royal-flush shim. Intuitively, he decided against the city. He wanted a nice easy one, no *series* of doors to open, just one big door with a Mickey Mouse spring latch, or maybe a patio door, those patio doors were like opening a rip-top beer can. He decided he might need a screwdriver if he came up against a patio door, so he stopped in a hardware store on Sixth Avenue and bought himself one. And since there was a deli right next door, he went in and helped himself to a few toothpicks from a container on the cashier's counter. The cashier glared at him, and he thought Fuck you, lady. That was all he'd need, the screwdriver, the royal-flush shim, and the toothpicks.

He rented a car, drove up the West Side Highway and onto the Cross County, and finally got off in White Plains. He had been to White Plains before, had taken Kitty to a movie up there and then checked into the Roger Smith Hotel with her. But he'd never done a job there, so he just kept driving around now, looking for a neighborhood with big expensive houses. There was no urgency to this job, if he didn't find anything that looked good, he'd just call it a day. But he hoped he found something. He wanted to get in somebody's house. He wanted to open a door and get in there and start rummaging around. He wanted to find all their hiding places.

The neighborhood he ended up in—this was all hit-or-miss, he didn't know White Plains from a hole in the wall—had houses he guessed were in the $80-100,000 range, set way back from the street. There were a lot of old trees on the winding roads, none of them in full leaf yet; this was still only April. But most of the houses had good foundation planting around them, and the evergreens had grown quite tall over the years and would afford him good cover from the street. He drove through the neighborhood leisurely, looking for signs that would tell him a particular house was empty. He didn't expect anyone to be away on vacation in April, so he didn't bother looking for newspapers on the front porches, or bulging mailboxes, or a lawn that badly needed cutting, or a house with all the drapes and blinds closed, or even a house with lights burning in the upstairs windows at one in the afternoon. He saw one house with the garage door open and no cars in it, and he marked that down as a definite possibility; and he saw another house with a note tacked to the front door, and he figured this one had potential, too. But both houses were in the middle of the street, with houses on either side of them, and he preferred a corner house, if he could find one, where his chances of being noticed would be cut in half. He wrote down the names on the mailboxes anyway, continued driving around, and suddenly got lucky.

The street he was on ended in a T-shaped intersection. On his right, there was a big English Tudor house, with good cover shrubbery near the front door. The name on the mailbox outside was R. Nichols. On his left, there was a house with a six-foot-tall Walpole fence surrounding the entire property. Across the intersecting road, he could see the greens of a golf course. This meant that the front of the English Tudor was facing the fence, and its right-hand side was facing the golf course. He backed the car up past the Tudor and then parked at the curb, reached over to the glove compartment, and pulled out a map. Pretending to study it, he looked instead at the stand of pines that separated the Tudor from the next house up the street. In effect, the Tudor had *three* blind sides. He lowered the hand brake, inched the car forward so that he could see up the driveway, and that was when he got lucky.

As he watched, a woman came out of the house, locked the door behind her with a key, and then walked swiftly to the connecting garage. She rolled up the garage door, and he saw there was only one car in there. Then she went into the garage, started the car, and backed it out into the oval in front of the house. She left the garage door open. As the car moved out of the driveway, Alex drove his own car to the full-stop sign on the corner, stopped there briefly, and then made a right turn and continued driving past the golf course.

There was one thing that looked bad about the house, but several things looked very good indeed. The woman had used a key to lock the door when she came out; this meant that the lock on the front door wasn't a spring latch, which would have locked simply by pulling the door shut. It was probably a lock he couldn't force with either the shim or the screwdriver—that was the *bad* news. But the *good* news was that she'd bothered to lock it at all. If a woman leaves her house, and there's a housekeeper inside there, she doesn't go to the trouble of locking the front door with a key. This indicated to Alex that the house was empty; this and the fact that there'd been only one car in the garage. Hubby was off to work, and now the lady of the house was on her way, and the place was empty. And there were three blind sides. That's the way he read it, and it looked very good. But to play it safe, he stopped at a drugstore and looked up R. Nichols in the phone book and found a listing for Robert Nichols. He dialed the number and let it ring ten times. Then he hung up and drove back to the street.

He drove directly into the driveway and backed the car around so that its front end was facing the street. He wasn't worried about anyone spotting the rented car, even though he'd had to show his license and sign for the car with his own name. Anyone saw the license plate and reported it to the police, he'd tell them Yes, that's the car I rented, all right. Left it on the street for a minute, and somebody drove off with it. Brought it back just a little while ago, and left it right where I'd parked it. Must've been your fuckin burglar.

Turning off the ignition, he put the keys in his pocket, looked around, and then walked to the front door. At the front door, he listened for a moment. He heard a radio going inside, but he knew a great many people left radios going as deterrents to burglars, and that didn't bother him either. He had seen the lady of the house leaving, he had seen her locking the door behind her, he had seen her taking the only car from the garage, and he had let the phone ring ten times without getting an answer. Boldly, he rang the front doorbell now. If he'd been mistaken, if there *was* a housekeeper inside there, he'd tell her he was selling lightning rods or storm windows or whatever the hell, and she'd tell him to come back another time, when the lady of the house was home.

He kept on leaning on the bell, and he heard it ringing loud and clear inside the house, but no one came to answer the door. He checked the windows on the front of the house for any stickers that would tell him the house was wired, but he found none. Swiftly, he walked to the connecting garage, and into the garage, and then to the door on the back wall of the garage—the door that led directly to the inside of the house. He didn't know what it was, you'd find people with expensive deadbolts on every door of the house except the fuckin door that led in from the garage. What you usually found on an interior garage door was a cheap, five-pin cylindrical lock, with a keyway on the garage side and on the other side a button you either pushed in or twisted to lock the door. That's what was on this door, and Alex slipped the bolt in thirty seconds flat, using the ace of hearts loid. He stepped inside the house, quickly closed the door behind him, and stood stock still, listening. All he heard was the radio.

Using that as a directional beam, since he had first heard it while standing outside the front door, he moved through a narrow hallway that went past the kitchen, a bathroom, and a television den, and then opened into the foyer. A wide doorway led into the living room. He could see the stereo setup across the room, the tuner and amplifier on, playing music loud enough to wake the dead. Moving instantly to the front door, he unlocked it, broke off a toothpick in the keyway outside, locked the door again, and then went up the carpeted steps to the second floor of the house, where he expected the bedrooms were. He was looking for the master bedroom because that's where the valuable stuff would be, if there *was* any valuable stuff. He would look for a wall box first, taking down pictures and mirrors to see what was behind them, and then checking out the closets to see if a box was mounted inside one of them. If he couldn't find a box, then he'd go through the dresser drawers looking for jewelry, cash, or credit cards, which he'd stuff in his pockets. Then he'd go back to the closets again and take any furs that were in them. If he ran across just a single fur, he'd probably carry it out on his arm. If there happened to be three or four of them, he'd look around for a suitcase and pack them inside it, together with whatever else looked good. Cash was the best, of course, you didn't have to share cash with anybody, you didn't have to go to a fence with cash. Credit cards were almost as good as cash, but they were hard to come by. Coin and stamp collections were good, too, but he didn't expect to find any of those in the bedroom—you usually came across those in a library or a den. He planned to check the house out thoroughly before he left it, going through it room by room, but first he wanted to find the master bedroom and give it a good working-over.

The stairs opened onto a long, carpeted, second-floor corridor with three doors in it. The first door in the corridor was open, and he looked in at a child's room with animals parading on the wallpaper. There was a single bed in the room and a dresser painted yellow, and on the dresser a piggy bank. He would bust open the piggy bank later, not because he was interested in pennies, but only because sometimes Grandma stuffed a five or a ten in there when she came visiting. He figured that the closed door at the end of the hall led to the master bedroom; for some reason, the master bedroom was usually at the end of the hall. But there was another closed door just past the child's room, and he went to that now, and twisted the knob, and opened it.

A woman was in there.

He froze in the doorway, he felt needles prickling along his spine and racing up into his skull. The woman had white hair, she was maybe seventy-five, eighty years old, she was sitting up in bed propped against the pillows, reading a book. Alongside the bed, there was a night table with a glass of water on it, and a box of Kleenex, and a whole collection of pill bottles—he had stumbled across a fuckin sick old lady in bed. She turned toward the door the minute he opened it and stared across the room at him, and neither of them said anything for several moments, and then he saw her mouth beginning to open, saw the scream forming on her mouth, and knew that she would scream in the next instant.

He turned, almost turned to run, and then wondered if he could get down the stairs and out the door and into the rented car before her scream brought down the whole neighborhood. He found himself walking into the room instead, moving swiftly to the bed, the scream about to erupt, the woman's eyes round and frightened, his own heart pounding as he reached the side of the bed and clamped one hand behind her head and the other hand over her mouth.

She smelled of medicine, she smelled of old age, she was a sick old lady in a house that should have been empty, why the hell hadn't she answered the phone when he'd called here? He saw now that there was no telephone in the room, the lady was bedridden, she couldn't have got up to answer a phone even if she'd wanted to. He still had his hand clamped right over her mouth, he didn't want to let go of her mouth because the scream would sure as hell follow. But he couldn't stay in here all day long either, with his hand over her mouth and her daughter or her niece or whoever it was maybe ready to come back to the house any minute. There was a sick person in the house, she wouldn't be gone long, she'd maybe run down to the drugstore to get some more medicine, she'd maybe gone to the same drugstore he'd made the call from, and that was only four blocks away, he was beginning to sweat. The sweat broke out on his forehead and under his arms; it was sweat that stank of fear, and it mingled with the medicinal old-age stink of the woman and made him sick to his stomach. He wanted nothing more than to get out of there, but if he let go of her mouth she would scream.

"I'm not gonna hurt you," he said.

The old lady nodded. Her head moved under his hand, he kept his hand clamped over her mouth, pressing hard. He could feel the outline of her teeth against his hand and the wetness of her lips, but he did not remove his hand, he kept pressing it against her mouth, his other hand at the back of her head. He thought for an instant that her skull would shatter between his hands, and he quickly said, "I don't want to hurt you, I just want to get out of here. If I take my hand off your mouth, and you scream, then I'll have to hurt you," he said. "You hear me?"

The old lady nodded again.

"If I take my hand off your mouth, and I start out of here, and I hear you screaming even if I'm downstairs in the living room, even if I'm on my way out the front door, I'll have to come back up here and hurt you. You understand that? I want you to understand that, because I'm not taking my hand away till you understand it. You understand it?"

The old lady nodded again. She was wearing a pink comforter around her shoulders, and it slid off one shoulder now, and she reached to readjust it with one bony hand, but she made no move to bring her hand to his, made no **try** for his wrist, just adjusted the comforter and kept nodding with her eyes wide.

"Okay," he said, "just so we understand each other," and he moved his hands from her head, but he did not budge from her side. His fists clenched, he waited for her to scream, waited for her to show any sign that she even *intended* to scream, because if she did he would hit her. He did not want to hit her, but he would do it if she screamed. He would have to.

In a very low voice, almost a whisper, the old lady said, "Please go," and Alex turned and bolted for the door. In the corridor outside, he tripped and fell to his knees, and picked himself up in almost the same motion, his hands pushing against the carpeted floor as he rose. He grabbed the bannister post at the top of the stairs, swung around it, and came racing down the steps to the front door. The radio was still blaring, a disc jockey was selling an amusement park in New Jersey. He unlocked the door, threw it open, ran to the car, and got in behind the wheel. Reaching for the ignition, he remembered he had put the keys in his pocket and clutched for them now, his sweaty hand reaching down into the loose change and finally extricating the keys. He was trembling as he inserted the ignition key, and twisted it, and started the car. He pressed the accelerator to the floor, and the wheels kicked back gravel before the rubber caught with a squeal and the car leaped forward. He came racing up the long driveway, braked only partially when he came to the street, and then turned right and went through the stop sign on the corner and made another right, and drove past the golf course, slowing the car only when he reached the next intersection.

He was still breathing very hard when he got on the Hutch and started the drive back to the city.

There was a note Scotch-taped to his door. The note had been written with a red marking pen, it virtually screamed at him from the door. He took it down and read it before putting his key into the lock.

Dear Alex:
I've been trying to reach you, but your
phone's unlisted. Some friends are coming
in for drinks tonight at 5:30.
If you'd like to join us, come on down. I
think you'll enjoy them.
                                        Jess

He unlocked the door, went into the apartment, and read the note again, standing in the entrance foyer under the ceiling light. He didn't want to go downstairs to drink with any of her friends, they'd probably be publishing people, and they'd start talking about books he hadn't read. Still, if they were coming at 5:30, they wouldn't be hanging around that long, and maybe there was a possibility he and Jessica could pick up where they'd left off Saturday night. Hell with her, he thought, what do I want to get involved with a cock-tease for? Unless they were invited for dinner, in which case they'd be there all night. And in which case why hadn't she also invited *him* for dinner? No, it was probably just for drinks, and they'd sit around bullshitting about Russian writers, the hell with it. And she'd be parading around without a bra and flashing those long legs, inviting him in and then slamming the door in his face. Thanks a lot, he thought. *Keep* your fuckin drinks. And don't go leaving notes on my door, okay? You want me to get ripped off? You want some burglar to go strolling by, and see the note, and realize right off there's nobody home? Jesus!

He was getting ready to shower when the telephone rang. He crossed the bedroom in his jockey shorts, sat on the edge of the bed, and lifted the receiver.

"Hello?" he said.

"Alex, this is Archie. How you doin', man?"

"Okay," he said. He did not want to tell Archie about the close call he'd had in White Plains. He was always riding Archie about the risks of nighttime burglaries, he could just imagine what Archie would say if he told him about the old lady. Jesus, that was scary. Walking in on her like that. He could not get the smell of her out of his nostrils, the stink of the medicine, and the suffocating stench of her age and her bedclothes. He had blown his nose repeatedly on the way back to the city, trying to rid himself of her smell, unable to relax until he'd hit the toll booths just north of Mosholu Parkway, when at last he'd stopped looking in the rearview mirror. But her stink had pursued him all the way home and was still with him now.

"What's up, Arch?" he said.

"This is bad news, man."

"What is it?"

"Kitty got busted."

"When?"

"This morning."

"She's been busted before," Alex said. "She'll pay the fine and be out on the street again tonight."

"Uh-uh," Archie said. "This wasn't no bullshit vice arrest."

"Then what was it?"

"Narcotics."

"She told me she was off the stuff."

"They caught her *pushing* it, Alex. She was holding half a dozen nickel bags. I don't know how much that could weigh, I don't think it could be *too* much, do you?"

"No, I don't think so."

"Even so, let's say it was less than an eighth, okay? She could *still* get a year to life, depending on how tough they want to get. That new drug law is a bitch."

"I hear they're easing up on it," Alex said.

"For users, yeah, but not dealers. If it was less than an eighth, that's an A-III felony. Even if she gets paroled, it'll be for life. They could send her back up anytime."

"Well, who told her to start *pushing* the damn stuff?"

"I hear she was in trouble with some cheap racketeer, took off with his roll. That's what they're saying on the street. She was trying to make some bread fast. Pay the guy back, you know?"

"Yeah," Alex said.

"Something, huh?"

"Yeah."

"What are you doing tonight?"

"I don't know yet."

"You feel like coming up here, I think I can get us in a game. There's a regular Tuesday night game, but two of the guys can't make it tonight. One of them's in the hospital with a prostate, the other one had to go to the Coast. I think I can get us in it, if you're interested?"

"Big stakes, or what?"

"No, no, a buck and two. Most you could lose is a few

bills. It's a good game, I played it once, some good players. And whoever's house it's in, the guy springs for the booze, and they take a break about eleven, he serves coffee and cake. You feel like playing?"

"Well, I don't know yet. Let me call you later, okay?"

"Not *too* late, though."

"You gonna be playing, anyway?"

"Yeah, I thought I'd make a call, see if I can get in. If you want to play, I'll tell them I got two of us, they can close out the game."

"I don't know if I feel like playing," Alex said.

"Well, it's up to you. It's a good game, though."

"I don't think so, Archie. Another time maybe."

"What's the matter with you? You sound down, man."

"No, I'm okay."

"Well, if you change your mind, give me a ring. I probably won't be calling for a half-hour or so. If you change your mind."

"Okay, thanks, Archie. And thanks for telling me about Kitty."

"Yeah, something, huh?" Archie said, and hung up.

Well, it wasn't *my* fault, Alex thought. I told her I wanted my two grand back, but I didn't tell her to get out there on the street and start pushing dope. That was *her* decision, she made it free and clear, it's *her* responsibility she got busted. And anyway, there's no chance she'll get life. She's never been busted for dope before, they had her in a dozen times on vice busts, but never on dope, so this is a first offense for her. Most she'll get is a year, she could do that standing on one leg. Time off, she'll be out in four months. They'll probably send her up there to Bedford Hills, that's not a bad place. Still, the idea of *anyone* being sent up troubled him. He simply could not visualize Kitty in jail. Not Kitty. Put that girl in jail, she'd go out of her mind. Well, she *was* in jail, she was in jail right this *minute,* in fact, and that was just the start of it, though he was sure they'd never hit her with a life sentence, not for a first offense. Either way, it wasn't his fault.

He got off the bed, looked at the clock on the dresser, and decided it was still too early for a drink. He didn't know what he wanted to do tonight, maybe he'd call Archie back and tell him Yeah, go ahead, get him in the game. He didn't much feel like playing poker, though. He didn't know what he felt like doing. *Jesus,* that old lady had scared him. He wondered if she'd known just how scared he was, and smiled now, remembering how scared he'd been, and thinking if only the old lady had realized it, she'd have jumped out of bed and hit him with a hammer. Man, the *stink* of her, he could still smell her, couldn't wait to get in that shower and wash the stink off, blow the stink out of his nose. He looked at the clock again, decided he'd rather have a nice long bath instead of a shower, and went into the bathroom to turn on the water.

Sitting on the edge of the tub, he watched the water pouring from the spout, and thought about Jessica's note, and wondered if he should go down there for at least a few minutes. He *did* read books, he probably could talk about books if that's what the conversation got around to, though probably they'd be people who read different kinds of books than he did. He liked to read a book after he had seen the movie; that way he could visualize the scenes all over again. He got very restless in a book where there were just pages of description. Who the hell cared about fields of flowers, or what kind of furniture was in a room, or anything like that? In real life, people went around *talking* to each other, and that's what he liked in books, too, when people talked to each other. Whenever he got to a section where it was supposed to be what somebody was thinking, he usually skipped that part because how could a writer know what anybody was thinking—he sometimes didn't even know what he *himself* was thinking.

Once, after reading a book where the character did a lot of thinking, Alex had tried to think about thinking. He had tried to examine his own thinking process, find out for himself how people thought. He discovered that he didn't think in long paragraphs or even in sentences, he usually thought in pictures, like in the movies or on television, a thought usually came into his head as an *action*. So what was all this bullshit in books where the person was doing all this heavy thinking in long sentences that could put you to sleep? That wasn't true to life, and books were supposed to be true to life, weren't they? Otherwise, why bother writing the things? Or reading them, for that matter.

Maybe he *should* go down, have a quick drink and then split, go up to Harlem later, get in Archie's poker game. Or look up Daisy instead. He wouldn't mind having a go at Daisy, be something to write home to mother about. Dear Mom, Guess what *I* did tonight? He laughed aloud at the thought, visualizing his mother reading the letter to Mr. Tennis Pro in his white shorts and shirt, fuckin dope probably took a tennis racket in the bathtub with him. Stay a half-hour maybe, tell her he had an appointment, sorry he had to leave so soon, it was nice meeting all of you. Stick it to *her* the way she'd stuck it to him Saturday night—I've had a lovely time, Alex, but really it's getting very late. Maybe he *would* go down there, just for the hell of it.

He took a nap after he got out of the tub, and when he woke up, the clock on his dresser read ten to six. He hadn't called Archie about the poker game, and it was too late to do that now, so he decided to go downstairs after all, see what her publishing friends were like. He put on a simple blue cardigan sweater. He put on the sports shirt he'd bought at Battaglia's, and over that he put on a simple blue cardigan sweater. He debated whether the new patent-leather Gucci whites would go with what he was wearing, but put on a pair of blue socks and black loafers instead. Then he took the fire stairs down to the fifth floor and listened outside her door. He could hear voices in there, and music, and someone laughing, a girl laughing, it didn't sound like Jessica. He almost changed his mind about going in, but then he pressed the bell button on the side of the door, and heard the chimes going off inside, and he waited, and heard someone coming toward the door, and the door opened.

"Alex," she said, and leaned forward to kiss him on the cheek. "I'm *so* glad you could come." She took his hand, and drew him into the foyer, and then closed the door behind him, not bothering to lock it. The kiss had surprised him, and her holding his hand now, as she led him into the living room, made him feel uncomfortable. But he couldn't pull his hand away without looking foolish, so he allowed himself to be dragged across the living-room floor and over to the couch where a man and woman were sitting.

"Alex," she said, "I'd like you to meet two very good friends of mine, Paul and Lena Epstein. This is Alex Hardy."

"How do you do?" Alex said, and extended his hand to Paul, and shook it, and then became embarrassed when he realized Lena had her hand out, too. He took her hand now, shook it briefly, and then backed off a pace, looked around for a chair, and found one near the piano. He sat quickly, and Jessica said, "What are you drinking, Alex?"

"Scotch on the rocks," he said.

Paul Epstein was a hawk-faced man going bald. He

combed his air sideways to disguise this, and he had on thick eyeglasses with enormous black frames. He was wearing a dark gray business suit, a white shirt, a blue tie, black shoes and socks. Alex assumed he had come there directly from work. Lena Epstein was a short, dark brunette, her hair clipped close to her face like a French whore's. She had brown eyes and a wide mouth, a she was wearing a brown turtleneck shirt with a short suede skirt, pantyhose—he knew they were pantyhose because he could see almost clear up to her ass—and low-heeled shoes with fringed tongues. He figured *she* had just come from work, too; there was a grimy look about her that a woman didn't have if she'd dressed especially for a party.

"Alex lives right upstairs," Jessica said.

"I wished he lived right upstairs from *me*," Lena said, and wiggled her eyebrows like Groucho Marx.

"Listen to *that*, will you?" Paul said, and laughed. "And she's sitting not two feet away from me."

"Here you go," Jessica said, and handed Alex the drink. She wasn't wearing a bra, of course, that was her specialty. No bra, blue cotton T-shirt, tight-fitting slacks, sandals. He was in a room with a cock-tease, a Jew girl who did Groucho Marx imitations, and a jerk of a husband who thought it was funny when she flirted with a strange man. Great. He had sure made the right decision coming here.

"Is this up too loud?" Jessica asked.

"It's only *ear*-shattering," Lena said.

"How's that?" she said, turning down the volume on the stereo unit. "Is that any better?"

"*Much*," Lena said.

"Lena has a delicate ear," Paul said.

"The lass with the delicate ear," Lena said.

"Ouch," Paul said.

"Or the lass with the delicate ass, if you prefer," she said, and winked at Alex. "How do you two know each other? Did you meet in the elevator or something?"

"We met in the lobby," Jessica said, and walked to where Alex was sitting, and stood beside his chair, and put her hand on the back of it.

"All you meet in the lobby of *my* building," Lena said, "are perverts and muggers."

"And an occasional burglar," Paul said.

"No New York atrocity stories, please," Jessica said.

"Listen," Paul said, "if that drink's boring you . . . "

"No, the drink is fine," Alex said.

"What I'm saying is I have some very fine grass here, if you'd prefer that. Got it from a fellow in the office, it's Mexican stuff. Isn't it very fine grass, Lena?"

"It's very fine."

"I don't smoke," Alex said, "thanks. Jess, you ought to lock that door, if you're going to smoke grass in here."

"Cops don't bother about grass nowadays," Lena said. "They probably smoke it themselves. When they're not asleep in their patrol cars."

"Well, who'd like to share a joint with me? Jessica?"

"Thanks, I don't care for any," Jessica said.

"He's higher than a kite now," Lena said, "and he wants to bust another joint."

"Hard day at the office, honey," Paul said, and smiled, and reached into his pocket. He took out a Sucrets tin, opened the lid, and then put the tin on the coffee table. There were four neatly rolled joints inside the tin. He took one out, lit it, toked on it, and passed it to his wife. Lena took a long hit and then offered the joint to Alex.

"Thanks, I have the Scotch," he said.

"How *is* that stuff, huh?" Paul asked, taking the joint from his wife again.

"Grass never affects me," Lena said.

"It affects you, sweetheart."

"Never. *You* get silly as hell. Me, I just sit there watching you."

"Bullshit. It affects you, sweetheart, take it from me."

"I don't mean *that* way."

"What she does when she's smoking," Paul said, "she becomes recording secretary to the world at large. She keeps going back over the conversations, trying to make certain everyone knows *exactly* what was said two minutes ago."

"I never do that," Lena said.

"You sure you don't want some of this?"

"Thanks," Jessica said, and shook her head.

"Have you ever tried it?"

"Yes, I have."

"She's afraid she might lose control," Lena said, and shrugged.

"Where's your son, Jess?" Alex asked. "Isn't your son here?"

"He's with my mother-in-law. She picked him up this afternoon."

"Come back here, find us flying around the room," Paul said.

"He won't be back till tomorrow afternoon. She's keeping him till then. I get along very well with my mother-in-law."

"Who said you didn't?" Lena asked.

"It's Michael who's the prick," Jessica said. "I don't want to divorce my mother-in-law, just Michael."

"I *like* Michael," Paul said. "He's a nice man."

"Make up your mind," Lena said. "You just said he was a prick."

"*Jessica* said he was a prick."

"Who said it, Alex?"

"I'm sorry, I wasn't listening," Alex said, and looked at his watch.

"Trains are all running on time, don't worry," Lena said.

"You have to catch a train, Alex?"

"No, no. I live right upstairs."

"Very convenient," Lena said.

"What do you do, Alex?" Paul asked. "Besides smoke dope all the time?"

"I'm a theater electrician," he said, and thought Here we go with the fuckin *theater* electrician again.

"I'm a lawyer," Paul said. "You ever electrocute anyone in the theater, just look me up."

"I'll do that," Alex said.

"This stuff doesn't affect me at all," Lena said.

"She's stoned out of her mind," Paul said.

"Shall I freshen that for you?" Jessica asked.

"No, I'm fine, thanks," Alex said.

"Things get very clear for me," Paul said. "Very sharp outlines. When I'm smoking grass, I mean. Very sharp details. I can see you very clearly right now, Alex."

"How do I look?"

"Very clear."

"You said that already," Lena said. "I don't see things any differently, this stuff has no effect on me whatsoever."

"Getting down to a roach here," Paul said. "The good stuff burns very fast."

"The good stuff burns *slow*," Lena said.

"This is good stuff, and it's burning fast."

"You said the *good* stuff burns fast."

"We'd better get out of here," Paul said. "It's almost six-thirty, we're supposed to be there at seven."

"We walk out of here this way," Lena said, "we'll get arrested."

"No, cops don't make pot busts anymore."

"That's what *I* said. Isn't that what *I* said?"

"Come on, come on," Paul said, and closed the lid on the Sucrets tin, and then rose from the couch and carried the tin to where Jessica was sitting. He dropped the tin into her lap, and said, "A present, Jessica."

"Take it with you, Paul. I don't use the stuff," she said.

"Where are we going, anyway?" Lena asked.

"The Keelings."

"Whose idea was *that?*"

"*You're* the one who made the date."

"Who said I didn't?" Lena asked. She bent over to kiss Jessica on the forehead and picked up the Sucrets tin from where it was resting in her lap. "It's a shame about your dope habit," she said, and giggled, and then looped her hand through Paul's arm. Jessica let them out of the apartment and then came back into the living room.

"Whoo," she said, "I'm glad *that's* over. I'm sorry, Alex, they used to be such nice people. Let me freshen that for you. Or are you in a hurry? Do you have other plans?"

"No, no."

"I thought we'd talk a while," she said, taking the glass from his hand and walking to the bar with it. "Now that the pothead contingent is gone."

"Sure," he said. "What'd you want to talk about?"

"You're still angry about Saturday night, aren't you?"

"Why should I be angry?"

"Well . . . because I left so early."

"Girl has to leave, she has to leave," Alex said, and shrugged.

"I was worried about the sitter."

"Yes, I know that."

She brought him his drink and then went to sit on the couch, leaning over to take a cigarette from the box on the coffee table, lighting it, and letting out a stream of smoke. She looked fresh and young and beautiful, and he thought suddenly of the old lady in White Plains—had there been a long white hair sprouting from her cheek, just above where he'd clamped his hand over her mouth? Or had he imagined it? The stink of her, the stink of medicine and old age . . . no, *death*. Death was what he had smelled on her. He looked at Jessica now as she shifted her body on the couch, and wanted to reach out to touch her, believing if he could touch her face, touch the smooth skin of her face, he would forget in an instant the old lady's parched and wrinkled flesh, and the stink of her. But he sat where he was, on a chair across the room from her, remembering again that she'd walked out on him last Saturday night, and resenting her for it and wondering again just what the hell he was doing here.

There was no way of understanding squares. What right did squares have to smoke pot, or to make jokes about cops, what the hell did any of them know about what it was really like? Ask *Kitty* what it was really like, he thought, Kitty who'd been hooked clear through the bag and back again, and who just got busted for narcotics, a serious bust at that, an A-III felony, shit, ask *Kitty*. Ask *me* about cops, you want to ask somebody, ask *me*, and don't come around telling me jokes in your dumb square way about cops smoking dope. Cops *stole* dope, if you wanted to know. They arrested pushers and sent them to prison, and they stole the dope from the pushers and then they sold it on the street to junkie burglars, *that's* what cops did, and don't get me started on cops.

" . . . only invited them as an excuse to get you down

here," Jessica said. "The Epsteins think they're very hip, but . . . "

"Why'd you need an excuse?" Alex asked.

"Well . . . because of Saturday night. I really *was* worried about the sitter, you know, but that's not the only reason I left."

"What were the other reasons?"

"One. Just one other reason. What I thought was that my husband might have put a detective on me. That occurred to me while I was in the bathroom. Do you remember, after we were dancing, when I went to the bathroom . . . ?"

"Yes," Alex said, "I remember."

"That's when it occurred to me. That he might have put a detective on me. That maybe all the while we were eating in that Chinese restaurant, a detective was watching us. And followed us back here. Because I was afraid of losing Peter, you see. My son. If a detective was watching me. Of losing custody, you see, if it ever got to push and shove. Do you understand what I'm saying?"

"No, I don't think so."

"Well, I just wouldn't put it past Michael to claim I'm an unfit mother or some such shit, and try to take Peter away from me. Do you understand?"

"No," Alex said.

"Well, let me see how I can put this," she said, and looked up at the ceiling, and then sighed and said, "If a detective *had* followed us back here from the restaurant, and if he'd seen me go into *your* apartment instead of my *own* . . . and if we were in there together for any substantial period of time, then he might possibly come to the conclusion that, well, we weren't in there just listening to jazz or playing chess, do you know what I mean?"

"Yes, I think I know what you mean," Alex said.

"He might draw the inference, you know, that something was going *on* in there. And if Michael wanted to get nasty about it, why then he could say I was an unfit mother, and take my son away from me. Which I couldn't let happen. So it occurred to me, while we were dancing, that things were getting, well, a little out of hand, you know, so when I went to the bathroom I started thinking what if there's a detective out there in the hall. But my lawyer said in today's climate it's very difficult to prove a mother is unfit. He knows of a case where a woman was an actual *prostitute,* would you believe it, and the courts wouldn't take the child away from her. That's what he told me. When I called him."

"You called your lawyer?" Alex said.

"Yes. To ask him if I could have men friends without jeopardizing my position."

"And what did he say?"

"He told me about the prostitute. And he said he didn't think there was really too much to worry about in this day and age. As concerns custody."

"When did you call him?" Alex asked.

"Yesterday morning. I would have called him sooner, but it was the weekend. So there we are," she said, and shrugged, and put out her cigarette.

"Where's that, Jess?"

"I love it when you call me Jess."

"Where, exactly, are we?"

"I think you know where we are," she said. "I don't think I have to spell it out for you."

It started in anger.

He wanted only to punish her and humiliate her, make her realize how deeply she had hurt him last Saturday night, even though he could understand her reason for walking out on him, in fact considered it a good and valid reason—if a stupid one. Any moron in the world knew they couldn't pin anything on you without pictures and witnesses, but Little Miss Farm Girl here, Little Miss Dairy Queen had to call her lawyer to find out about it, wonder she didn't call the Mayor, too. Good morning, your Honor, is it okay to . . . you see, there's this terribly attractive young man lives in my building, just two flights up, your Honor, and I was wondering . . . I'm in the middle of a divorce, you see, and I just thought I'd check to see if it's all right, if he makes advances or anything, if it's all right to . . . well, you know, get to know him a little better than I know him now, would that be all right, your Honor, sir?

He was angered by her stupidity, and angered too that she hadn't shared her fears with him on Saturday night, right after she'd come out of the bathroom, told him straight out what was bothering her instead of giving him all that bullshit about the sitter, though she'd probably been worried about that, too, *that* part of it was probably true, too—and yet he was angry. In his anger, he forgot that it was she who'd made the first painful approach that day in the park, forgot that she had blushed immediately afterward, forgot how well everything had been going on Saturday night, how much they'd been enjoying each other, how really special everything had been—until she walked out. That was it, of course. She should not have walked out on him. What*ever* the hell she'd thought, she should have *told* him about it, *trusted* him enough to have said Look, Alex, this is where it's at, this is what's bugging me, it's got nothing to do with how much I want you or don't, it's just *this*. Instead, she walked out. Left him standing there like a fool. Good night, Jess. Good night, Alex. Good night, Mrs. Calabash, wherever you are, she should *not* have left him standing there like a fool. He was no punk you could do whatever you wanted to. He was a man in his own right, and he was entitled to respect.

So it started in anger, there was not the slightest thought of making love. "Love" had nothing to do with it in the beginning, not for him, anyway. He stripped her in anger, pulling the blue T-shirt up over her naked breasts, and then unbuckling the belt at her waist, and taking off her sandals, and lowering the slacks over her thighs and the long length of her legs, and pulling them free of her feet, and tossing them across the room. She was wearing pale blue bikini panties, and he pulled them down, and she lifted herself to help him, and he was suddenly excited. In haste, he lowered the panties over her thighs, and down below her knees, and she worked them past her shins and kicked them free, and spread beneath him on the couch, and opened her arms to embrace him.

His anger became threaded with doubt as he lowered the zipper on his pants—he did not want to take off his clothes, he wanted her naked and open beneath him but he wanted to be fully dressed—doubt about his size, doubt about whether she would consider him adequate, he had told Daisy he'd read a book and Daisy had said the book was full of shit. He hesitated a moment, remembering the showers at Sing Sing, the cons going into the showers, the different sizes of the other men, he had not looked at them except from the corners of his eyes, he did not want any of them thinking he was on the make, thinking he was ready to be turned out as a penitentiary punk. You showed them you were weak, that was the end of it, that was what Tommy had told him.

The doubt and fear all but smothered his anger. Her eyes were closed, she lay beneath him with her arms wide and her legs wide, waiting for him to fall upon her, and at last he dared release himself from the prison of his pants, fearful that she might open her eyes and belittle him, make some kind of wise remark. Oh is that a *cock,* I thought it was a cock*roach,* something smart-ass like that, you could not trust squares. The whores he'd fucked, the whores were always pro enough to look at a man and roll their eyes in appreciation and say Oh, *baby,* you're not going to stick *that* fuckin engine in me, are you? That monster's gonna rip me in half, have mercy on a poor working girl, the hookers knew what they were doing. But Jessica lay back with her eyes closed, her arms still waiting to enfold him in embrace, he was afraid she would open her eyes if he did not do it soon.

He crouched on his knees above her, he did not want to soil his expensive trousers, but neither did he want to take off his clothes, she had to know who was the daddy here, who was the jock, who was the fuckin *stud!* He would not take off his clothes, it was different with a whore, a whore knew what she was doing. He was afraid he'd go soft, afraid that once he was inside her she would open her eyes and look up at him and ask Is it *in?,* afraid that he would come too soon, before he even *got* inside her, afraid of all these things that shattered the anger and caused him to tremble. He told himself he was trembling in excitement, and then became more afraid he would come too soon and began trembling more violently.

He eased himself into her, and she gasped slightly as he entered and he felt a sudden thrill of accomplishment—it was all right, he wondered why he'd been fearful at all, he was certainly as big as any of the fuckin jocks soaping themselves in the shower, Hey, kid, how'd you like to suck my joint? He pushed deeper into her, and she moaned, he heard her moan, the moan encouraged him and at the same time made him fearful again of coming too soon. She raised her hips to meet him and he thought Don't *move,* you'll bring me off, and he thought of, tried to think of, forced himself to think of anything but what they were doing, thought of roller skates and tennis rackets, thought of Mr. Tennis Pro, and then suddenly and unbiddenly thought of him on top of his mother, and thought of doors, opening doors, doors opening, loiding them, picking them, punching them, jimmying them, doors opening on secret places, caskets revealing jewels he could pour through his fingers, rubies and diamonds, emeralds and pearls, he reached for her breasts, he clutched both breasts in his hands, free show she gave to every fuckin guy in the world, fuckin cunt parading without a bra like a cheap whore. The slopes of her breasts were dusted with freckles like the bridge of her nose, the nipples were pink, he'd thought only virgins had pink nipples, you fuckin' mother, don't *move!*

Afterward, she lay watching him lazily from the couch as he took off his clothes and carefully draped them over the back of the chair near the piano. She asked him for a cigarette, and he took one from the box on the coffee table, and put it between her lips, and lit it for her, and she dragged on it deeply and exhaled the smoke on a sigh, and then smiled at him. He asked her something he had never asked any woman but Kitty, asked her if it had been all right, and she said Couldn't you tell, Alex? and touched her fingers to his lips, and said You didn't kiss me. Don't you want to kiss me, Alex? He kissed her then. The anger was gone, he kissed her gently and lingeringly, exploring her lips with his own, touching her tongue with his, kissing the full lower lip and the tip of her nose, gliding his lips over her cheeks and onto her forehead, and then kissing the hair at her temple, damp with perspiration, and her closed eyes, and then lowering his mouth to her breasts, and kissing each nipple, and then the smooth round hill of her belly and then her navel. And then he did something he had never done with any other woman, not even Kitty, he kissed her there, he put his lips there, and became frightened for a moment because he wondered if he was queer, wondered if this was the same as going down on a jock. But her hands were at the back of his head, her slender fingers stroked the hair at the back of his head, gentling him, and he felt suddenly at ease.

Later, in her bedroom, they made love for the first time. And afterward, he cried. He put his head on her breasts, and cried, and she said only Yes.

THREE

They were in Daisy's apartment.

This was Thursday night, and she had just come back from Post Mills. The apartment was scrupulously clean, she told them she had a woman come in twice a week. Daisy was wearing a long nylon dressing gown, and when she was standing you couldn't tell she had only one leg. Only when she sat, and the robe flattened out on one side, were you aware of it. She told them to help themselves to the booze, and then made herself comfortable on the couch. Archie was sitting opposite her, Alex beside her. She smelled of soap.

"First of all," Archie said, "did you get in the house?"

"I got in," Daisy said. "It wasn't easy, but I got in."

"What happened? The old guy raise a fuss?"

"He wanted to know *why*. I told him I'd never seen the inside of the house, was he ashamed of letting me in there? He said No, he wasn't ashamed, why should he be ashamed? I said me being a one-legged whore and all. He said that had nothing to do with it, he just didn't want his wife coming home and smelling me in the house. I wear this perfume, you know, when I go up to see him. He likes me to wear this fuckin cheap perfume, it makes me sick to my stomach. So I told him I could take a shower first, he's got a shower out there in the studio where he paints, and that way she wouldn't smell nothing, and he said Well, why don't you take the shower, and we'll see how the day goes, and maybe later we'll run on over there, huh?"

Daisy smiled suddenly and radiantly.

"I ain't a whore for nothing, I always get paid *first*. So I went in the bathroom out there in the studio, and I *locked* the door and took my shower and then put on all my clothes again, and when I come outside he said What are you doing all dressed? and I said I want to see the house, you said you'd show me the house. We can see it later, he said, now come on, Daisy. I told him I washed off all the perfume, I smell as sweet and innocent as the day I was born, and I want to see the inside of the fuckin house. Unless he was afraid I'd contaminate it or somethin, in which case maybe we ought to forget about my coming all the way out there every Thursday, I have hay fever, anyway, and all that stuff beginning to bloom is making me sneeze. So he said All right, all right, it's just a house, I don't know what the big deal is, and I told him it was important to me. I was like playing the square girl who wants her man to prove he *values* her, you know?" Daisy said, and laughed.

"So he took you over there," Archie said.

"He took me over."

"Any stickers on the windows?" Alex asked.

"Doors *and* windows both," Daisy said. "He's got these glass panels on the side of the front door, and there's stickers on them, and also stickers on the glass sliding doors, and on all the windows around the house."

"What'd it say on the stickers?"

"Provident Security."

"These premises protected by Provident Security?"

"Yeah."

"Provident Security. That mean anything to you, Alex?"

"Never heard of it."

"I asked him what the stickers were, he said an alarm system. So I began joking about that, did a big bell go off if you opened the door, and he said No, it was a silent alarm, it was tied in someplace. I asked him where it was tied in, did it go off at the police station or what? He said there *ain't* no police station in Post Mills, it's the state troopers cover the town. So I asked him was the alarm tied in to the troopers, and he said No, a man named Charlie Duncan, who also runs a taxi service up there, has a dozen houses or so wired into his place, and he runs right over if one of them goes off."

"Reed didn't get suspicious, all these questions, did he?"

"No, no, I was just making jokes about the whole thing," Daisy said. "This was when we were going in the house, it all sounded very natural." In her watermelon accent, she said, "I'se jes a dumb li'l whore, you see, ain't *spected* to know nothin bout no burglar larms."

"Charlie Duncan, that's the guy's name?"

"Yeah."

"And he has a taxi service there in the town, huh?"

"Yeah. Calls it Duncan's Livery."

"Duncan's Livery, right."

"This is a one-horse town, you understand," Daisy said.

"Yeah, we been up there."

"No police force, volunteer fire department, like that."

"We got the picture," Archie said. "So what's the house like?"

"Gorgeous," Daisy said.

"Describe it," Alex said. "You come in the front door . . ."

"Yeah, you come in the front door, and it sort of goes off into two wings. It's a very modern house, you know, glass and stone and wood, its really something, Arch, I'd give my *other* leg to live in that fuckin place. There's stone on the floor just inside the front door, and what you're facing is the back of the living-room fireplace. The living room's about as big as a football field, with the fireplace on one end and these sliding glass doors covering the entire wall on the other end, looking out over the lake."

"Did you get a look at those doors?" Alex said.

"Yeah, they've got stickers on them too. I told you that already."

"What kind of locks on them? Your crappy patio door locks?"

"I don't know anything about locks," Daisy said.

"Were the doors glass or plastic?"

"I don't know."

"Was there a safety bar across them?"

"I don't know what you mean."

"A crossbar, about waist high. With a chain and a catch on it."

"I didn't see anything like that."

"Okay, go on. Where are the bedrooms?"

"The house is all on one level," Daisy said. "Behind the entrance, like divided from the entrance by the fireplace, is the living room. Then, going off to the right of the entrance, there's the dining room and past that the kitchen. And on the left of the entrance, there's three bedrooms. One of them is theirs, the Reeds, and the other one is a guest room, and the third they keep for when their daughter comes up. She's thirty-four, but she ain't married, she comes up weekends sometimes."

"Where's the master bedroom?"

"There's this very wide hallway, and first there's the daughter's room for when she comes up, and then there's the guest room, and then the master bedroom. The hallway is all stone like the foyer, the entrance foyer. In fact, all the floors in the house are stone."

"Did you go in the master bedroom?"

"Yeah, he showed me the whole house. He didn't want to take me in the house, but once we got in there, you'd think he was trying to *sell* me the place."

"So off the left of the entrance, you come in this wide hallway, and first there're the two rooms, and then the master bedroom at the end of the hall, is that it?"

"Yeah. The master bedroom looks out on the lake, too."

"Start with the door," Alex said. "You open the door to the master bedroom . . ."

"Yeah, and what you're facing is this window wall that looks out on the lake."

"Patio doors again?"

"One section of it, yeah. The rest is windows. Set up high on the wall."

"What's outside the doors?"

"A stone terrace, steps leading down to the lake."

"Okay, we're standing just inside the bedroom door now," Alex said. "What's on our right?"

"On the right is a wall of closets. Sliding doors on them."

"Did he open the closets for you?"

"I opened them myself."

"What's in them?"

"The closets are Mr. Reed's, that's where he keeps his clothes. His wife has a separate dressing room. That's between the bedroom and the john, it's as big as this room we're sitting in."

"Okay, on the right are closets full of his clothes. Keep going around the room now, counterclockwise."

"Counterclockwise?"

"Yeah. It's six o'clock where we came in the room. The closet wall is six o'clock. Now what's on the wall that's three o'clock?"

"The bed. This big king-size bed. A painting over it."

"Okay, that's three o'clock," Alex said. "Now what's on . . . ?"

"There's more on three o'clock," Daisy said.

"What else?"

"The door that goes in the wife's dressing room."

"Okay, fine, we'll get to the dressing room later."

"And the john," Daisy said. "On the other side of the dressing room, there's a door goes in the john."

"Okay, we'll get to that later. What's at twelve o'clock?"

"These windows set high up on the wall, and under them a row of dressers. And to the left of the dressers, the doors that open up on the terrace."

"Good. And at nine o'clock?"

"That's just a wooden wall, this paneled wooden wall, and in front of it a very low bench with a plant on one end of it and a piece of sculpture on the other end. Jack O'Malley did it, the sculpture. It's a statue of a very long, skinny man. Mr. Reed said it was a Jack O'Malley."

"Anything hanging on that wooden wall?" Alex asked.

"Nothing."

"No paintings, nothing like that?"

"Nothing."

"Were there any other paintings in the room? Besides the one over the bed?"

"No, just that one."

"Any mirrors?"

"Over the dressers, yes. The whole wall over the dressers is a mirror that goes up to the windows. Those high windows I was telling you about."

"Screwed to the wall?"

"I didn't see no screws, but it's attached to the wall, if that's what you mean. It doesn't have a frame around it or anything, it's not *hanging* on the wall."

"Okay, what about the dressing room?"

"You should see the stuff that broad has," Daisy said, and rolled her eyes. "She's got dresses in there . . ."

"Never mind the dresses. Any furs in there?"

"Six of them."

"What kind?"

"Two minks, I'm sure of. The rest, I couldn't tell you what kind. I asked Mr. Reed could I try on one of the minks, he said he thought that wasn't such a good idea. I never had a mink on in my life. I sure wish I could've tried one on."

"Any mirror in there? A *hanging* mirror, I mean."

"There's a full-length mirror, but it's attached to the wall, like the one in the bedroom."

"Any paintings in the dressing room?"

"No."

"So where the fuck's the box?" Archie said. "Man wouldn't hide a box behind a painting over the *bed,* would he? Be too hard to get at."

"Yeah," Alex said. "Daisy, let's get back to the bedroom, okay? Tell me about that paneled wall. What kind of wall is it?"

"Panels. Wooden panels," Daisy said, and shrugged.

"Running vertically?"

"Up and down, right."

"With joints?"

"Well, yeah, if I'm following you."

"Can you *see* where the panels are joined, that's what I'm asking you. Do they look like separate planks of wood?"

"Yeah, about six or seven inches wide, each plank."

"What are you thinking, Alex?" Archie asked.

"I don't know, maybe there's a touch latch there, maybe you press on one of the panels, it springs open. Did you see any hinges, Daisy? On that wall, I mean."

"Was a touch latch," Archie said, "you'd have piano hinges, Alex."

"Yeah, but piano hinges'll show, too."

"I didn't see any hinges," Daisy said.

"What about Reed's closet? Did you get a look in there behind the clothes?"

"I fingered a couple of his suits, moved some of them aside on the hangers. I didn't see any safe on the wall back there, if that's what you want to know."

"So where's the box?" Archie said.

"Maybe there ain't any," Alex said. "Maybe he thinks the alarm system's enough."

"Man goes to the trouble of installing an alarm, nine times out of ten he's got a box, too."

"Yeah," Alex said.

"So where is it?"

"Those dressers against the wall," Alex said. "On the twelve o'clock wall. What'd they look like?"

"Dressers," Daisy said, and shrugged again. "What dressers look like. They're white, I guess they're Formica or whatever, and they got drawers in them—they're *dressers,* Alex, what the hell you *think* they look like?"

"All drawers? Or were there some plain panels?"

"I didn't notice."

"Man wouldn't stick a box behind a panel in a *dresser,* would he?" Archie asked.

"I run across lots of boxes I could just pick up and carry off," Alex said. "I had one box, must've been a hundred-fifty pounder, it was just sitting there between two shelves, had a sliding panel in front of it was supposed to look like books, you know. I slid the panel over, the box was just sitting loose between those shelves, a square-door box. I picked it up and carried it home with me."

"What was in it?" Archie asked, momentarily distracted.

"Six thousand in cash. It was one of the sweetest scores I ever made. I took that little box home with me and peeled it at my leisure, it was one sweet fuckin score."

"Maybe Reed's got his box in the living room," Archie said, getting back to business. "That's possible, ain't it?"

"Yeah, but a woman getting dressed, she doesn't like to run out to the living room to get her good ring. It's possible, look, *any*thing's possible, but most of them are in the bedrooms. That's my experience, anyway. If I've run across three boxes in the living room, all the time I been working, that's a lot. And usually, it ain't even a living room, it's like a library or a den or something, and then it's a fire box, with papers in it. Your money box, that's in the bedroom. I'm talking *usually* now. That's where it usually is."

"Well, maybe there ain't a box," Archie said. "Maybe it's as simple as that. You get a chance to open any of them dresser drawers, Daise?"

"Yeah, I told him I wanted to see his wife's underwear. He said why? I told him it'd turn me on."

"Anything in the drawers? Besides his *wife's* drawers?" Archie said.

"No jewelry, if that's what you mean. But there's big stuff in that house, Arch, that's for sure."

"How do you know?"

"There's pictures of her all over the place, and she's dripping diamonds in every one of them. There's one picture in a glass frame on the dresser top, it was taken at her son's wedding, they got two kids, the Reeds, the son is married and lives in South America someplace. He's a doctor down there. In this picture she's giving her son a kiss, and she's decked out like the Queen of England, with a diamond tiara in her hair, and this diamond necklace, and diamond bracelets all over her arm, clear up to her elbow. She's a walking Tiffany's, that lady. I said to Mr. Reed, I said Man, where does your wife *keep* all this stuff, over in the bank vault?"

"What did he say?"

"He just laughed. Then he asked me did I want to take a pair of her panties over to the studio with us. He was beginning to get itchy by then, I figured it was time we got out of the house."

"He sounds like a fuckin freak," Archie said.

"No, he was just pickin up on my cue, the bullshit I gave him about being turned on by her underwear. So we went out to the studio."

"How far is it from the main house?"

"I paced it off on my crutches," Daisy said. "There's a path runs from the house into the woods where he's got the studio, it took me ninety-four swings to get out there. You got to figure I cover about three, four feet with each swing."

"So that's about a hundred yards, give or take," Alex said. "When you're out there, Daisy, can you hear any sounds?"

"Just heavy breathing," she said.

"I mean, from the outside. Can you hear cars on the road, anything like that?"

"Every now and then, yeah. But the studio's closer to the road than the house is, you know. The house is set way back but the way the property's shaped, the studio is in the woods but closer to the road. That's how come you can hear cars."

"Now what about this five in help? Are you *sure* they're all gone on Thursdays?"

"Positive. Mr. Reed took me in the house, didn't he? He

wouldn't have done that if there was even a chance of any-body being around."

"That's right, Alex."

"Yeah. Now listen, Daisy, we plan on looking over the house next Thursday. Is there any way you can get him out of there? Away from the place, I mean."

"I don't see how."

"Ask him to take you for a ride in his car, something like that."

"He don't bring me up there so he can take me for a ride in his car."

"What time do you usually get up there?"

"Around noon."

"And what time do you get started out there in the studio?"

"Twelve-oh-one," Daisy said.

"Come on, I'm serious."

"So am I."

"How long do you stay out there in the studio?" Archie asked.

"I'm there at twelve, I leave about three. He phones up a taxi for me at two-thirty. Taxi comes from Stamford."

"Can you see the house from the studio?" Archie said.

"No, it's too far back in the woods."

"Well, you just make sure he *stays* out there in the studio while we case the joint. Say between 1:00 and 2:00. You just keep him out there and busy."

"I'll keep him real busy," Daisy said, and smiled.

"I mean, he wants to go back in the house for anything, you just keep him nailed to that fuckin bed."

"Don't worry."

"You said this guy Duncan runs a taxi service," Archie said. "Who's sittin the alarm when he's out driving?"

"I got no idea," Daisy said.

"Can you ask Reed? I'm thinking maybe we knock out the Duncan end of it, we don't have to worry about whether it goes off or not."

"That's already another man on the job," Alex said.

"Yeah."

"I think we just find some way to get in there, that's all," Alex said. "There's got to be some way to get in without the alarm going off."

"Whyn't we just haul Reed out of bed? He lets us in, turns off the alarm, and then calls this Charlie Duncan to tell him everything's okay."

"That means we got to show face," Alex said. "I don't want to show face, do you?"

"No, I don't want to show face," Archie said, "but . . ."

"You better *not* come in that studio," Daisy said. "I don't want Reed to think I had anything to do with settin this up. Fact is, once it's over, I'd like to keep right on going up there every Thursday."

"We won't come in the studio, don't worry about it," Alex said.

"Just so you understand."

"We understand, so shut the fuck up already," Archie said.

"I don't want to go to jail because of something dumb you guys do."

"You won't go to jail."

"Cause the first thing Mr. Reed's gonna think *any*way, is I showed her the house, she musta had something to do with it. Soon as it's over, I'm gonna tell him I'm scared, he better get me a taxi and get me out of there fore he calls the troopers. He's got to do that, anyway, cause otherwise his wife'll find out what he does out there every Thursday."

"That's good, that'll give us plenty of time to get far away before he blows the whistle."

"And me, too," Daisy said, *"I* want to be far away, too."

"Sure, don't worry."

"Okay, then. So you guys comin up next Thursday, one o'clock, is that it? And you'll be there an hour or so, that's when I got to keep Mr. Reed busy."

"That's right."

"Okay, then. If there's nothin else, I got a john due in fifteen minutes."

"Alex?"

"Nothing."

On the sidewalk outside the building, Archie said, "So what do you think?"

"We'll see how it looks next Thursday," Alex said.

"You interested in anything meanwhile?"

"Like what?"

"I got a supermarket, I need me a lay-in man."

"A nighttime job?"

"Yeah."

"Forget it."

"I just need somebody stay in there, rewire the alarm."

"What kind of system?"

"Bell alarm."

"Whyn't you just knock out the bell? It's outside the building, ain't it?"

"Yeah, but it's high up on this wall faces an apartment house. I'd need a ladder to get at it, and anybody could see me from their window. All I want is somebody to stay inside the market, get at the wiring for me."

"What kind of wiring is it?"

"Got to figure a combination system, don't you think? On a supermarket? You'd have all the time you need, though. I watched the place last night, there's no doorshakers on the beat, a squad car comes by only twice, at midnight and 2:00 A.M. Makes a circle of the parking lot, shines a light on the windows, that's about it."

"How much you expect to find in there?"

"Got to be at least a day's receipts. Two grand or more."

"What kind of box?"

"Big old single-door mercantile on the floor in the office."

"Where's your lay-in man going to hide himself?"

"There's a room in back where they stack all the empty cartons. I figure he'll go in just before closing, hide himself in that back room. Cartons piled all over the place back there."

"Still . . . nighttime."

"Well, you think about it."

"When you plan to go in?"

"Soon's I can find me a lay-in man."

"I think you better count me out," Alex said.

But on Friday he found himself thinking about Archie's supermarket. He wouldn't have dreamt of doing a job *alone* at night, but maybe with a full partner it wouldn't be too bad. Also he'd be going in during the day actually, or at least while it was still light, and once he knocked out the alarm and let Archie into the place, the two of them working on the box could knock it off in no time. Peeling a box was all muscle, anyway, they could probably be in and out of there in just a few hours, two of them taking turns on the chisel and sledge. Might even get lucky and find a box they could punch, Archie said it was an old square-door Mosler, maybe it had a spindle they could punch.

The scent of Jessica was still in his bed. She had left him at a little past midnight because today was a school day, and she hadn't wanted to keep Felice up too late. They had talked about possibly going away for the weekend together, and now, without getting out of bed, he dialed Jessica's number and asked her if she'd talked to her mother-in-law yet. She told him it was all set, and they arranged a time, and then he put the receiver back on the cradle and began thinking about Archie's job again.

He didn't know why he was thinking about it. He had scored only last week, and he was in the middle of setting up what could be a really big one up there in Post Mills, so why the hell was he thinking about maybe going out again? He threw back the covers and swung his legs over the side of the bed, but then instead of getting out of bed, he just sat there on the edge and looked at the phone, and wondered whether he honestly wanted to spend the entire weekend with Jessica. Maybe he'd been hoping all along her mother-in-law would say no. Didn't know what kind of mother-in-law *she* was, anyway, her son fighting a divorce, and she agrees to stay with the kid while Jessica runs up to Massachusetts. Jessica hadn't *told* her she was going up there with anybody, of course, but still a person should be able to put two and two together and realize a good-looking girl, even if she went up there alone, the odds were she wouldn't *be* alone too long.

Squares had a strange way of thinking it was "civilized" to just look the other way and make believe something wasn't happening. See a guy dancing with your wife, he's got his hand on her ass, do you take him outside and beat the shit out of him? Hell, no, you look the other way, you make believe it isn't happening. That was "civilized," that was the way squares handled things. Your daughter-in-law comes to you, says Hey, Mom, I want to get away for the weekend, do some heavy thinking about this whole thing, maybe decide *not* to divorce your son Michael the prick, what do you say,

Mom, will you stay with the kid? Yes, my darling daughter. Squares.

He didn't know where Stockbridge was, he'd never been up there, and it made him nervous that there was a theater up there. Jessica had told him there was a theater, maybe he'd know some of the people. Fat chance of that. But suppose she asked him to take her over to the theater, see if there were any famous actors he knew? What would he do then? Walk over to Cary Grant, say Hello there, Cary, long time no see?

The rented car kept pulling to the right, and he figured it had something to do with the balance of the wheels or the alignment, he didn't know which. He was a total idiot when it came to automobiles, and it bothered him that the car kept pulling to the right for reasons he could only guess at. The more the car kept pulling—it did it only when he stepped on the brake—the more he found himself thinking of Archie's supermarket and the possibility of making himself a quick thou just for crossing a few wires. The countryside was in bloom with trees and shrubs he couldn't identify, and when he asked Jessica what they were, it annoyed him that she could reel off the names so easily. That and the car pulling to the right. And Archie's supermarket. He was a fool even to consider going in at night, with or without a full partner. Hell with Archie, let him find himself another boy.

When they got to Stockbridge late that afternoon, he registered them as man and wife at the Red Lion Inn, a place Jessica recommended. The bellhop carried their bags up, and he tipped the kid a dollar, and then looked around the room, and heard Jessica asking if the theater was open for the season yet. The kid told her No, it was still too early, and Alex said nothing, but he handed the kid another dollar, as if the kid was the one responsible for the theater being closed. Jessica suggested that they take a stroll through the town and then drive over for dinner to a place she knew where the owner was a piano player who taught accompaniment. A lot of theater people stopped in there, she said, and sometimes they got up to entertain, it was really a lot of fun. That was just the kind of fun Alex needed, theater people, but he said Sure, whatever she wanted to do, and he watched while she freshened her lipstick, and he thought again of Archie's supermarket.

As they walked through the town, a bunch of long-haired kids turned to look at her, and one of them whistled after they went past, and Alex wanted to go back and punch the little shithead in the mouth. It was beginning to annoy him that Jessica never wore a bra. It annoyed him, too, that she seemed so familiar with the town, knew just where all the shops were, could tell him about all the things going on even in the nearby towns—classical music and ballet and experimental theater and even rock concerts. That was *during* the season, of course; she'd somehow had the feeling the season started earlier than it did; she didn't know why. Maybe because they began advertising Tanglewood in the *Times* each year long before the first concert started, though she hadn't yet seen any ads this year. Maybe she'd just *wanted* the theater to be open, *wanted* the season to have begun already so that she could share it with him.

"Yeah," he said.

They stopped in an antiques shop in town, and all around the place, on the shelves with little glass objects and brass things and medals and the like, there were these hand-lettered index cards that said:

> *If you plan to steal it,*
> *let's talk it over instead.*

Jessica asked the owner of the shop if the signs had helped cut down on shoplifting, and he said Oh, you'd be surprised. He was a jolly old fart wearing a lavender shirt with a checked vest over it, and dungaree trousers, and black loafers without socks. He explained to Jessica that there was a definite cycle involved in thefts of this sort, which he supposed fell under the general heading of burglary, he supposed shoplifting was a form of burglary—a lot the fuck *he* knew. They had made studies on burglary, he told Jessica, and whereas he didn't wish to bore her with a lengthy response to her simple question, they'd discovered that burglars had the same needs as noncriminal people (No kidding, Alex thought), such as the need for money, or the need for peer-group approval, or even the need for thrills, or in many cases the need to rebel against the man in the gray flannel suit, if Jessica knew what he meant.

"This is fascinating," Jessica said. "Isn't it fascinating, Alex?"

"Yeah," Alex said.

"Now this need has to be coupled with an opportunity to steal," the owner of the shop said, "*and* a recognition of that opportunity. The person then makes his choice; will he, or will he not steal to satisfy his need? If he *does* steal, and if he gets away with it, if he's successful, in other words, why then he'll gain a feeling of satisfaction from having stolen, and the cycle will repeat itself over and over again—he'll just keep right on stealing to satisfy his need."

The owner of the shop smiled broadly, said something that sounded like "Norks," and then spelled it out for Jessica. "N.O.R.C.S.S. Need, Opportunity, Recognition, Choice, Success, and Satisfaction. Now what I've done here, I've tried to step in at the 'Choice' stage of the cycle. A man comes in here with a need to steal, and he sees an opportunity to steal, and he recognizes this opportunity as a means of filling his need, why then he must make his choice. Well, my little signs allow him a freedom of choice. He doesn't *have* to steal, he can come talk it over with me instead."

"Do they ever talk it over with you?" Jessica asked.

"Oh, you'd be surprised," the man said. "Had a fellow in here some months back, said he didn't know what came over him but he just *had* to have a little figurine he saw on the shelf, and he knew he didn't have the money for it, and was tempted to steal it. We talked it over, and I allowed him to buy it on a sort of installment plan. He gave me five dollars—the piece cost fifty—and I let him take it home with him, and he's been sending me five dollars a month ever since. That was in November, it should be all paid up by August. Oh, yes, the signs have worked very well indeed."

Outside the shop, Jessica said, "He's got a good idea there, don't you think, Alex?"

"Unless a guy really *wants* to steal something, in which case he'll steal it," Alex said. "He won't go up there and talk to the owner. The guy who went up to him, he didn't want to steal that piece, he just wanted to buy it on time."

"Maybe you're right," Jessica said, but he could tell she *didn't* think he was right.

He was surprised by the place she took him to. It had really good French food, he hadn't expected to find anything so good up here in the sticks. And the man who ran the place was a very good piano player, who besides singing and accompanying himself, also played very good jazz. He wasn't Monk or Jamison or Shearing, but he knew what to do with a chart, sounded a lot like Powell, in fact, must have been influenced by the early bop piano players. After dinner, sitting in the small room with the piano in one corner, and candles flickering in round red holders on all of the tables, the sound of jazz flowing through the room, the taste of good cognac in his mouth, Alex found himself relaxing for the first time that day. And later, in the big double bed back at the hotel, he and Jessica made love, and he held her close and forgot about Archie's supermarket or any of the other things that had been troubling him all day long, including the little speech about burglary in the antiques shop.

But in the morning, while he was showering, he thought of the supermarket again, and when he came out of the shower and saw Jessica pulling a T-shirt over her head, he said, "Hey, don't you have any brassieres?"

"What?" she said.

"Don't you ever wear a bra?"

"Well, yes, sometimes."

"Well, whyn't you put one on now?"

"I don't have any with me," she said.

"What'd you do, go out in the street and burn them all?"

"I'll buy one, if you like," she said. "We'll find a shop, and I'll . . ."

"I don't care whether you wear one or not," he said. "You want to look like a whore, that's your business."

"Really, Alex, hardly any young girls . . ."

"You're not *that* young," he said, "you're twenty-nine. And also you're married and you've got a kid."

"I didn't realize it bothered you," she said.

"It doesn't bother me, you can do whatever you like."

"I'll buy a bra," she said.

But after breakfast, when she bought herself a bra in a shop on the town's main street, and came out of the dressing room wearing it under the T-shirt, he became annoyed again.

"You don't have to do everything I tell you," he said.

"I want to please you," she said.

"I'm not the kind of man forces a woman to do anything she doesn't want to do."

"I know that, Alex."

"Woman who does that is nothing but a whore."

"Alex . . ."

"Let's forget it, okay? You can wear a bra or not wear a bra, you can do whatever you like."

"Well, I'm wearing one. I bought one, and I'm wearing it."

He nodded briefly, and said nothing more about it, but he was still annoyed. If she was a square, then why didn't she dress like one? He didn't know what he was doing up here in the sticks with a square, anyway, but as long as he was here with her, he didn't want her parading around like a whore. A girl like Kitty, you went anyplace with her, people immediately knew she was a whore. There was no way of disguising it, that's what she was, and at least that was honest. It was like those square friends Jessica had, smoking pot and making jokes about the fuzz, what the hell did they know? It was the same thing here. Girl puts on a thin cotton T-shirt, nothing under it, what's *that* supposed to be? Girl's either a whore, or she isn't, and if she isn't she shouldn't go around trying to look like one. Those long-haired kids yesterday, he should have cleaned the street with them. Still, you couldn't blame them, thinking what they were thinking. Surprised they didn't come over and ask her how much. It bothered him that she'd knuckled under that way, ran right out to buy a bra. Girl's supposed to know her own mind, she doesn't *want* to wear a bra, then the hell with what anyone else says, just *do* it, get out there and do your own thing. Like that guy in the antiques shop with his stupid little signs. Did he really think that was going to stop anybody from doing his thing?

Serve him right somebody went in there one night and wiped out the whole fuckin shop, *including* the signs.

They spent all day Saturday looking at antiques. It was a beautiful day, he didn't mind driving around from shop to shop, but he was bored silly once he got inside the places. Jessica loved antiques, he should have figured that from the way her apartment was decorated. His own taste ran to severe modern, he liked things clean and simple, with swift lines, like a racehorse. He had heard guys in prison describing your high-priced call girls that way, as racehorses. He didn't suppose Kitty was a racehorse. You turned out Jessica, she'd be what you called a racehorse. Damn that fuckin Kitty, getting busted that way. Now he'd *never* get his two grand back.

He didn't see one thing he liked in any of the shops they went to, not one single thing. If he'd walked into any of those places planning to steal something, there wasn't anything he'd take. It reminded him of a story he'd heard, about a burglar who went into somebody's house and then left a note behind saying, "You cheap bastards, you got nothing here worth stealing." There was plenty *worth* stealing in all the shops they went to, that wasn't the point. The price tags told him the stuff was valuable, but if he'd walked into a living room brimming with the stuff, he wouldn't have known which was good and which was crap, and his own taste would have told him to leave it all there.

It was different with jewels. He could tell a piece of glass from a real diamond with only a casual glance, no need to scratch a window with it. He was sort of eager to get into that Post Mills house and get a crack at the Reed woman's diamonds, though he couldn't imagine where the box might be, and he knew he'd have to wait till they actually went in to even begin a search for it. He was eager to get in there for another reason, too. He wanted to *see* the place. He wanted to see what you could do with racehorse furniture if you had all the money you could ever hope to spend. Maybe this would be the one. Maybe this would be the big score he'd always been looking for, pull out after it, buy *himself* a house maybe, furnish it with good clean stuff, invest in the market maybe, or just sock it all away in the bank and let it draw interest. Still, a man could get restless, he supposed. Itch for a little action.

Archie's supermarket. It seemed like a simple job, get in there, knock out the alarm, open the box in no time at all. Still, it would have to be at night. *A dwelling's a building in Burglary Two, unless it's at night, like in Burglary One.* This wouldn't be a *dwelling* at night, a supermarket was only a building. So it would still be only Burglary Three, unless they ran into somebody inside there and had to hurt him. Neither of them would be carrying guns, he'd make sure of that; anyway, Archie didn't normally work with a gun, so there'd be no problem about it. It was the nighttime that bothered him, even if the rap was just the same as going into an apartment during the day. Something about the nighttime spooked him. You had to work with a flashlight, there were fuckin shadows all over the place, the hell with it, he'd tell Archie no.

They went to a lobster joint for dinner that night.

He liked the way she ate. She had a truck driver's appetite, it was a wonder she didn't weigh a thousand pounds. She hardly talked at all while she ate, she was busy dissecting lobster all the time, she scarcely even *looked* at him except when she paused occasionally to lift her glass of Muscadet and her eyes met his over the rim. There were things he liked about this damn girl. He liked the look of her, the clean, swift racehorse look, and the way she moved, whether it was picking up a fork or ripping the cellophane strip off a package of cigarettes, or just lifting her arms to untie the lobster bib. He liked her sense of humor, too, though at first he'd thought she was essentially humorless, like most square girls, but maybe that was because people who were in it joked about different things, things the squares could never hope to understand. But he found her picking up instantly on things he said, like when a lady came into the restaurant with a chihuahua in a little pink basket, and Alex took one look at the dog and said, "Used to be a Great Dane before she washed him," and Jessica burst out laughing, her mouth full of strawberry shortcake, and immediately grabbed for her napkin. And when she laughed at anything he said, he then found himself elaborating on the initial joke, expanding it into an anecdote, a short story practically, making it up as he went along, the crazier the better.

At one point during the meal, while they were sitting there over their second cups of coffee, he got into a routine that had her in stitches for a full five minutes, a thing about two bank robbers who got locked inside a vault and who started playing poker with the bank's money and one of them was winning six million dollars when the manager opened the vault the next morning, and by that time the thief actually believed the money was *his,* the six million he'd won, and asked the manager if he could open an account with his winnings, and the manager was so thrilled to be getting such a big account that he forgot for a moment there were two *thieves* inside his vault.

Alex didn't know where the story came from, he was certain it had never happened, never been told to him by any of the cons up at Sing Sing. It had just popped into his head—he couldn't even remember what either of them had said to trigger it—and he'd begun snowballing it, encouraged by her

laughter, falling into street jargon when the two thieves were
supposed to be talking, and then beginning to feel totally ex-
hilarated by the zany freedom of inventing something that
was causing her to fall off her chair, as though the two of
them were building a high together without benefit of dope.
She was laughing helplessly by the time he finished the
story, and she rose swiftly and put her napkin on the table,
and said, "I'm going to wet my pants," and walked immediately to the ladies' room. He'd liked *that* about her, too, her
remark about wetting her pants; there were things about this
girl he liked a hell of a lot.

In the car, on the way back to the Red Lion, she put her
head on his shoulder, and hummed along with a song Sinatra
was singing, and then broke into the lyrics where she remembered them, and suddenly he was singing with her, they were
both singing softly and probably out of tune, the car windows were open, there was a brisk snap to the air. The song
reminded her of another song, and she turned off the radio,
and he began singing *that* one with her, too, and he just continued driving past the Red Lion, turning right at the corner
there, one song recalling another, "Remember this one,
Alex?" or "How about this one, Jess?"—each of them beginning a song in turn, the other joining in immediately, sometimes just humming when either one of them didn't know the
lyrics. Singing, they drove all the way to Pittsfield and back,
Jessica's head on his shoulder, his arm around her, and after
he'd parked the car in front of the Red Lion, they went into
the lobby arm in arm and then upstairs to the room. She un-
dressed as shyly as a bride and then put on a nightgown she
had brought along, he had never seen her in a nightgown before. Outside the room, they could hear the trucks lumbering
past on Route 7, an occasional laugh on the street below, and

once, as they lay side by side in breathless silence, the clicking of the traffic light hanging over the main street.

In the middle of the night, she woke up and said, "Alex?"

"Yes?" he said.

"Alex," she said, "I think I'm in love with you."

It was then that he decided to go in with Archie on the supermarket job.

He went into the market alone on Monday morning and bought a shopping cart full of groceries while he looked the place over. It was a privately owned neighborhood market, small in comparison to the chain stores, but it seemed to be doing a brisk business even at ten in the morning. Archie had told him a day's receipts at *any* supermarket were usually in the two to three thousand dollar range, and that the receipts were almost always in the box at night because the market closed too late to get to the bank with them. In some of your markets, on Thursday nights when they stayed open late, you could sometimes beat them for five, six grand, but Archie didn't want to wait till Thursday, and anyway they had to go up to Post Mills on Thursday to case the Reed house. Besides, the place was a sitting duck, and he wanted to get in there before somebody else got the bright idea of knocking it over.

So they decided to do it on Monday night, provided the setup seemed okay to Alex once he'd had a chance to look it over. They had discussed all this on the phone the night before. While Jessica sent her mother-in-law packing, Alex phoned Archie from his own apartment and told him he wanted to go ahead with the job. Jessica rang him a half-hour later to tell him the coast was clear, and then he went downstairs. Jessica made dinner for them both, and then she put the kid to bed, and they made love again in her bedroom, and again she told him she thought she was falling in love with him, and just before he went upstairs again, she said, "I love you, Alex," without any *thinking* about it this time, just "I love you, Alex," straight out.

He spent less than a half-hour in the market, and while he was there he went into the manager's office and told him he was moving some of his stuff to his sister's house and would need some empty cartons, did the manager have any he could spare? The manager told him where the cartons were kept and Alex said he'd be back later in the afternoon with his station wagon, all he had outside right now was a small car. He asked the manager what time the store closed, and the manager said six o'clock. He thanked the manager, told him he'd see him later, and then paid cash for the groceries and carried them out to the rented car. He had spent $46.10 in the place, but he expected to get that back tonight, plus a little bit more. They didn't plan to use the rented car tonight. Tonight, they'd be using a car Archie would borrow from his Jewgirl social worker. The square wouldn't know they'd be using the car in a burglary, of course; squares never thought of things like that.

He drove back home, put the groceries away, and then phoned Archie to tell him the place looked just the way he'd described it, and he'd already set up getting into the room where they kept the cartons, it all looked fine. He told Archie he'd taxi up to Harlem around four-thirty and then they'd drive up to the Bronx together, and he'd plan to go in around a quarter to six. Archie asked him if he wanted to come up to Harlem right now, have a few beers together, but Alex told him no, there were some other things he had to do before tonight. Actually, there wasn't anything he had to do, but he liked to be well rested before a job, and he planned to take a little nap before heading uptown.

He didn't call Jessica. He had told her he'd be out job hunting all day long and probably wouldn't be home till late. He'd only told her that because he knew she'd be asking questions, squares were always asking their stupid questions. But even so, he'd made it clear he wasn't accounting to her for his time, he didn't have to account to *anyone* for his time. He'd told her that on the phone, early this morning, before he'd left for the Bronx. There had been a long silence on the line, and then she'd said in a very low voice, "I wasn't asking you to account for your time, Alex," which had made him feel like apologizing or something, he didn't know what *for*. It had finally ended up with him promising to call her when he got in tonight, though he told her one of the jobs he was looking into was way out on Long Island, for a summer theater out there ("Oh, which *one?*" she had asked immediately. "The one in East Hampton?"), and he might be getting in *very* late. No, *not* the one in East Hampton, he had said just before hanging up.

He took off all his clothes now, and pulled back the covers on the bed, and then opened the window a little so that he could hear the lulling sounds of the traffic far below. He set the clock for three, then lay down on the bed and stared up at the ceiling for a while, and then closed his eyes and tried to sleep. But he couldn't seem to drift off, so he got up and went naked into the living room, and put on some Charlie Parker and listened to that, lying on the couch, the speakers up full until he suddenly realized Jessica might check to see if he'd come home early, and hear the speakers blaring and knock on the door. He got up from the couch and turned down the speakers, but this wasn't the way you were supposed to listen to jazz, you were supposed to feel you were right in the *middle* of the band, right in there playing with them. He lay down on the couch again, barely able to hear one of the greatest alto sax solos ever recorded, and unable to enjoy it because it was so low. Like why the hell should he care if she knocked on the door? Knock on the door, he'd open it bare-assed and say Sorry, kid, I'm busy. He was tempted to turn the volume up full again, but suppose she *did* come upstairs on the off chance he might be home, suppose she *did* knock on the door, he'd have to let her in, wouldn't he? If only to give her another alibi about where he'd be tonight while he and Archie were ripping off the market.

That was the thing about square girls. You took your ordinary whore, you said to her I'll be out awhile, honey, she didn't ask you where you were going, what you were going to be doing, she knew you were a burglar and where you were going was to steal somebody blind, *that's* where you were going. Your square girl automatically figured you had some unexplained time, why then you had to be cheating on her. Thing with a whore, she gave you any trouble, you smacked her one. She was used to that, you couldn't find any whore who hadn't spent at least *some* time hustling for a pimp, she was used to getting smacked around. Smack around a square girl, she's on the pipe right away, calling the police. Law comes up there, says All right, folks, what's the trouble here? Square girl is all smiles by then. She's got a black eye, but she says No trouble at all officer, there must be some mistake. Cops had a rough job with squares. Squares were trouble for *every*body, even the fuckin cops. He didn't know why he'd started up with a square, and what was this about loving him? She hardly knew him, for Christ's sake! How could she be in love with him?

There was no use trying to sleep, and no use listening to jazz with the volume all the way down like that. He got off the couch and was walking to the bar to pour himself a drink when he remembered he'd be working later in the day. He made it a rule never to touch a drop before a job. Never. He'd heard stories about burglars going in a place and making a really heavy score, and then sitting down to celebrate with a bottle of the guy's Scotch. Man comes home, finds two drunken bums rolling around his living-room floor. Alex had never touched anything inside a place, not booze and not food either, except that one time when he knew the people were on vacation and he decided to make himself a sandwich and found the thousand bucks inside the loaf of bread. He smiled now, thinking about that time. Those were the times he liked best, when he came upon something unexpected like that.

So what the hell was he supposed to do now?

He decided to go uptown after all, sit around and chew the rag with Archie till it was time to go to the Bronx.

He hadn't expected to find Kitty up there.

He'd gone first to Archie's place, and when he'd knocked on the door and got no answer, he went looking for him in the bars along Lenox Avenue. Kitty was sitting on a stool in the third place he tried. He thought for a minute he was seeing things. But it was Kitty all right, sitting on the stool and drinking a crème de menthe over ice, watching the television set above the bar. He took the stool next to hers, and then said, "Hi, I thought you were in jail."

She turned away from the television set, the stool swiveling around, a fixed smile on her face, a hooker smile, a square-john greeting. Then she saw it was Alex, and the smile turned to something more personal, and she said, "You never sent me so much as a candy bar."

"How you doing, Kitt?"

"Okay," she said.

"When did you get out?"

"Just this morning. Transit went for my bail."

"Oh," Alex said.

Transit was a white pimp who'd been trying to get Kitty in his stable even when she and Alex were still living together. His real name was Travis Croft, but he'd worked for the Transit Authority years ago, when he was still a square john, and he'd picked up the nickname in prison, after everybody found out what he was in there for. He was in there for grand larceny because one day he'd decided he was fed up with sitting in the change booth on Eighty-sixth Street and Lexington Avenue, and he'd simply packed $300 in quarters, dimes, and nickels into his lunch pail and walked off the job. No way of getting away with it, no *possible* way of making it work. A typical square-john caper.

While he was in prison, though, he met a black pimp from Schenectady who told him how to start a stable, and as soon as Transit got out—he was serving one-to-three and had plenty of time to learn all about pimping—he got himself a few girls and set himself up in business. He had maybe half a dozen girls now, all of them black, and he dressed like a spade pimp himself, with the big hat and the high-heeled shoes and the flashy suits and dark glasses. Transit was five feet ten inches tall and built like an oak tree. He had a reputation for severely beating his girls if they didn't turn what he considered a respectable number of tricks every day of the week. You could always tell one of Transit's girls standing on a Sixth Avenue street corner. She usually had a split lip or a shiner, and Alex had even seen one of them hustling with her arm in a cast. He was a stupid ox of a man, Transit was, and a sweetheart besides. And now he'd sprung for Kitty's bail.

"He's got me a good lawyer, too," Kitty said. "Man named Aronberg, do you know him?"

"No," Alex said.

"He thinks he may be able to get me off with a suspended sentence."

"Is Transit doing all this out of the goodness of his heart?"

"Well, we have a sort of deal,"

"Why the fuck did you go to Transit?"

"He come to me," she said. "Well, you know, he's *always* been after me."

"So now he's got you."

"It's just a temporary arrangement," she said. "Till I can pay him back what he gave the bondsman."

"Why didn't you go to a bondsman direct?"

"Fuckin judge set bail at five thousand, said I was a bad risk. I just couldn't raise the five hundred for the bondsman's commission. Transit went the five."

"How're you gonna pay him back, Kitty?"

"Well, Transit's got a fine book. I won't be one of his scaly-legs standin on Forty-ninth, don't worry about that. I'll be turnin hundred-dollar, two-hundred-dollar tricks."

"Transit must be coming up in the world."

"He's got a fine book. Out-of-town johns comin in, you know."

"Is that what he told you?"

"It's the truth, Alex. I *know* it's the truth. Anyway, he came up with the five, and he's got me a good lawyer, and maybe I'll beat the fuckin rap. Or maybe we can get it reduced. Either way, I'm ahead."

"How much is the lawyer costing?"

"I don't know. Transit's takin care of that."

"Great. He owns you now, huh?"

"Nobody owns me," Kitty said, and looked into her drink.

He went into the supermarket at a quarter to six and walked directly to the room where the cartons were stacked. A kid was back there sweeping up. He looked at Alex when he came in.

"Manager said I could have some cartons," Alex said.

"Okay with me," the kid said, and shrugged, and went back to his sweeping. Alex spent two or three minutes looking over the cartons, selecting those he wanted, noting at the same time that there were several very large toilet-tissue cartons he could use later, when he stashed himself. He put three cartons into a larger carton, and then said to the kid, "I'll be back, I'm going to need more of these," and went out of the room and past the checkout counters and then to the parking lot where the Jewgirl's car was parked. He put the cartons on the back seat and then looked at his watch. It was eight minutes to six.

He wondered how long that kid would be in there sweeping, but he couldn't waste any more time, he had to get in there again before they closed the front doors. He took the car keys from his pocket and put them into the ignition. As he walked back to the market, he saw Archie coming around the corner and heading for the car. Archie would drive off with it and come back later, at nine o'clock sharp; they figured Alex would have knocked out the alarm and unlocked the back door by then. Archie would park the car, kill the lights, and then just shake the door to see if it was unlocked. If it wasn't yet unlocked, he'd come back a half-hour later, and keep coming back every half-hour till he *found* it unlocked.

Alex went past the checkout counters again and walked through the market, past the meat counter, and into the room where the cartons were stacked. The kid was still in there sweeping.

"Lady out there needs some help," Alex said.

"What?" the kid said. "What lady?"

"Wants you to carry some bundles out to her car."

"Where's Jerry?" the kid asked. "Jerry's supposed to do that."

"Don't ask me," Alex said. "I'm just telling you what the lady wants."

"Shit," the kid said, but he put his broom in the corner and went out.

The moment he was gone, Alex swiftly checked the room to see which parts of it had already been swept, chose a corner farthest from the door, and picked up two of the large toilet-tissue cartons. He laid one of these on its side, so that the open end was facing the wall. Then he turned the other one upside down and put it in front of the first carton. Quickly, he began stacking a row of cartons on top of each other around the larger cartons. It was three minutes to six when he went around behind the barrier he'd created and crawled into the carton he'd laid on its side. The fit was tight, his shins and feet were sticking out. But they were facing the wall, and hidden by the mound of cartons he had stacked around his little cave.

A moment later, he heard someone coming into the room. Then he heard the sound of the broom. A little while after that, someone else came into the room.

"Hey, Jerry, you see a lady out there?" the kid asked.

"What lady?" Jerry said.

"Some lady needed bundles carried."

"What the hell are you talking about?"

"Guy said some lady needed bundles carried."

"I didn't see no lady. It's six o'clock. Finish up, and let's get out of here."

"Hold the dustpan for me, will you?"

He listened as they finished the sweeping. There were voices outside in the market now, employees wrapping up for the day, walking past the room in which he was hidden. The front doors were probably locked already, it would take them maybe another half-hour to tally the registers and put the money in the box. Maybe the manager would stay another half-hour after that, checking over the books, who the hell knew what? Alex was counting on all of them being out by seven; Archie had said they would all be out by seven. But to play it safe, he would stay hidden till eight.

"How's that?" the kid said.

"Beautiful. You want a fuckin medal for sweepin the floor?"

The kid and Jerry both laughed, and together they went out of the room. Alex waited. From somewhere outside, he heard a man say, ". . . those beef sides in tomorrow, better try to get here early."

"Yeah, good night, Sam."

"See you in the morning."

There was a water tap dripping someplace. He lay inside the carton, curled like a fetus in its womb, listening to the steady dripping of the water tap and the ticking of his own watch. He remembered when he was a child living in the Bronx, hiding under the dining room table with his cousin Cecily, the tablecloth his mother had tatted coming almost to the floor. Shoes going by. They could see shoes going by below the edge of the tablecloth. "Where are the kids?" his aunt asked. "Have you seen the kids?" Putting his hand on Cecily's thigh in the gloom of their hiding place. "They must have gone downstairs," his mother said. In the kitchen, the sound of a cabinet door being opened, a chair being scraped back from the enamel-topped table. "Too early for a pick-me-up?" his mother asked, and his aunt replied, "Never too early, Demmy." His mother's name was really Demetria, but everyone called her Demmy. Greek women weren't supposed to drink a lot, but his mother did. His aunt was Irish, like his father, and there were statistics on the Irish being big boozers, belligerent too when they got drunk. His aunt was his mother's good steady drinking companion. Under the dining room table, he slid his hand up under Cecily's skirt and into her cotton panties.

Alex looked at his watch. It was only six-fifteen, it was going to be a long night. He had already thought of what he would say if someone came back there and found him curled up inside the carton—provided it wasn't the manager, who already knew him. He would simply pretend he was drunk, a drunken bum who had stumbled in there and curled up for a good night's sleep. They'd just kick him out of the store, unless it was the manager, who'd remember him asking for cartons, and who might put two and two together. But even if it *was* the manager, he wasn't expecting too much intelligence from a machine who ran a fuckin supermarket. Maybe the drunk act would work even if it was the manager. Anyway, he hoped *nobody* would come back there, why *would* anyone come back there? Check out a bunch of empty cartons? No way.

He heard more voices outside, but he couldn't distinguish what they were saying. Probably on the other side of the store, near the manager's office. Maybe the cashiers were bringing the receipts back for him to put in the box. Cecily's box under the dining room table, his hand easing up under the elastic legband of her panties. Cecily trapped, a partner in crime already, unable to protest without giving away their hiding place and ruining the little cocktail hour out there in the kitchen. Enjoying it besides, wriggling as he explored. In the kitchen, his mother and his aunt drank their booze and laughed softly, the sounds of summer coming through the open kitchen windows and wafting into the dining room where in the cool shade Cecily wriggled beneath his questing hand and murmured something he could not hear for the pounding of blood in his ears. "Good night, Josie," someone called in the market outside, and he heard the sound of high heels clattering across the tiled floor, echoing in the high-ceilinged room. He looked at his watch again. It was six-twenty; only five minutes had passed since the last time he'd looked.

By seven, the room was becoming dim, the market had grown still except for the steady clatter of what he assumed was an adding machine in the manager's office. Nighttime was coming, he felt a sudden chill. Lying curled inside the carton, his arms crossed over his chest, his knees up, his shins and feet exposed to the encroaching darkness, he hugged himself and thought of how empty the Bronx apartment had seemed after his father left, the sounds in the night, water pipes usually, or sometimes toilets flushing, or occasionally a mouse in the walls, gnawing at the plaster lath with all the fury of a jungle beast. But most often, the sound of his mother weeping or swearing in the kitchen as she drank herself into a stupor. The room was getting darker and darker, the hands of his watch were luminous the next time he looked at them. Twenty minutes past seven, and still the fuckin adding machine was going. Cecily's teeth chattering in the darkness on the roof of the building. "We're cousins," she whispered. He had sawed through the shackle on the roof door's padlock, and they had gone around to the other side of the peaked structure into which the door was set. This was October, she was wearing a cheerleader's white sweater with a huge red R between her breasts, a pleated maroon skirt, white bobby sox and loafers. She squirmed against the brick wall to which he held her pinned, and whispered again, "We're cousins," and he listened for the sound of the door opening, knowing it could be opened now, knowing some- one might find the sawed-off padlock, and open the door, and find them in the darkness, his hands up under the pleated skirt.

The adding machine stopped suddenly.

He listened.

He heard a door closing. The door to the manager's office had a knob-operated drop bolt lock on it, but the upper panel of the door was glass, which meant the lock wasn't worth a shit. He could not hear any sound coming from across the market now, but he assumed the manager was locking the door to his office. The next thing he'd do, if Alex knew any- thing at all about alarms, he'd test to make sure everything was all locked up, and then he'd turn on the alarm and leave.

All the alarm systems Alex had ever seen, no matter how crude or sophisticated, were composed of three basic units. You had your protective circuit, your control box, and your signaling device, that was all. Your protective circuit was an electrical current which, if you disturbed it, flashed a signal to the control box. Your control box was the brain of the sys- tem; the minute a window or door or whatever was opened, disturbing the electrical flow, the brain immediately trig- gered the signaling device. The signaling device was either a bell outside, like here at the market, or else something that flashed or rang at a remote station. That's all there was to it.

The control box here was just inside the rear door of the market, no larger than the switch plate for a light. The face of the recessed box had on it a red light, a white light, and a slot into which you put the alarm key. When you were ready to activate the alarm, you locked all your doors and windows, and if the white light stayed on, that meant something was still open. So you looked around for it, closing everything till that white light went out. That meant the place was now secure. Then you put your key into the slot on the face of the box, and you turned it to the right, and the red light came on, telling you the alarm system was now set. With these alarms that had the control box on the *inside* of a place, there was usually a thirty-second delay that allowed you to open the door and go outside without the alarm going off. After that thirty seconds, though, if anybody opened a window or door, a skylight or transom—*bang* went the bell on the wall outside. Very nice—unless somebody was already inside waiting to fuck up the wiring.

The market was still.

He waited till eight, and then he crawled out of the toilet-tissue carton, and stretched his legs which had got stiff from his curled-up position. He listened just inside the door before he went out of the room, and then he walked past the meat counter in the dark, and went directly to the manager's office. In one pocket of his jacket, he was carrying a screwdriver, a knife, a pair of pliers, a compass, a six-inch piece of electrical wire, and a hacksaw blade. In the other pocket, he was carrying a fifty-cent glass cutter and a suction cup. Tucked into the waistband of his trousers were a hammer and a cold chisel. Strapped to his right thigh with adhesive tape was the hacksaw itself. He pulled on his gloves, walked directly to the control box on the right of the rear door, and then spread his tools on the floor, leaving only the glass cutter and the suction cup in his pocket. He had to lower his pants to get at the hacksaw, and he thought how comical it would be if the law arrived just then, found him with his tools all over the floor, and his pants down around his knees. He pulled up his pants again, fastened his belt, and inserted the blade into the hacksaw. The red light on the alarm box was glowing; the alarm was alive and well and living in the Bronx.

On his trip here this morning, he had not seen any exposed wiring, which meant all of it was in the walls. There were no exposed screws on the control-box plate, nor had he expected to find any there. He didn't plan to mess around with the brain, anyway; it was much simpler to fuck up the wiring. He knew that *wherever* the wiring was inside those walls, it eventually had to feed into that control box, so he picked up his hammer and chisel and began chipping away at the plaster around the box, trying to locate the BX cable. By law, any inside-the-wall wiring had to run inside the BX, which was a piece of twisted steel tubing. He began working just above the control box, at twelve o'clock, and then he worked his way around to three o'clock and finally hit the cable at six. He kept chipping until he had a clear area all the way around the cable, and then he hooked it with his pliers and began working on it with the hacksaw. As he came closer to sawing through it, he became extremely cautious, not wanting to saw right through the wires that were inside it. Do that, and the fuckin bell would go off.

There were four wires inside the BX. Just as he and Archie had expected, this was a combination system. Basically, you had only three different kinds of alarm systems—your open-circuit, your closed-circuit, and your combination. The open-circuit system was the cheapest kind and the easiest to knock out. It was nothing more than the kind of wiring you'd use on your front doorbell. Gap in the wiring, press the bell button outside, it closed the gap and allowed the current to pass through, ringing the doorbell. When you used this kind of wiring for an alarm, the gap got closed whenever a door or a window was opened, and this allowed the current to run through and trigger the bell. A pair of shears could knock out an open-circuit system, because all you had to do with it was cut the wires, and that was that, the current never *could* run through wires that had been cut.

Your closed-circuit system operated in exactly the opposite way. A mild current ran through the wires at all times, and when a door or a window was opened, it broke the current and caused a relay to jump out, and this triggered the bell. If you cut the wires in this system, it was the same thing as opening a door or a window; you'd break your current and the bell would go off. The way you beat *this* system was to crosscontact the wires, so that the current would continue running through no matter how many doors or windows you opened later. He had been taught how to beat both of these systems by a con up at Sing Sing, who'd explained it to him in the simplest possible terms. For that bell to ring in an *open*-circuit system, the circuit had to be *closed;* in the *closed*-circuit system, the circuit had to be *opened*. To beat them, you just made sure the open stayed open and the closed stayed closed. Simple. As for the combination system, that was exactly what it sounded like—a combination of open and closed. To beat it, you had to cut one set of wires and cross-contact the other set, and the only thing you had to be careful about was cutting the wrong wires. You couldn't cut the ones carrying the current, or the bell would go off.

Which is why Alex was carrying a compass.

With the wiring exposed, he put the compass against each wire in turn and when the needle jumped he knew which two were carrying the current. Using the knife, he stripped a section on each of those wires, exposing the copper through which the current ran. Then he stripped both ends of the six-inch piece of wire he had brought with him. He twisted one end of this small section around one of the current-bearing wires, and the other end around the second wire. If he'd done his cross-contacting right, he should now be able to knock out the entire system, simply by cutting *all* the wires inside the BX. He had no reason to believe he'd done anything wrong. Swiftly he cut the wires. The red light on the face of the control box went out, as effectively as if he'd put a key in the slot to turn off the alarm. He looked at his watch. It was twenty minutes to nine. He still had twenty minutes before Archie would try the back door. He decided not to unlock it until close to zero hour, just in case a cop came around and shook the door. Instead, he took the suction cup and the glass cutter from his jacket pocket and went to the door of the manager's office.

He spit into the suction cup, wetting it, and then pushed it hard against the glass panel on the side of the door closest to the lock. He tested the cup to make sure it was holding securely to the glass, and then took the glass cutter from his pocket. In less than a minute he had cut almost a full circle in the glass. He grabbed the suction cup with his left hand, tested it to make sure it was still holding, cut away the remainder of the circle, and pulled the glass free of the panel. He put the glass circle on the floor, away from the door so that he wouldn't step on it by accident, and then reached into the hole with his left hand and turned the knob on the drop bolt.

At three minutes to nine, he unlocked the back door of the market. Archie came into the place at nine sharp, carrying the heavier tools they'd need to open the mercantile. As it turned out, all they needed was a sledge and a punch because that broad form box must've been an old one even when Hector was a pup. They knocked off the dial, and then punched the spindle shaft clear back through the gut box, and broke the lock nuts, and opened it in less than four minutes flat.

There was $3,500 in cash inside that sweet old box.

On Tuesday, the idea came to him that maybe it wasn't necessary to do a dry run on the Reed house. He took a taxi over to Grand Central Station, where he knew he could find a Westchester-Putnam telephone directory. In the yellow pages at the back of the book, he looked up *Burglar Alarm Systems* and came across a quarter-page ad that read:

PROVIDENT ELECTRONIC SECURITY
INVISIBLE
SILENT ALARMS

- Homes & Apartments
- Offices & Showrooms
- Cash & Vault Areas
- Wireless Hold-up Alarms

SPECIALIZING IN:
- Automatic Telephone Police Dialers
- Low-Cost Temporary Alarms

- Thin-Line Window Security
- Area Surveillance

RESIDENTIAL AND COMMERCIAL

Free Estimate and Consultation

The company was on Mamaroneck Avenue, in White Plains. Alex jotted down the phone number and then flipped through the yellow pages until he came to a heading for *Taxicab Service*. He checked out the companies under that heading, but could find no listing for Duncan's Livery. He then looked up *Limousine Service* on the off chance Dun-

can's setup was a very exclusive one, but there was no listing
there, either. Finally, he tried to find a listing for Duncan
under *Livery* but there was only a heading for *Livery Stables,*
and under that it said "See Stables." So he had to figure Duncan was a nickel-and-dime operator who couldn't even afford an ad in the yellow pages. In the white pages, he looked
up Duncan's Livery and found three telephone numbers, one
under the other:

Duncan's Livery Service	Cross Rdge Rd	Lngston	LA 4-7210
		Post Mls	PO 8-3461
Duncan Charles	Cross Rdge Rd	Lngston	LA 4-7210

The two Langston listings were identical, and they told
Alex that Duncan was running his business out of his home.
There was no address for the listing in Post Mills; Alex had
to assume it was a telephone answering service. He turned to
the area-code map at the front of the directory and saw that
Post Mills and Langston were about a quarter-inch apart.
There was no scale on the map, but he knew the mileage
from Post Mills to New York City, and by comparing the
distances, he estimated that Langston was a good ten miles
from Post Mills. This meant that even if they *did* trigger the
alarm in the Reed house, it'd take Duncan at least ten minutes to get there, doing sixty miles an hour.

Alex then flipped through the directory pages to the NEW
YORK-STATE OF listings, and under *State Police,* he found
telephone numbers for substations at Brewster, Croton Falls,
Hawthorne, Peekskill, Taconic State Parkway, and Tarry-
town. Nine towns were lumped together under the heading
Calls For. These were Armonk Village, Katonah, Langston,
Lewisboro, Mount Kisco, Post Mills, Pound Ridge, Somers,
and South Salem & Vicinity. For state police assistance to

any of these nine towns, the number was BE 4–3100. Alex turned to the front of the book again and learned that BE was the dialing prefix for Bedford. Looking at the area code map, he estimated that Bedford was approximately fifteen miles from Post Mills.

He wrote Duncan's two telephone numbers on the same slip of paper with the Provident number, and then he made change at the cigar stand and went into the closest phone booth. A young girl answered the phone at Provident, and Alex told her he was interested in having a burglar alarm installed and would like to talk to someone about it. The man who came on the line a moment later said, "Yes, sir, may I help you?"

"This is Mr. Cunningham," Alex said. "Who am I talking to, please?"

"Mr. D'Amato," the man said.

"Mr. D'Amato," Alex said, "I'm purchasing a home in Post Mills, and the real estate agent up there said I should contact you about a burglar alarm system. There's no police force up there, as you may know, and it seemed to me . . ."

"Yes, a security system *would* be a wise investment."

"Now, I didn't quite understand this, but she said something about a man named Charles Douglas, who runs a taxi service up there . . ."

"Duncan," D'Amato corrected.

"Yes, Duncan, that was the name. Is *he* the man I should be contacting?"

"No, this is the sales office for Provident."

"Doesn't he work for you?"

"Yes, he does. We have a private arrangement with him, whereby he monitors our system up there."

"A *taxi* driver monitors your system?" Alex said.

"Yes."

"I see. Well, thank you very much, Mr. D'Amato. Actually, I had something a little more . . ."

"I know that sounds a bit odd, Mr. Cunningham," D'Amato said, "but it's proven quite effective for us. We have fourteen houses wired into our system in Post Mills, and we've found . . ."

"I thought you were hooked into the police, you see. The real estate agent led me to believe . . ."

"Well, there *is* no police force in Post Mills, as you know. And when we made our initial tests up there, we found that the state trooper response was inadequate—not that they aren't doing a very good job, it's just that they have so much territory to cover. Response time is the key factor in any burglar alarm system."

"Well, if the alarm goes off, if the bell rings, who . . . ?"

"It's a silent alarm, Mr. Cunningham."

"I don't know anything about burglar alarms, I'm sorry. Would you explain what that means?"

"It's very simple. If anyone enters any of the houses we've wired—this is assuming the alarm is *set*, you understand—then the telephone rings in Mr. Duncan's office, and a recorded message announces that there's an intruder at such and such a subscriber's house. Mr. Duncan immediately phones the state police and then goes over to the house himself."

"What if he's on the road? If he runs a taxi service . . ."

"There's always someone answering his phone. If he's out, an answering service in Post Mills picks up."

"What good will an answering service do if somebody's in my house?"

"Mr. Duncan's cars are all equipped with two-way radios."

"Suppose he's out at Kennedy Airport or something?"

"He employs six drivers. One of them is always some-where in the vicinity of Post Mills."

"I see," Alex said. "Well, let me think about it. It'll be some time before I take title . . ."

"Mr. Cunningham, why don't we do this?" D'Amato said. "I hate to give such a sketchy picture on the telephone. A telephone conversation just doesn't suffice, really, when we're talking about the protection of your family and your personal property. You'll be making a sizable investment up there in Post Mills, I know the houses up there, Mr. Cun-ningham. I naturally want to sell you one of our systems, I happen to feel we're installing the best burglar alarm system in Westchester County. I also want you to understand it com-pletely. I can make an appointment for you here in White Plains or, what would be more fruitful, actually, we could meet at the house you're buying in Post Mills, go over the terrain and the interior together, and at the same time discuss more fully . . ."

"Well, let me talk it over with my wife," Alex said. "Thank you very much, Mr. D'Amato."

He put the receiver onto the hook and smiled. He had learned all he needed to know about the alarm system in Reed the Third's house. It was a telephone dialer, and it wasn't worth a shit. However it was rigged—open, closed, or combination circuit—what happened if you tripped it was that it activated the telephone. Instead of an alarm going off, the telephone automatically dialed a number that had been fed into it, usually a police station, but in this case Duncan's Livery. Whoever picked up on the other end got a recorded message saying there'd been a break-in. Usually, if it was a police station, the message gave the address of the place. With Duncan sitting the system, though, and with only four-teen houses on the wire, there probably was no need for that, the message would just say Break-in at the Jones house, or the Smith house, or the Reed house. Your telephone dialer was silent, the burglar never even knew he'd disturbed the electrical flow that activated the phone. But it was almost worthless because in order for the phone to dial out, there had to be telephone wires. And wherever there were telephone wires, they had to feed into the house someplace. In order to knock out the alarm, all you had to do was cut those wires. Burglar trips the alarm, so what? Phone can't dial for help with the wires cut.

It looked nice.

It looked very nice indeed.

When they told Daisy they wouldn't be up there on Thursday, she misunderstood them.

"Good," she said. "I was *hoping* you'd call off the job."

"Who said we're calling it off?" Archie said.

"You just told me . . ."

"We just told you there's no reason to come up there, we know what kind of alarm Reed's got."

"Oh," Daisy said.

"What do you mean you were hoping we'd call it off?" Alex said.

"I been worrying about it, that's all. I don't want it to get back to me."

"How's it gonna get back to you?"

"Cause Mr. Reed knows I been inside the house."

"So what? Must be dozens of people go in and out of that house all the time."

"It's just he might think I set it up."

"Even so, you're protected. He can't involve you cause then the wife finds out."

"You never can tell," Daisy said. "He might all at once get

religion, decide to tell his wife all about it. You steal a man blind, he can get religious mighty fast."

"You've got nothing to worry about," Archie said. "Just relax, will ya?"

"I still wish you'd call it off," Daisy said.

The kid knew him now. "See?" he said, and held up his stuffed bear.

"That's some bear you got there, Peter. That bear's almost bigger'n you are."

"Bear," the kid said. "Fuzzy bear."

He was sitting in the middle of the crib surrounded by the stuffed bear and a half dozen other toys. From the bathroom down the hall, Jessica called, "It's almost bedtime, Peter."

"Fuzzy go seep," the kid said.

"You have to go to sleep, too," Alex said.

"No, no," he said, and shook his head.

"Get a good night's rest, so you can wake up tomorrow and play with the bear."

"No," the kid said, and shook his head again.

"Alex would you get his things out of the crib and tuck him in?" Jessica said.

"You hear your mommy?" Alex said.

"Just leave the bear," Jessica said. "He likes to sleep with it."

"You like to sleep with the bear, Peter?"

"Fuzzy bear," the kid said.

"Okay, let's just get these other things out of here, okay? Then you can go to sleep with the bear."

"Okay."

Alex took the other toys out of the crib and put them on one of the shelves in the unpainted bookcase. When he went back to the crib, the kid was already lying down, the bear clutched to his chest, his thumb in his mouth.

"Don't suck your thumb, Peter, it'll make your teeth crooked," Alex said.

"Mmm," the kid said, but he went right on sucking his thumb.

"I think you're gonna need a blanket tonight," Alex said. "Little chilly. Here you go now, let's just tuck it up right here, right under *your* chin and *Fuzzy's* chin, too. Okay?"

"Okay."

"G'night now, Peter," he said, and almost reached over the crib railing to kiss the kid, but he didn't.

"Night," the kid said.

"G'night."

"Night."

He went out of the room, and the kid called after him again, "Night," and he said, "G'night, Peter," and again the kid called, "Night."

"That's a ritual with him," Jessica said. She was standing in the hallway wearing a white terry robe, belted at the waist. Her hair was wet. In her hands, she was holding a portable hair dryer. "He'll keep it up all night if you let him."

"Well, he's a good kid," Alex said.

"Can you fix this thing for me?" she asked.

"What's wrong with it?" he asked.

"Search me," she said, and shrugged. *"You're* the electrician."

She kissed him on the cheek, handed him the dryer, and then went into the kid's room. Alex carried the dryer into the living room with him, put it down on the coffee table, and then sat on the couch and stared at it. Has to be a dryer, he thought. Couldn't have been a lamp, something like that, simple wiring like in an open-circuit system. No. *Has* to be a fuckin hair dryer. In the hallway, he heard Jessica exchanging three or four good-nights with her son, and then she came into the living room and went directly to the cigarette box on the coffee table, and took one from it, and lit it. Then she looked at the dryer.

"What do you think?" she said.

"Have you got a screwdriver?" Alex asked. "I'll have to take it apart."

"I'll get you one," she said. "Do you want a drink? Fix yourself a drink."

"A Phillips, I'll need."

"What's a Phillips?"

"With the little cross on the head. I'll need that to get these screws off."

"I'll see what I have out there," she said, and left the room. When she came back, she was carrying two screwdrivers. One of them was a Phillips. She put both on the coffee table, and said, "He *is* a nice kid, isn't he?"

"Oh, yeah."

"He likes you a lot," Jessica said. "This is a very difficult time for him. He keeps asking me where his daddy is. Where Daddy, he says. But he likes you a lot, Alex."

"Mmm," Alex said, and began unscrewing the four screws that held the dryer together. He didn't know what he was going to find inside there, it was something like peeling a safe without having any idea of the contents. She was watching him intently, the way people watch an autmobile mechanic when he's fooling around under the hood, no idea what the man is doing with the engine there, but fascinated, anyway. She was watching him that way now.

"How'd you make out today?" she asked.

"No luck," Alex said.

"Where'd you go?"

"Stage electrician's union," he said.

"Must be awful for you," she said.

"Well, I've got a little put aside," he said. "In this business, I know there'll be stretches when I'm not working, so I plan for those. I'm in good shape, Jess, really. You don't have to worry about it." He had taken the dryer apart now, it lay in two halves on the coffee table. He made a show of studying the wiring.

"It just won't go on," Jessica said. "I turn it on and nothing happens."

"Mmm," he said. "This is a foreign dryer, huh?"

"German," she said, and nodded. "It's supposed to be a very good one."

"Cause the parts in here look different than ours."

"What do you mean?"

"Ours are different," he said, and immediately began putting the dryer together again. "You'd better take it back where you bought it. There's a warranty on it, isn't there?"

"Yes, but that means I won't *see* the damn thing for another month."

"Can't help you," he said, and smiled.

"Some electrician," she said, and returned the smile. "Meanwhile, my hair's wet. Let me get a towel, Alex. Fix me a martini, would you? I feel like a martini."

He screwed the dryer together while she was gone, and then he went to the bar and mixed a pitcherful of martinis. When she came back into the living room, a white towel was wrapped around her head. He had already poured two drinks from the pitcher. She picked hers up immediately, said "Skoal," and then drank. "Ahhh," she said. "Good. You're better with martinis than you are with hair dryers."

"What can I tell you?" he said, and smiled again.

"Felice'll be here at eight," she said.

"I didn't know we were going out."

"I thought you said . . ."

"I thought . . ."

"I can call her, tell her to . . ."

"No, no."

"If you'd prefer staying home."

"No, let's go out," he said.

"I thought you said you wanted to go out tonight. When we talked on the phone this morning . . ."

"Yeah, that's all right, don't worry about it."

"If you're short of cash or anything . . ."

"No, I'm fine. Come on, Jess, I'm fine."

"It really ought to be *my* treat, anyway," Jessica said, and smiled. "I've got something to celebrate tonight, Alex."

"Oh? What's that?"

"Well . . ." she said, drawing out the word, still smiling, "I went to see Samalson again this afternoon. My lawyer, I told you I was going to see him, didn't I?"

"Yes."

"So guess what?" she said. She was still smiling. She looked like a kid with a secret, sitting there on the couch with her legs tucked under her, bundled in the terry robe, the white towel wrapped around her head. A little kid with a big secret. He knew what the secret was, he could guess what it was, but he didn't want to spoil it for her.

"What?" he said.

"Michael's agreed to a settlement," she said in a rush.

"Great," he said. "That's great, Jess."

"Now how's *that?*" she said, grinning.

"Great," he said again.

"That means once we sign the agreement, I can go down to Haiti or the Dominican Republic and get a divorce in twenty-four hours."

"Are they good, those divorces?"

"Good as gold."

"I mean, will they stand up?"

"They'll stand up and *cheer!*" she said, and burst out laughing, and suddenly said, "Let's get smashed." She moved swiftly to the pitcher, and poured herself another drink. "I feel like getting smashed tonight. Let's just sit here and get smashed, the hell with going out. I'll call Felice and tell her to forget it. Would you like to get smashed?"

"If you want to, sure."

"I'd like to see you smashed. You're a very controlled person, Alex, I'd like to see you when you're really totally and completely smashed out of your mind."

"I never get *that* smashed," he said.

"Let's get you that smashed, okay? Let's both get smashed out of our minds."

"Whatever you say," he said.

"I'll call Felice. All I have to do is change Peter later, I can do that blindfolded. Let's not worry about anything but getting smashed, okay? I feel terrific, Alex. I feel so goddamn terrific, I can't tell you. I'm going to be free of that prick at last, do you realize it? Do you know how much that means to me?"

"I know you've been wanting it, Jess."

"Yes," she said, and nodded. "Yes." She looked into the mouth of her glass for a moment, thoughtfully, and then suddenly grinned. "Jesus," she said, "I can't believe it," and immediately went to the phone and dialed Felice's number. As she waited for the phone to ring, she gestured for Alex to drink up, and then blew a kiss across the room.

He had no intention of getting drunk, not with her or any other square. Moreover, he didn't know how much he liked the idea of *her* getting drunk. He had seen his mother drunk on far too many occasions, and he knew there was nothing attractive about a drunken broad. So he listened as she made her apologies to Felice, but he was already planning to go easy on the sauce, and maybe to call out for some food later, there was a place up on Broadway that delivered. She finished her second martini shortly after she got off the phone, and then she poured herself another from the pitcher, and filled Alex's glass at the same time. There was something almost manic in her mood, something that smacked to him of imminent danger, but he told himself he was in complete control of the situation. She could drink herself falling-down drunk for all he cared; *he* was going to stay sober. There were too many secrets to protect, and drinking with a square was not the same as drinking with somebody who was in it.

But in spite of his resolve, and perhaps because he too had something to celebrate—the supermarket score on Monday, the newly acquired knowledge that the Reed house alarm could be knocked out simply by cutting the telephone wires—or perhaps because he truly *did* feel more relaxed with her than with any square girl he had ever known, he found himself drinking along with her, not as much as she was drinking, pacing himself so that he was always at least a drink behind her, but drinking nonetheless. When she started getting a little silly—this was after her fourth martini, he was beginning to think the girl had a hollow leg and the drinks would *never* affect her—he told himself it was no good sitting with somebody who was getting high unless you were getting a little high yourself. And partly because he didn't want to be left behind when the fun started, partly because she kept urging him to catch up, he decided another one or two wouldn't hurt, so long as he kept the situation well in control, so long as he remembered there were secrets to guard, this girl was a square, he must never forget she was a square.

He found this difficult to remember after they'd finished the pitcher of martinis and were making love on the living-room sofa, Jessica opening the robe but not taking it off, the towel falling loose from her head, he found it very difficult to remember that she wasn't a practiced whore. He told her this, told her in an unguarded moment (though he was still in complete control, even if they *were* both laughing a lot), told her she was better than half the whores he'd ever laid, and she laughed and said Oh, have you laid a lot of whores? He told her he'd laid a thousand of them at least, and they both laughed again, and she asked him to tell her the things whores did, and he started to tell her, and then remembered she was a square, and quickly said I'm putting you on, I've never laid a whore in my life.

He felt good making love to this girl, he'd actually told her the truth (though in an unguarded moment), it really *was* better with her than with the whores. But their lovemaking took the edge off the good fine high they'd been building, and when she suggested that he mix them another pitcherful of martinis (The idea is to get *smashed,* Alex, you're forget-ting the whole idea), he got off the sofa and went to the bar, and began pouring gin into the pitcher, and she told him to go a little easier on the vermouth this time, You've got a very heavy hand with the vermouth, Alex. Stirring, he lis-tened to the ice rattling in the pitcher, and felt the sides of the pitcher growing colder and colder under his hand, and re-membered the time he'd lost his gloves, it was a job he was on in the wintertime, he'd lost his gloves, his fuckin hands got so cold he almost couldn't pick the lock on the front door—and quickly put this out of his mind because it was a secret, he had to be very careful about guarding his secrets.

He carried the martini pitcher back to the sofa and poured their glasses full again, and Jessica drank a toast to her husband Michael the prick and said Dear God, now please make him *sign* the agreement, and Alex clinked his glass against hers and said Amen. They got into a discussion about God then, whether they believed in God, whether they considered themselves religious or not, a very serious solemn discussion in a boozy way, and then Jessica asked if he thought God was a woman, and Alex replied that God was probably a *Polish* woman, and this reminded Jessica of the latest Polish joke she'd heard. This Polish man comes home, finds his wife in bed with his best friend, runs to his dresser drawer, pulls out a gun, and holds it to his own head, planning to shoot himself in the head. His wife bursts out laughing. He looks at her, the gun still to his head, and he says Don't laugh, *you're* next! Alex burst out laughing and then poured her glass full again when she held it out to him. He swallowed what was left in his own glass and then poured himself another drink. Tell me about all those whores, Jessica said. What do all those whores do, Alex?

He wasn't about to tell her anything about the whores, hell with her. He glanced down at the way she was sitting, and suddenly and impulsively said The Open Robe, by Seymour Hair, and Jessica laughed and said Oh, do you know book-title jokes, I *love* book-title jokes, and then told one of her own, The Russian Revenge by I. Kutcha Kokoff. Alex said *Some* kind of publishing business *you* must've been in, and then said The Yellow Stream by I. P. Daley, and Jessica said Hawaiian Paradise by Awana Lei-A Hua, and Alex said The Chinese Lament by Wun Hung Low, and Jessica said I just made one up, The Rapist's Tale by Dick Daring, and they both burst out laughing again.

Come on, Jessica said, tell me about all your whores. He

told her again he didn't know any whores, but he said a *guy* he knew, an electrician in the theater, had told him about a one-legged whore up in Harlem, the guys were always after her, it was a remarkable thing. Jessica wanted to know did she do it standing up on crutches, and Alex said he didn't know how she did it, he had never had the pleasure, though she was supposed to be something special. Am *I* something special, Jessica asked, and he told her she was something very special indeed, and she asked *How* special am I? and he said Very, very special, and then she said Do you love me, Alex? and he said Sure, I love you. Then tell me about your whores, she said.

He poured himself another drink instead of telling her about the whores, and she held out her glass for him to fill, and they sat there drinking, and suddenly he found himself telling her his mother was an alcoholic, did she know his mother was an alcoholic? Jessica said No, she hadn't known that, and again got very serious in a boozy way and asked Alex to tell her about it, and he just shrugged and said Well, she's a drunk, she was a drunk even when I was a kid, even before my father left home; I think that's *why* he left, in fact, cause she was always drinking all the time. And then, without warning, he certainly hadn't planned to tell her this, he'd felt in fact that he was in complete control of the situation (he hadn't told her about the whores, had he?) he heard himself telling her about the first burglary he'd ever committed. He told it to her in detail, it had been a very crude burglary, he'd just gone in through the window, climbed the fire escape and gone in through the window, this was in the Bronx, a building maybe six blocks from where he lived at the time. He was only seventeen, all he got out of it was a portable radio and $30 in cash, didn't even know about fences then, kept the radio in his room, told his mother he'd won it at a church bazaar.

Jessica didn't seem shocked by the revelation, didn't even seem to understand completely that he'd just admitted to a burglary, said instead she used to steal things when she was a kid, too, went into the five-and-ten with a friend of hers, stole things from the counter. And then, maybe because it annoyed him that she hadn't quite understood what he'd just told her (Was he talking to the goddamn wall?) he heard himself telling her all about the burglary that time he got busted, that time the Hawk busted him. And then he told her all about Sing Sing, and about meeting Tommy Palumbo up there, and about the things guys did in prison, though they'd never got to him, he wasn't one of your penitentiary punks, he wasn't weak like some of the other guys. Jessica laughed and said Come on, you got that out of a book, and he said *What* book? I could *write* a fuckin book on the subject, *that's* the book I got it out of. And he went on to tell her about the Rothman burglary he'd done just two weeks ago, and about running into that old lady in White Plains—Jesus, she stunk of death, do you know what that smells like, do you know the stink of death? Jessica said he got *that* out of a book, too, that was in Ernest Hemingway's book (she had a little trouble pronouncing his name, it came out more like Erns Hemway) where Pilar is telling about death, about kissing the women in the marketplace, *that's* where he'd got *that* one. Alex said No, this happened only last week, I went in there and this old lady was sitting there in bed, I nearly shit my pants, I'm telling you. Then he told her about being lay-in man on Archie's supermarket job, and he told her all about the job they were planning for next Thursday, about how simple the job was, all they had to do was cut the telephone wires, though finding the box once they got inside there was another matter, they *still* didn't know where the box was. He mentioned the one-legged whore again, mentioned her by name, said Daisy, the one-legged whore I was telling you about, and this time Jessica looked at him through her lidded eyes, and she hiccupped, and then kept right on looking at him, and finally said Oh, *come* on. He told her it was true, would he lie to her, for Christ's sake? And she said he was just making all this up, the way he'd made up the story about the two bank robbers when they were up in Stockbridge (she had a little trouble with the name of the town, too, pronouncing it Starbridge), she'd had such a good time that weekend, wasn't that a great weekend, Alex?

He told her it had been a very good weekend, and he apologized for having forced her to run out and buy a bra, it was just that he knew so *many* whores, he didn't want anybody thinking *she* was a whore, too. Jessica said What do they do, these whores? Tell me what they do. Give me a few pointers, Alex. He said No, no, whattya wanna know about whores for, you think it's good to be a whore, it ain't good to be a whore. It ain't good to be a burglar either, you think it's good to be a burglar? What I'm gonna do after the Reed job, I'm gonna pull out, buy myself a house someplace, this is gonna be a terrific score, Jess, I can afford to pull out after this one. This is the one I been lookin for all along, I knock this one off, I'm gonna get out of it, that's the truth. Well, good, she said, you get out of it, and I'll get out of it down in Haiti, and then we'll *both* be out of it.

That's *right*, he said, we'll *both* be out of it.

I feel like dancing, she said, and got up off the sofa and without turning on any music began dancing, using the robe like a stripper, opening and closing it, twirling it around her, and then beginning to giggle helplessly. She collapsed in the middle of the living-room floor, still giggling, sitting there

with her legs crossed Indian fashion, and then she asked
Alex to bring her her glass, and he brought it to her and sat
down beside her, and they clinked glasses, and she said
Here's to getting out of it, and solemnly they drank. Though
I don't believe a word of what you told me, she said.

In the morning, she remembered all of it, and believed it
then, and phoned up to his apartment and said Oh, Alex,
what are we going to do?

His head was pounding when he put down the phone.
They had talked for close to ten minutes, and she confirmed
for him the uneasy suspicion that had kept him awake half
the night—he *had* told her everything, it had *not* been a
drunken fantasy, he had told her and she knew. He stumbled
out of the bedroom and went directly to the bathroom to
brush his teeth, thinking Jesus, I told her. Bending over the
sink increased the throbbing at the back of his head, but he
brushed his teeth vigorously, trying to obliterate the taste of
dead liquor and the memory of what he'd done, the fuckin
stupidity of it. She had cried on the phone just now. I love
you, Alex, we'll work this out. Tears. Work *shit* out, he
thought. I'm a burglar. You don't like what I am, tough.

But as he showered, he remembered some of the other
things he'd told her last night. About pulling out. About getting out of it if the Reed job shaped up as big as it looked.
Buy a house someplace, maybe ask Jessica to move in with
him. They didn't have to get married, that could wait. They
could get married later, if that's what they decided, but in the
meantime they could just live together, there were plenty
people just living together these days, even squares. The kid
liked him, she'd said herself the kid liked him. Settle down,
what the hell. Reed job turned out to be a really good one,

he'd have plenty to sock away, live on that a while, on the interest, maybe even get a nine-to-five later on.

Well, he wasn't so sure about that, putting on a monkey suit and going to an office every day, but there were other things a man could do. Maybe look for a house down there in Miami, where his mother lived with Mr. Tennis Pro, get himself some kind of job that wasn't a desk job, something outside maybe, the weather down there was terrific, you couldn't knock the weather down there. And then, you know, he could tell people, he could say, This is my wife, Jessica, this here's my stepson, even *before* they were married he could do that. Lay around in the sun half the day, he wouldn't even mind if she went around without a bra down there in Miami, it was different down there, you expected people to dress for the climate, she'd look terrific down there. He'd say This is my wife, and all the squares would shake her hand and say How do you do, Mrs. Hardy?, wanting to get her in the sack but of course they wouldn't, couldn't. Go to the races a lot, the fronton, maybe even buy a boat, maybe Lauderdale was the place to go, all those canals down there in Lauderdale, get himself a little boat, park it right outside the house. Kid would love a boat, just see him sitting there holding his bear up to the wind. It was possible. If the Reed score turned out to be what he hoped, why then it was possible.

He'd talk it over with her. Soon as he was dressed, he'd go downstairs and talk it over with her. Well, no, he didn't want her thinking she owned him or anything, give a girl the idea you were doing all this for *her,* no, that put her in a position of power, no, he didn't want to do that. Square girls, you let them think *they* were running the show, they started holding out on you, it was different with whores. Still, it wouldn't hurt to just, you know, get his thoughts out in the open.

Sober. Tell her *sober* he was seriously thinking of pulling out after this one, find a house in Lauderdale, go down there with her and the kid. Maybe even go with her when she went to Haiti for the divorce. No strings, there'd be no strings on either one of them, they'd just try it a while, see how it worked out. He wouldn't even mention marriage to her, not yet he wouldn't. Anyway, she was just about to get out of *one* marriage, she probably wouldn't be in such a hurry to jump into another one. Give it a little time, see how they liked living with each other, that was the way to do it. Girl like Jessica, she'd understand that. He liked that girl, he really liked that goddamn . . . had he told her he loved her? Last night, had he said I love you, Jess? He supposed he had. He supposed he loved her.

He took two aspirins when he got out of the shower, and then he went into the kitchen, poured himself a glass of tomato juice, and drank two cups of coffee black. He was dressed and ready to go downstairs when the doorbell rang. He went to the door, and threw back the peephole flap, and looked outside. There were two guys standing out there in the hall; he had never seen either of them in his life.

"Yeah, what is it?" he said.

One of them held up a shield. "Police officer," he said.

The Thirteenth Precinct was on East Twenty-first Street, between Second and Third Avenues. Alex knew the building because the Hawk had taken him there the time he got busted good. It was one of the newer station houses in the city, backing onto the Police Academy, which was on Twentieth Street. Twenty-first was lined with gun shops, and there were always hundreds of rookies in the area; you wandered down there around Gramercy Park, you had the feeling you were in the middle of an enemy army. The building was constructed of white brick, glass, and a polished metal Alex assumed was steel. Even the lettering to the left of the entrance doors was done in the same metal trim: 13th Precinct, it was supposed to read, but the "th" had fallen away from the brick, leaving only its outline. The green lights on either side of the entrance doors were tubular, unlike the globes you found on some of the older precincts. The paint on the one to the right of the doors had chipped away so that there appeared to be one green light and one white light. A huge American flag hung on the outside of the building.

The detectives who'd picked him up led him through the doors, and past the muster desk, and directly to the elevator. Inside the elevator, one of the detectives pressed the button for the second floor. Neither of them said anything to Alex. When they got out of the elevator on B-deck, they went down a corridor Alex remembered well, that fuckin sign on the wall reading DETECTIVES, with a black hand-drawn arrow under it. The blue doors at the end of the corridor opened onto the office of what was called, in the new police setup, the Thirteenth Precinct Investigating Unit. A detective in shirt sleeves sat at a folding table just inside the doors. He was wearing a clamshell shoulder holster, and he was typing. He scarcely looked up as they came in.

The room looked different to Alex. There were three doors on the wall to his right, they had been there when he'd got busted years ago. But a row of gray metal filing cabinets divided the larger room now, and a hand-lettered sign Scotch-taped to the cabinets read First Detective District, Homicide Squad. As they led him into the room and past the filing cabinets, Alex saw a detective printing a black girl, and it seemed to him that he'd been printed in a different part of the room that time he'd got busted. Everything looked different except the doors to the three offices, and one of them was marked Homicide, and that was the one they were leading him to, and for a minute he got scared because he thought they'd dragged him in here on some fuckin homicide he'd had nothing to do with. But then he saw Detective Hawkins sitting inside the office there, and he knew Hawkins wasn't in Homicide, so he figured the guys up here were just cramped for space and using whatever offices they could lay their hands on. As he went into the office, in fact, one of the detectives turned over a cardboard sign hanging on the door. On the one side of the sign there was only a lieutenant's name, but stenciled on the other side were the words INTER-ROGATION IN PROGRESS. Which meant they didn't even have an interrogation room up here, he sometimes wondered how cops managed to get *any* work done at all. One of the detectives closed the door behind him.

"Sit down," Hawkins said. "You want a cup of coffee or something?"

"What is this?" Alex said.

"It's a social visit."

"What kind of social visit, you send two bulls to drag me down here?"

"I wanted to talk to you," Hawkins said.

"Then why didn't you come uptown?"

"I couldn't leave the office, Alex. I'm expecting the D.A., we'll be doing a Q and A on a guy killed his wife with a hatchet. I didn't think you'd mind coming here."

"You should have called me on the telephone, *asked* me to come down. I don't need two bulls knocking on my door early in the morning."

"Well, you're here now, so why don't you just relax?"

"Yeah," Alex said. He was still angry. He didn't believe for a minute that any D.A. was coming in. The Hawk just wanted to get him here in his own territory, that was all.

Some more bullshit cop psychology. You drag a man in a station house, he's supposed to start shaking all over. The Hawk should have known better than to pull that on him. "So what is it?" he said. "Did somebody else do a job you can't dope out? Only time you want to see me is when you're trying to hang a job on me."

"No, Alex, nobody did a job."

"Then what is it?"

"Well, I wanted to talk to you."

"Yeah, what about?"

"Have some coffee, all right?"

"I don't want coffee. I've got things to do, I just want to get this over with. *Whatever* it is."

"Alex, do you know a woman named Daisy Williams?"

"No," he said. "Who is she?" With cops, you never admitted to knowing anybody, even if it was your own mother. Besides, he was halfway telling the truth. Until this minute, he hadn't known Daisy's last name.

"She's a one-legged hooker up in Harlem. You sure you don't know her? She's pretty well known up there."

"I don't know her. How come *you* know her, Mr. Hawkins? You been changing your luck up there in Harlem?"

"I didn't say she was black, Alex."

"If she's a hooker in Harlem . . ."

"There are white hookers up there, too."

"Anyway, what about her?" Alex asked, and shrugged. He wasn't about to go around the dance floor two or three times with Hawkins. Cops always liked to think they'd tripped you up on something. Ah, but only *you* could have known the pistol was hidden in the garden because none of *us* mentioned it, and it wasn't in the newspapers, and besides there's a rose sticking out of your ass. Cops automatically figured everybody but themselves was dumb.

"Daisy got involved in a little fracas last night. I thought you might have heard about it."

"If I don't know her, how could I hear anything about her?"

"That's right, you don't know her. I forgot that."

"Yeah," Alex said, and sighed.

"Stabbed a man," Hawkins said.

"Too bad for Daisy," Alex said offhandedly, but inside he was suddenly alert. Had she really stabbed somebody, or was this just more of Hawkins's bullshit? Why hadn't Archie called him? If Daisy was really in trouble . . . ?"

"Sailor was trying to make time with her in a bar up there, didn't know she was a hooker. When she told him how much it would cost, he got insulted, grabbed one of her crutches, and started beating her with it. Daisy pulled a knife out of her bag, sliced him up."

Alex said nothing. He was wondering why Hawkins was telling him all this. There was something very strange in Hawkins's manner, he had never seen him like this before. He could not put his finger on what it was. He waited. There had to be something more behind this than a D.D. report in triplicate on what Daisy had done or hadn't done.

"She was plenty scared, Daisy was. Saw the sailor going off in an ambulance, and *she's* in a squad car heading for the Two-Eight. She practically started plea bargaining right in the car, while they were driving her in."

"Well, I don't know her," Alex said, "so it doesn't matter to me what . . ."

"Detective up there named Fields, black cop, started talking to Daisy. She's hysterical by now, doesn't know how bad she hurt the sailor, figures we'll throw the book at her. Fields smelled something, he's a good cop. Strung her along, told her how bad this looked for her—you know the tricks, Alex, he pulled them all."

"I don't know what you're driving at, Mr. Hawkins," Alex said. "I don't know this hooker, I couldn't care less about what trouble she's in."

"Strung her along, Fields did. She'd already made a call to a lawyer, and Fields knew he was flirting with Miranda-Escobedo, but he kept stringing her along, anyway, fishing for whatever he could get before the lawyer arrived. He got something, Alex."

"What'd he get?"

"A few names, for one thing."

"What names?"

"Yours. And Archie Fuller's."

"I guess she must know Archie then. If she mentioned his name . . ."

"Yeah, she seemed to know Archie. Seemed to know *you*, too, but of course you don't know her."

"Never heard of her."

"Also seemed to know you and Archie are burglars."

"I only *was* a burglar, Mr. Hawkins. I'm out of it now."

"Yes, I know that," Hawkins said dryly.

"So is that it? Hooker stabbed a sailor, mentioned me and Archie? Is that why you dragged me down here?"

"There's more, Alex. You sure you don't want a cup of coffee?"

Alex shook his head. He was really worried now and wanted to get out of there as fast as he could. But at the same time, he wanted to know what Daisy had told the bull up in Harlem.

"Daisy said if they'd go easy on her, she could tell them all about a burglary you and Archie were planning."

"Is that right?" Alex said. "She must have some imagination, this Daisy." But his heart was pounding.

"Up in Westchester County," Hawkins said.

"Is that right?" Alex said again. His throat was suddenly parched, his voice sounded strange even to himself.

"Yeah, that's what she told Fields. This was all before her lawyer got there. The minute he got there, he wanted to know if she'd been advised of her rights, told her not to say another word, threatened to bring charges against Fields— you know how these lawyers are."

"Yeah, I know how they are," Alex said. "If it wasn't for them, you'd *still* be using rubber hoses in the back room."

"What makes you think we aren't?" Hawkins said, and smiled his Burt Reynolds smile.

"So, the way I understand this, a one-legged hooker named Daisy Williams stabs a sailor in a bar, and then cops a plea by telling you Archie and I are planning a burglary in Westchester County. You're making this up, am I right, Mr. Hawkins? I mean, like, *come* on. A one-legged hooker? You think I was born yesterday?"

"Alex," Hawkins said, "if you go ahead with this job, I'm going to get your ass."

"Thanks for the warning. I don't know what job you mean. Where's Westchester County, anyway? Someplace in Pennsylvania?"

"Alex, I'll find out which town in Westchester County, and I'll be waiting there for you."

"Oh, then you don't *know* where it is, huh? I guess your one-legged hooker didn't pinpoint it for you, huh?"

"No, we don't know where it is, I'm telling you the absolute truth, Alex. I'll tell you something else. When Fields got your name from the hooker, and looked up your B-sheet, and found out I was the detective who'd busted you, he naturally called me. I was about ready to believe you by then, Alex, I was thinking miracles never cease, maybe here's one stupid bastard who's finally wised up, maybe's *really* out of it. Then Fields called me, and Alex, I've got to tell you, my heart sank."

"Where are the violins, Mr. Hawkins?"

"I'm telling you the truth," Hawkins said flatly.

"Well, if you're worried about me committing a burglary up there in Westchester County, you're wasting your sympathy. Your one-legged hooker's probably a junkie, made this all up while she was sto . . ."

"She's not a junkie. She was scared, Alex, and trying to save her own skin."

"Well, like I said, thanks for the information. I'll file it away for future . . ."

"You understand what I'm telling you, Alex?"

"What are you telling me, Mr. Hawkins?"

"Don't do the job."

"I don't know what job you mean."

"Okay," Hawkins said. "Play it your way. Be a wise guy." He sighed heavily, shook his head, and then said, "Get out of here, I'm busy."

They searched for her all that weekend.

Late Friday, they located the bondsman who'd gone her bail, and he told them she'd been sprung not two hours before, but he had no idea where she was now. It didn't seem possible to them that a one-legged whore could disappear completely from sight, even in a city as big as New York, but by Sunday night they were ready to give up. She *had* to be hiding from them, afraid Archie would break her in half once he found out she'd snitched.

It was Transit who put them onto her.

Transit came into the bar where they were sitting over their drinks. It was well past midnight, they'd already decided Daisy was a lost cause. Archie had even made a joke about it, and they'd managed to laugh at it, but neither of them thought the situation was at all comical.

"What's the fastest thing in the world?" Archie had asked.

"What?" Alex said.

"A one-legged whore heading south on the Jersey Turnpike."

They'd laughed their hollow laughter, and then ordered another round, and were sitting there nursing the drinks when Transit walked in with his spade pimp threads and his big sombrero and decided out of the goodness of his heart to share his company with them.

"Fuck off, Transit," Archie said. "We're busy here."

"Doin what?" Transit asked, and squeezed himself into the booth alongside Archie. Both men were huge, they filled almost the entire seat.

"Man's deaf," Archie said to Alex.

"Anybody interested in a good lay?" Transit said. "I've got a Chinese virgin, anybody's interested."

"The last time you saw a virgin," Archie said, "was just before you fucked your ten-year-old sister."

"Nice talk," Transit said, and laughed. "Nice talk on the man, huh, Alex? What're you guys doin here, anyway, looking like somebody died? Who died, Arch? Somebody die?"

"Somebody's *gonna* die, he doesn't get the fuck out of here," Archie said.

"Well, okay, I can take a hint," Transit said, but he made no move to get up. "What're you drinkin there, Alex?"

"Horse piss," Alex said.

Transit burst out laughing, slapping his hand on the table top and almost knocking over Archie's glass.

"You trying to win a popularity contest?" Archie asked.

"Come on, come on, I'll buy you a round, what're you drinking?" Transit said. "I'm feeling good tonight. I got a new girl, she's gonna make me a millionaire. Last night was the best Saturday I've had since New Year's Eve. Kitty. You remember Kitty, Alex? Man, she's taking in a fortune. You remember her?"

"I remember her."

"You know how much she took in last night? Guess how much she took in?"

"I got no idea," Alex said.

"You wouldn't believe it if I told you," Transit said. "Daisy didn't even believe it. I told Daisy how much . . ."

"When'd you see Daisy?" Archie asked.

"Huh? Couple of hours ago. She got in trouble Thursday night, you know. Carved up a sailor. She's out on bail now, I think they charged her with Assualt Two. She'll beat it, though, it was self-defense. That sailor was crazy, from what I hear. Kept hitting her with a crutch, can you feature that? More crazy bastards out on the streets than inside."

"Where'd you see her?" Alex asked.

"Who? Daisy? She's staying with one of my girls. She's afraid the sailor might come after her again, wants to lay low for a while."

"What girl?" Archie asked.

"The Chinese virgin I was telling you about," Transit said, and laughed, and then suddenly stopped laughing when Archie grabbed his tie and twisted it into his collar.

"What girl?" Archie said again.

"Helen Barker, hey, leggo my tie!"

"Where does she live?"

"On a Hun Twelfth and St. Nicholas. You crazy or something?"

"The address."

"One thirty-four West a Hun Twelfth."

"Thanks, Transit," Archie said, and let go of his tie. "Now get out of the booth."

"Think you're a fuckin big shot, don't you?" Transit said, but he got out of the booth and let Archie by.

There were no nameplates in the lobby mailboxes, so they decided to go right through the whole building, starting with the ground floor and knocking on every door as they worked their way upstairs. In one of the apartments, a drunk threatened to shoot Archie, told Archie to just wait right there while he got his gun, and Archie told him to go back to sleep or he'd throw him down the stairs. Archie was beginning to think Transit had lied to them; there'd be one sorry pimp tomorrow morning if he'd lied to them. But when they knocked on the door to Apartment 6A, a woman called out, "Who's there?" and Archie said, "I'm looking for Helen Barker. Transit sent me," and she opened the door. Daisy was sitting at the kitchen table, a glass of beer in front of her. She saw the two of them and reached for her crutches, but it was too late, they were already in the apartment.

"What *is* this?" Helen said. She was a dark-skinned girl in her early twenties, and she kept looking back and forth from Daisy to the two men. "You know these guys, Daise?"

"I wish to hell I didn't," Daisy said.

"Go down and buy yourself some cigarettes," Archie said to Helen.

"I don't smoke," Helen said.

"Just get lost," Alex said.

"You be all right, Daise?"

"Yeah, yeah, go on."

Helen looked at her dubiously, picked up her handbag, and

then went out of the apartment. The minute the door closed behind her, Archie said, "So how's the big mouth?"

"I didn't tell them nothing," Daisy said.

"You told them about the job."

"Not *where*," Daisy said.

"You told them Westchester County."

"But not where."

"You fuckin whore, you told them Alex and me . . ."

"They don't know it's Reed, they don't know anything about it. All I said was Westchester County."

"To save your ass."

"Damn *right*, to save my ass," Daisy said. "You'da done the same, Arch. Anyway, they don't know nothin anyway, so what difference does it make?"

"How much do they know?" Alex said.

She told them everything she'd given Fields on the night she was busted, repeated to them essentially what the Hawk had told Alex. They listened to her intently, trying to determine whether the job still had a chance. They were both aware that Westchester County was a very large place; if that's all the Hawk knew, if that's all the cops knew was Westchester County, why then it could be *anyplace* in Westchester County.

"Are you sure you didn't tell them where?" Alex asked.

"I'm positive. I wouldn't have told them that unless they made some promises, which they didn't. Man, I was *scared,* man. I cut that sailor up near his neck, I wasn't sure whether I hit his jugular or what. He was bleedin like a pig, I thought I was facing a homicide rap there, way they carried him off in that ambulance. I'da told them my own *mother* was plannin to shoot the President, they'd have let me off."

"But you *didn't* tell them what day."

"No, sir, I did not."

"Or what town."

"No, sir."

"And you didn't mention Reed's name."

"Uh-uh. You think I want to blow my steady Thursday trick?"

"So all you told them was that me and Arch were planning a burglary up in Westchester County."

"That's all."

"That's *enough,* you fuckin whore," Archie said.

"You'da done the same," Daisy said again.

"So what do you think, Alex?"

"I think it's still worth a shot," Alex said.

"So do I," Archie said.

"Without me," Daisy said.

"What are you talking about?"

"I don't want any part of it. I'm in enough trouble as it is."

"You hear this?" Archie said.

"I hear it."

"I hope you hear it good," Daisy said, "cause that's where it's at."

"How many good legs you got, Daise?" Archie asked conversationally. "You want us to break that good leg of yours? You want us to make you a basket case?"

"I don't care *what* you do," Daisy said, "you can't force me to go on that job next Thursday."

"I don't think you understand," Archie said. "There *ain't* no job without you. If you don't get Reed out there to the studio . . ."

"What you need me for, man?"

"To make sure he's in the studio. We don't want to walk into that house, find him *there* stead of in the studio."

"You understand that, Daisy?" Alex said.

"No, I don't."

"What the hell's so hard to understand?" Archie said. "We don't want to show face, we don't want the man to see us."

"Well, *I* don't want the man to go suspectin *me*," Daisy said. "First thing you know, I'll have troopers on my doorstep wantin to know this and that, they find out I'm already in trouble for stabbin that sailor, how's *that* gonna look? They'd know sure as shit I set the thing up. No, sir, I don't want any part of it."

"You got no choice," Archie said. "You don't go up there next Thursday, we'll break your ass."

"No way you can get me to go," Daisy said, and shook her head. Her hand, Alex noticed, was fiddling with the catch on her bag. He didn't know whether she had a knife in there, the cops had probably taken the knife away when they busted her. But that was Thursday night, and this was Sunday, and if Tommy had bought himself a fuckin cannon for two hundred and forty bucks, Daisy could have bought herself another knife for a nickel. He was more scared of knives than he was of guns. He knew what it felt like to be cut. Cut your fingers slicing a loaf of bread, he knew what that felt like. Guns were different, he'd only seen guns going off on television or in the movies, knew what they could *do,* but had no way of knowing what it *felt* like to get shot. Bang, hole in a man, he falls over dead. Hard to believe, almost. But a knife . . . He did not want to be cut by a one-legged whore, or by *anybody* for that matter. There were two of them in that room with her, he didn't think she'd try anything dumb unless they forced her hand. He hoped only that Archie was bluffing about hurting her; she was clearly scared of going up there next Thursday, and a person who's scared is liable to do anything. He was about to say The hell with it, let's call it off, when Daisy said, "I can get you somebody else, you so fuckin hot to do this job."

"What do you mean?" Alex said immediately.

"I can call Mr. Reed, tell him I'm sending another girl."

"You ever do that before?"

"Time to time. When I get the curse, I do it. And once I did it when I was sick with the flu."

"How does he feel about that?"

"He don't care, long as the girl is black. He thinks he's got the cab drivers fooled there's a maid comin in to tidy up the studio. They all know we're hookers, I turned a trick with one of them on the way back to the city one time. You want another girl, I'll get you one. That way, there's any heat, he don't even know who the hell she is, he can't blow the whistle on her."

"That's no good," Archie said.

"Why not?"

"Cause it means we got to let a stranger in on the job. We got to tell her we're in the house there, keep him busy in the studio. I ain't about to risk my neck on some strange whore."

"Why does it have to be a stranger?" Daisy asked.

Both men looked at each other. The name was on their lips before either of them gave it voice. Alex hesitated, not wanting to be the one who suggested it, not wanting Archie to think the only reason he might be suggesting it was that she owed him money—her share of the job would ensure payment of what she owed him, her share would enable her to pay off him and Transit both.

"Kitty," Archie said. "Why not use Kitty?"

It was raining on the day of the job.

"Fuckin rain's a hoodoo," Archie said.

"It'll help us," Alex said.

"How's it gonna help us, man? It'll get us wet, is what it'll do."

"Rain beatin on the roof, Reed won't be able to hear us over there in the house."

"He won't be able to hear us, anyway," Archie said. "Rain's a fuckin hoodoo jinx, all it is."

They had planned to use the social worker's car today, but at the last minute she'd called Archie to say her brother was coming in from California, and she had to pick him up at Kennedy. There was a greater risk with the rented car, but they were prepared with their alibi in case anyone spotted the license plate and reported it. The alibi was a variation of the one Alex had concocted that day in White Plains, just before he'd stumbled on the old lady in bed—Jesus, he hoped there weren't any sick old ladies inside the *Reed* house. If the police came knocking on Archie's door—he was the one who'd signed out the car—he'd tell them somebody had taken the car right from in front of his building, brought it back three, four hours later. Probably some kids joyriding, officer. Sure, the cop would say.

But let them try to *prove* Archie had been the one driving the car up there in Post Mills. They could come around from here to doomsday with their bullshit. If they didn't catch you inside there, or going in or coming out with tools or with the actual loot, why *ten* people could've seen your license plate, and all that did was put the cops onto you, which didn't mean they could bust you. Different if a lady picked you out of a lineup, said That's the man who was in my house. But a license plate? Still, it would've been safer with the social worker's car, cause then all the heat would go back to her, and Archie could claim he didn't know her from a hole in the wall. But it was all right this way, too. And anyway, they didn't plan on being spotted. Only person who could possibly spot them was old Reed the Third, and he'd be busy with Kitty out in the studio.

They had told Kitty about the job on Monday. They had sat in the kitchen of her Harlem apartment, and she had listened intently as they talked, and then a wide grin had erupted on her swollen mouth. Transit had given her the lip, she explained. He had booked her with a freak, and Kitty had walked out on the john when his demands became just a bit too bizarre, even for a hooker. Transit hadn't liked that. You're either a professional or you ain't, he'd told her, and then he'd begun smacking her around. She showed them a large purple bruise on her left breast, and then cursed Transit the way only a hooker could curse a man, wishing him pestilence and disease in all his private parts. They'd explained to her that Daisy would still want a piece of the action for setting up the job, and that this would have to come out of Kitty's end. Even so, she could expect to come away with more than enough to buy off Transit. They'd told her Daisy had already called Reed, and he was expecting her this Thursday at noon sharp. Reed would give Daisy a ring Thursday morning as soon as his wife left for the city, let her know the coast was clear. Meanwhile, all Kitty had to do was meet with Daisy and find out how she could best keep Reed busy and happy out there in the studio while they ripped off the house. Kitty said it sounded like a piece of cake.

The rented car nosed its way through the rain, they knew the way to Post Mills by heart now, like fuckin horses going to stable, Archie said. They had driven up to Post Mills on Tuesday, because it had suddenly occurred to Alex that the telephone wires at the Reed house might be underground. With a lot of new houses, especially the modern ones, people didn't want telephone or electrical wires coming overhead from the road to the house, spoiling the look of it. So they buried the wires underground, and the phone company's protector was installed someplace inside the house, instead of on an outside wall where it, too, would spoil the clean-lined look of the place. The protector was a small box with fuses and carbon inside it, and was just what it sounded like—a protector. Against lightning. Without that little box, you got a thunderstorm while you were talking on the phone, next thing you knew you were lighting up the whole house without benefit of electricity. The wires from the terminal pole led into the protector, and then the wires to the various phones in the house led out of it. If the wires to the Reed house were underground, then the protector was most likely inside the house someplace, probably in the basement, or else in the garage. If that was the case, they would have to first get into the house to cut the telephone wires, which made it ridiculous since the reason they wanted to cut the wires in the first place was so they *could* get into the house. They were ready to call off the job if the telephone wires were underground.

They'd driven up Pembrook Road watching the telephone poles, and when they saw the one outside the Reed house, and saw those wires up high above the stone wall, leading right toward where the house was, they turned to each other and grinned. Then, while they were on the road, they drove up and down it several times, trying to find a good place to park the car when they made the house. They didn't want to drive right up to the front door, because old Reed the Third might hear them coming in and jump right off Kitty and onto the pipe to the state troopers. They found a cutoff into the woods about a thousand yards from the Reed driveway, an old dirt road overgrown with weeds. There were two rotted wooden posts on either side of the cutoff, it might have been a logging trail at one time, they didn't know and didn't care. A rusted chain hung between the two posts. They got out of the car to examine the chain, saw it could easily be removed from one of the posts, and decided this was where they'd leave the car while they were looting the house. They drove back to the city then, and shook hands before leaving each other, as though they had already closed a five hundred thousand dollar deal and were congratulating themselves on their brilliance.

The wipers snicked steadily at the rain now, the defroster threw a gentle stream of warm air against the windshield. The dashboard clock read eleven-ten, and they had just passed the Greenwich tollgates. They'd be in Post Mills in twenty minutes, a half hour at most. Reed the Third had called Daisy at nine-thirty to say his wife was off and running. He had asked her a lot of questions about the girl Daisy was sending him, and she had given Kitty a real send-off and asked him to be real nice to her as she was a personal friend in addition to being a fine piece of ass. Reed had chuckled into the phone and warned Daisy to be careful, he might take a fancy to this other girl. There was something between those two that was almost like man and wife, it was really peculiar. Listening to the steady rhythm of the windshield wipers, Alex thought about Reed and Daisy, and then thought about himself and Jessica, and of the long conversation they'd had last night.

They had talked mostly about getting out of it. She would be getting out of a bad marriage, and he would be getting out of a life he had to realize was unrewarding. That had been Jessica's word. Unrewarding. He'd told her it wasn't unrewarding *financially,* he was after all expecting to figure sixty grand on this job. That's if they came away with half a million. Thirty percent of that would be a hundred and fifty thousand, and they'd give Daisy, say, ten for setting it up, and Kitty would get, say, another ten, which would leave the rest for him and Archie to split. That wasn't exactly unrewarding, he said. Yes, Jessica said, but what if you get caught, Alex, what'll happen to us if you get caught? He told her there was no chance of getting caught, they had researched this thing very thoroughly and it looked like a piece of cake. He had used Kitty's words in describing it—a piece of cake. I'd die if anything happened to you, Jessica said. I'd die if you got caught and sent to prison. And he'd told her again there was no chance of getting caught.

But now he wondered about it. In the closed and steamy near-silence of the automobile, the only sound the steady *whick-whick* of the wipers and the drone of the engine and the hiss of the tires against the wet roadway, he wondered whether there was even the slightest possibility of getting caught. Kitty was already on her way up there by taxi, she'd left her apartment the moment Daisy called to tell her everything was okay. They'd arranged for Vito Bolognese to fence the stolen furs, and for Henry Green to fence the jewelry. They'd told Henry they didn't know *exactly* how much they'd be taking out of the house, but according to the photographs Daisy had described, it looked like it would be a very big haul. Henry had wanted to know what they meant by very big, and they'd told him they were hoping in the neighborhood of half a million dollars. This was a figure they'd picked out of the air, a figure only sketchily arrived at on the basis of the photographs. But it was a figure they believed nonetheless. They had talked about the job so often that now the figure seemed real to them. Five hundred thousand dollars. This was the once-in-a-lifetime score they'd both been dreaming about, and the dream seemed within reach now, and they would not compromise the dream by reducing the scope of it. Henry shook his head and said he could probably come up with seventy-five thousand by Thursday afternoon, but that they'd have to wait for the balance till the early part of next week, if that was all right with them. They'd shaken hands on the deal and promised to deliver the goods late Thursday.

So that part of it was okay. There was no chance of them getting stuck with hot goods, they'd be rid of the stuff the minute they got back to the city this afternoon. And they knew Henry's reputation, he wouldn't try to screw them, he'd deliver the remainder of the cash just as he'd promised, early next week, you couldn't expect a man to have that kind of cash just lying around. There was no chance of them walking in on a house full of people either, because Reed would be out in the studio with Kitty, and besides they planned to ring the front doorbell before cutting the phone wires. Anybody answered the door, they'd give him a bullshit magazine-subscription pitch. Meanwhile they'd be looking all around, making sure nobody was mowing the lawn or painting the shutters or whatever the hell. Nothing unexpected. They saw anything out of the way, it was good-bye, nice knowing you. Kitty'd come out of it with a hundred-dollar bill for her trouble, and a free taxi ride back to the city, and they'd both go home and weep in their beer. No, he could see nothing wrong in their approach to the job, and nothing wrong in the way they planned to dispose of the hot goods afterwards.

As for the Hawk, Alex had to admit he'd worried about him quite a bit in the past few days, especially when he'd come from the trip to Post Mills on Tuesday and found fire engines in front of the building, people standing on the sidewalk, tenants he recognized. He knew the police sometimes pulled phony bomb scares or false-alarm fires, just to get a guy out of his apartment so they could put in a wire. But they usually did that in big investigations, like when they were after somebody in the rackets and had to bug his phone for incriminating evidence, or when they suspected a big hijacking was about to take place, something like that. It cost a lot of money, after all, to get the whole fuckin fire department out just so they could send a police technician in. He'd never been afraid of anything he'd said on the telephone because he knew the cops just wouldn't bother a burglar that way, they just wouldn't. No matter *what* they said, they had a lot of respect for burglars, they didn't consider them cheap mobsters, no, he'd never heard of a burglar whose phone had been bugged. But those fire engines outside had scared him, made him begin to think maybe the Hawk *had* gone to the trouble of bugging his phone, and when he talked to Archie that night, he told him to cool it, and Archie understood right away and they talked about the weather instead of the Reed job. This was after Jessica had already told him there really had been a fire in the building that day. Still, he'd been nervous.

And suppose, well, he didn't think this was likely to happen, but suppose the Hawk had Daisy picked up, dragged her down there to the Thirteenth, started throwing a lot of questions at her, she was scared shitless as it was, that assault charge hanging over her. And suppose he promised her a deal, told her he'd whisper in the D.A.'s ear, the usual cop bullshit, get the charge reduced, maybe get the charge dropped completely, if only she'd tell them where and when her two friends were planning to hit Westchester County. Well, he didn't think she'd tell the Hawk anything, even if he promised her the sky, because after all there was ten grand in this for her, a fuckin whore didn't come across ten grand every day of the week. Got to turn a lot of tricks to pile up ten grand. No, he didn't think

Daisy would tell the cops anything more than she'd already told them.

So he couldn't see any way of them getting caught, and yet the job troubled him, and he didn't know why. He kept telling himself it really *was* a piece of cake, it really would be the once-in-a-lifetime score he'd been hoping for ever since he'd first broken that window in the Bronx and come away with a portable radio and $30 in cash. And if it *did* turn out to be the kind of score they all were hoping for, why then of *course* he would buy that house in Lauderdale, take Jess and the kid down there, Christ, it would be beautiful. He'd told her that last night. He'd promised her this would be the very last one, even if it turned out to be a nickel-and-dime score. Go in there, find himself a piggy bank and a fried omelet, okay the hell with it. No more. They'd go south anyway, get themselves jobs—I promise you Jess, this is it, he'd said. This is the last one. And before she'd left him to go downstairs again, she'd made him promise to call her in the morning before he left for Post Mills. And this morning, on the phone, she'd told him she loved him, and she'd begged him to be careful, and made him promise that he would call her the minute he got back to the city, she'd be worried all that time, he had to promise he'd call her. Do you love me, Alex? she'd asked. I love you, he'd answered, I'll call you the minute I get back. I love you, Jess.

"Almost there," Archie said.

Alex glanced at the dashboard clock. The time was a quarter to twelve.

"Don't want to get there before twelve-fifteen," he said. "Give Kitty a chance to get started."

"Yeah. You want to stop for some coffee?"

"I think we better. Arch?" he said, and then hesitated.

"Yeah?"

"You worried about this job?"

"No," Archie said.

"Me, neither," Alex said.

They stopped for coffee in a luncheonette in Langston, across the street from the bank. They kept watching the traffic on the main street outside. The rain had let up a little, but most of the bank's business was still being done at the drive-in window. As they sipped at their coffee, they speculated that a bank in a one-horse town like this would be a pushover for somebody with a gun and a pair of balls— somebody like Tommy Palumbo. When the clock's hands were standing straight up, they paid for their coffee, and left the luncheonette, and started the drive to Post Mills. Archie seemed calm and relaxed. As for himself, Alex knew the juices wouldn't begin flowing till he started opening one of the doors. The front door, a patio door, it wouldn't matter; the juices would start flowing the minute he put a tool on one of those doors. The tools they would use were in a satchel in the trunk of the car. Archie had observed all the speed limits on the way up, and he drove carefully and slowly now. Neither of the men spoke. Alex was thinking that in two hours' time, give or take, they'd each be richer by sixty grand or more. When they got to Post Mills, they drove down Pembrook Road to the cutoff they'd spotted on Tuesday. Alex got out of the car, lowered the chain and then stood in the lightly falling rain while Archie pulled the car off the road. Archie drove it as far back as he could, so that it was almost completely hidden by the trees. He took the satchel of tools out of the trunk then and came to where Alex was standing just off the road.

"Fuckin rain," he said.

They walked down the road together and then scaled the wall around the Reed property. The rain pattered gently on the leaves as they worked their way through the woods toward the house; a faint mist was rising underfoot. They came out onto the driveway and walked directly to the front door of the house. There was no one in sight. Archie reached out and pressed the bell button. They heard chimes inside. They waited. No one came to the door. Archie rang again, and again, the chimes sounded.

"What do you think?" he whispered.

"Give it a few minutes," Alex said.

"Don't want Reed to hear the chimes over in the fuckin studio."

"Kitty's taking care of him, don't worry."

Archie pressed the bell button again. There was the sound of the chimes. There was the sound of the falling rain.

"What do you say?" Archie whispered.

"Let's hit it," Alex said.

They celebrated in Daisy's apartment that night.

There was whiskey and beer and deli they'd sent out for. They ate a lot and drank a lot, but mostly they went over what had happened that afternoon at the Reed house, telling the same stories two and three times over, and laughing each time. They were like a troupe of amateur actors at the cast party following a performance. Their stories were anecdotal, they were there less to inform Daisy than to relive for themselves the highlights of the action. They broke in on each other often, Kitty remembering something that had happened out in the studio, Archie interrupting with a story of his own, barely able to get it out before Alex broke in. Daisy sat there on the sofa, listening mostly. There was green eye shadow on her lids, bright red lipstick on her mouth. She looked like a great Egyptian whore or something, amber eyes darting from face to face as they told their stories, cat eyes, a faint smile on her mouth.

". . . we'd *never* find that fuckin box," Archie said. "First time I ever run across one like that," Alex said.

"I like that man you got out there," Kitty said. "I really do like him. He's a gentleman."

"Oh, he's a gentleman, all right," Daisy said. She held out her glass for Alex to fill, shifting her weight on the couch, her dress riding up on the thigh of her good leg. She caught his glance and lifted her eyebrows in surprise, and watched him steadily as he filled her glass, cat eyes, Egyptian whore eyes.

"Oh, shit," Archie said, and burst out laughing. "When you knocked over that vase, man, I thought I'd have a hemorrhage. Daise, you never heard anything so loud in your *life.* Thing hit that stone floor, sounded like a bomb going off. You didn't hear it out there, Kitty?"

"Man, we didn't hear *nothing* out there," Kitty said. "That Reed's got a one-track mind, you coulda been starting World War III in that house, he wouldn't have heard nothing."

"Wait'll he sees that bedroom," Archie said, and laughed.

"He's *already* seen it by now," Alex said.

"We made a mess in there, you never *seen* such a mess. Now *that* was your World War III, Kitty. We took that fuckin room apart looking for the box. You know where the box was?"

"You already told us where the box was," Kitty said.

"In the *floor!*" Archie said, as though revealing a fresh secret. "Had the box under one of the stones in the floor. Alex was the one found the box."

"No, you found it, Arch."

"No, all I did was say one of the stones was loose, watch you don't trip over it."

"That's what gave me the clue, though. You ever see anything like that? You ever come across a box in the floor?"

"Never."

"That was no cinch box either, I got to tell you."

Kitty suddenly began laughing, and then said to Daisy, "He says going, Reed does. Instead of coming, he says going. He asked me did I go? I said What you mean did I go? He says did I make you go? Then I realize he means did I come? I told him Why sure, honey, I went clear to California and back. What you got him thinkin up there Daise? You got him thinkin he brings you off?"

"He damn near did once," Daisy said.

"Got a new muscle on my arm, workin on that box," Archie said.

"Thought we'd *never* beat that fuckin box," Alex said.

"How come you don't know furs?" Archie asked Daisy.

"I know *mink,* man, that's what I know," Daisy said.

"That one mink in there, it was a black diamond mink, full-length," Archie said.

"That was sable on the collar," Alex said.

"That coat alone was worth six grand," Archie said. "You know how much them furs were worth altogether? How come you don't know about furs, Daise? Seventeen thousand bucks, those furs. Vito looks at them, he nods his head, he says Very nice, boys. He's like a fuckin college professor, Vito."

"Right, a college professor," Alex said, and laughed.

"Very nice, boys, and he hands us five thousand bucks, says he's rounding it off. Alex says Whutchoo mean, man, rounding it off? Those furs are worth seventeen grand, we want fifty-one hundred, never mind rounding it off. Fuckin Vito, tryin to short-change us a lousy C-note."

"We got it, though," Alex said. "How you doin there, Daise? You want a little more of this?"

"Sure," she said, and held out her glass. Alex got up from where he was sitting and walked over to the sofa with the bottle in his hand. Leaning over her, he poured into the glass, and she watched him steadily with her Egyptian cat eyes, and then said, "Easy, man. You get me drunk, I'll be no good to you."

"You gonna be good to me?" he said.

"Depends," she said, and smiled.

"Opened that box, near fell over dead," Archie said. "The *stuff* in that fuckin box! Man has to be crazy keepin stuff like that in the house."

"Well, where's he *gonna* keep it?" Alex said. "Wife wants to put on one of those bracelets, what's she gonna do, run over to the bank?"

"I couldn't believe that one bracelet. An inch wide, musta been five hundred round diamonds in the . . ."

"Was the marquise diamonds gave it the value," Alex said.

"Sixty-five grand, holy *shit!*" Archie said, and slapped his thigh.

"Sure, they totaled twenty-seven carats, those marquise diamonds."

"Job would have been worth it for the bracelet alone."

"The ring and the bracelet. Them two alone would've made it a big one."

"You shoulda seen that ring, Kitty," Archie said. "Three diamonds in it, an engagement ring. Two pear-shaped diamonds, each about two carats. Ain't that what Henry said, Alex? About two carats each?"

"Give or take."

"And this big round diamond in the middle, how many carats did he say that was?"

"Eighteen."

"Man!" Archie said.

"You know how much that ring is worth?" Alex asked Daisy.

"How much, honey?" she said.

"Seventy-five thousand. That ring and the bracelet, them two would've made it a big score all by themselves."

"Biggest score I ever made in my fuckin life," Archie said. "Even splitting it. Biggest ever. You ever make a bigger score, Alex?"

"Never."

"You girls'll be able to retire, your end of it," Archie said.

"Oh, yeah, sure," Kitty said.

"You think I'm foolin? You know how much we took out of that place?"

"How much?"

"The jewels was more than four hundred alone, and another seventeen for the furs . . ."

"It was four twenty-two total," Alex said. "Close to what we figured, Arch. Damn close to what we figured."

"Four twenty-two, right. So what's thirty percent of that?"

"Close to a hun twenty-seven."

"Right, and you girls get to split fifteen percent of that . . ."

"I thought you said we'd get ten thousand each," Daisy said.

"That's if it was half-a-million," Archie said.

"I was countin on ten thousand."

"That's when we were countin on half-a-million. But it's only four twenty-two, that's the fair count, we ain't shortchangin you like that fuckin Vito. Now what's fifteen percent of our end, Alex?"

"Give them the ten," Alex said.

"What for?"

"They're supposed to split close to nineteen grand. So make it an even ten each, what the hell."

"Man, you mighty generous with my money," Archie said.

"Break your heart, Archie," Kitty said.

"What the hell," Archie said, and laughed. "Give them ten each, you're right, what the hell. This is the biggest fuckin score I ever made, what the hell. We all worked for it, am I right? What the hell."

They sat around drinking and talking till close to midnight, and then Kitty asked if she could have her piece of the money, or at least her piece of what they'd got so far, cause she was anxious to go find Transit and pay off what she owed him, tell the son of a bitch he ever came near her again she'd have him busted for molesting her. They had received fifty-one hundred from Vito and seventy-five thousand from Henry, so they did a little arithmetic and decided they could let the girls have six thousand apiece right now, and another four when Henry paid them the balance. Kitty counted the bills and then immediately handed two thousand dollars to Alex.

"We're even now, right?" she said.

"That does it," Alex said.

"Okay," she said. "I got to run now, go tell Transit what I think of him."

"I'll go with you," Archie said. "I want to head uptown, see my social worker."

"Think I'll hang around, have a little nightcap," Alex said. "That okay with you, Daisy?"

"Yeah, fine," Daisy said.

She got up onto her crutches and went to the door to let Archie and Kitty out, leaving her money on the coffee table. Archie and Kitty said good night, and then went out, and Daisy locked the door behind them and put the Fox lock in place, wedging the buttress bar against the door. On the stairwell outside, Archie yelled something to them, but they couldn't understand what he'd said. In a few minutes, they heard Kitty's laughter on the sidewalk outside.

"Better put this away," Daisy said, picking up the money. "Next thing I know you'll be ripping *me* off." She hobbled toward the bedroom, and then hesitated in the doorway, and turned toward him, and said, "So you're gonna have a little nightcap with ole Daisy, huh?"

"That's my plan," he said.

"Mm," she said, and smiled. "Fix one for me, too, okay? I won't be a minute."

She went into the bedroom, and he heard a dresser drawer opening and closing. Daisy started humming something then, a tune he didn't recognize. He poured the drinks and listened to her humming in there, and then he sat on the sofa to wait for her. When she came back into the room, she was wearing a long silk robe belted at the waist. She sat beside him on the sofa and said, "That was nice of you, Alex. Going to the full ten, I mean."

"Well, we all worked for it," Alex said.

"What you gonna do with your share of it?"

"Who the hell knows?" he said. "It never lasts that long."

"That's right, it never does."

"This was a big one, but shit, it wasn't no once-in-a-lifetime score. It wasn't nothin' a man could retire on. Anyway, I get itchy," he said. "I sit around too long, I get itchy."

"Mm," she said. "Give me your hand, baby."

At two in the morning, he woke up in Daisy's bed, and for

a moment didn't know where he was. He sat up against the pillows and blinked into the room, trying to distinguish shapes in the darkness, and saw her crutches leaning against the foot of the bed, and remembered then where he was. And remembered, too, that he'd promised to call Jessica the minute he got back to the city. He debated getting out of bed and going into the living room, where the phone was, call her now, tell her something important had come up, tell her . . .

Fuck her, he thought, and lay down again beside Daisy.